# ST. MARTIN'S

# MINOTAUR
## MYSTERIES

Praise for the Mysteries of Susan Holtzer

### Better Than Sex

"[A] lively and humorous tale."

— *Booklist*

### The Wedding Game

"[S]olidifies [Holtzer's] position as a mystery writer to watch... Both mystery lovers and computer buffs will enjoy this imaginative romp in cyberspace."

— *Publishers Weekly*

"The best Haagen tale to date...the unique mystery has an intriguing twist since most of the characters have never met outside of cyberspace. This plot device works because of Ms. Holtzer's strong storytelling abilities."

— *Harriet Klausner*

"Anneke is the kind of friend with whom one gets comfortable, sinking into the sofa and sipping a brandy, quietly conversing until past midnight."

— *Alfred Hitchcock's Mystery Magazine*

### Black Diamond

"This relaxed, evenly paced mystery deftly entwines a century-old tale with a modern murder, and firmly unites three disparate sleuths in a common goal...Excellent....This satisfying story includes a surprising yet plausible finale."

— *Publishers Weekly*

"[This] promising series features appealing characters and skillful plotting."

— *Booklist*

"Enjoy the adroit intermingling of intrigue present and past as Holtzer bridges a hundred years to bring two generations of strong Swann women vividly to life."

— *Kirkus Reviews*

**Read these Susan Holtzer Mysteries**

# BETTER
## THAN SEX

*A Mystery Featuring Anneke Haagen*

## SUSAN HOLTZER

St. Martin's Paperbacks

## Author's Note

All characters and situations in this book are firmly rooted in my own imagination and are not intended to bear any resemblance to any person, living or dead. However, it makes no sense to write about food and San Francisco without mentioning some favorite restaurants. So a few of the restaurants praised by these imaginary characters are local favorites, the kind that often fall through the cracks of guidebooks. (Note: Any and all restaurants that are *not* praised are completely and absolutely imaginary.) Enjoy.

BETTER THAN SEX

Copyright © 2001 by Susan Holtzer.

Library of Congress Catalog Card Number: 2001019161

ISBN: 0-312-98005-1

Printed in the United States of America

St. Martin's Press hardcover edition / August 2001
St. Martin's Paperbacks edition / July 2002

St. Martin's Paperbacks are published by St. Martin's Press, 175 Fifth Avenue, New York, NY 10010.

10 9 8 7 6 5 4 3 2 1

# ONE

"...Big Nate's. Now that's the kind of barbecue that..."

"...terrible Wharf places. The ahi was so overcooked that..."

"...potato skins stuffed with goat cheese at the Potrero Brewing Company..."

Good grief, Anneke Haagen thought crossly. Did everyone in San Francisco talk about food *all* the time? She craned her neck to see around George McMartin, whose head was squarely between her and the fifty-four-inch TV screen. If they weren't interested in the football game, why did they bother coming to a sports bar in the first place?

"...is good, but Amici's has the right kind of thin, crisp crust. And they have pine nuts," Jeremy Blake said. On the screen, Anneke saw Wade Furlong, Michigan's freshman quarterback, take a quick three-step drop and fire the ball toward the end zone.

"...Mandalay. They do the best tampoi rice I've ever tasted," Blair Falcone said. Furlong's pass sailed over the receiver's head and bounced out of bounds. "Do you like Burmese food?" he asked Anneke.

"I didn't even know there was such a thing," she confessed. Michigan lined up on the Penn State 12-yard line, fourth and goal.

"What about P. J.'s Oysterbed?" Mimi Rojas asked Blair. Furlong took the snap from center. "Really good seafood, and they even do an authentic ceviche." She turned to Anneke. "There's a lot of good seafood in the city as long as you stay away from the Fisherman's Wharf tourist traps."

"Don't get sucked in by the views, either," Noelle Greene warned. "If you want a place with a great view and good food . . ." She stopped as the noise level in the dining room rose. All eyes turned to the TV screen, where Wade Furlong was scrambling out of the pocket. The shouting rose to a crescendo and then died into a chorus of groans as Furlong's desperate pass was picked off by a Penn State safety.

". . . or Louie's," George McMartin pronounced. "Simple, first-rate American food. Great brunches, and on a clear day you can see all the way to the Farallones. I've even seen whales from their window."

She was going to murder Richard Killian, she decided. Preferably slowly, and preferably with something food-related. Something nasty-tasting.

It had sounded like fun when Richard called them at the Ritz-Carlton. Come watch the Michigan game Saturday at the Maize and Blue, he'd said over the phone. Brunch is on the house—a wedding present, he'd said. Lots of other Michigan alumni to watch the game with, he'd said. And you can spend the entire game answering silly, intrusive, highly personal questions about your eating habits—he hadn't said.

Definitely a slow-acting poison. Anneke nibbled a croissant thoughtfully. She wanted to watch him die.

\* \* \*

"Would you say this is more than you normally eat for breakfast?" Lindsay Summers wrenched the conversation back to the immediate meal. Lindsay Summers had long, pale blond hair and a tiny, sinewy body and tiny, delicate hands. She wore pencil-thin khaki pants, and a clingy beige tank top over a clingy short-sleeved white tee. She sipped—delicately—from a glass of water that looked almost too heavy for her fine-boned wrist.

The question was addressed to the table at large, but her blue eyes fixed on Anneke.

"Good Lord, yes." Anneke wondered why she felt apologetic.

"It's not breakfast, it's brunch," George McMartin corrected Lindsay. "I'd say I ate about what I normally would for breakfast and lunch combined."

"Frankly, I never really thought about it." Blair Falcone, looking out of place in a beautifully cut Armani suit, responded shortly to Lindsay's look of interrogation. He sounded even more annoyed than Anneke felt. His glance flicked to Lindsay and then back to the television screen. "I'm not in the habit of analyzing what I eat."

"I see." Lindsay's large blue eyes regarded him thoughtfully.

"No, of course he doesn't." Elisa Falcone, beautifully if dressily clothed in a heavy white silk shirt, hand-painted silk quilted vest, and black wool pants, uttered a dramatic sigh. She waved a hand heavy with gold bracelets and rings. "He'd absolutely live on pasta if I let him," she told the table at large. "Do you know, he once ordered spaghetti and meatballs at Venticello's?" She smiled and rolled her mascaraed brown eyes, inviting the others to share her amusement at her husbands's peccadilloes.

First there'd been the questionnaire, which took up most of the first quarter of the game. ("How many meals do you eat in restaurants during an average week?" "Exactly what did you eat the last time you had dinner in a restaurant?" "Do you normally try to limit your intake of saturated fats?" "How many times in the last year did you eat a meal while watching a football game at a sports bar?")

Then there was the brunch buffet. Anneke, who was used to watching football at a decent afternoon hour, found it disconcerting to be faced with a kickoff at nine A.M. West Coast time, but she couldn't fault the food. There were scrambled eggs mixed with crumbled sausage, slivers of leek, and sprinkles of caraway seeds; there were miniature croissants with cream cheese fillings flavored variously with herbs, asparagus, and brandied cherries; there were cups of tiny melon balls and strawberries in a sour cream–cardamom dressing; and finally, there was a gourmet doughnut bar—crisp little balls and twists with drizzled caramel or orange glaze or cinnamon–sugar coating that had her altering her attitude toward doughnuts. Of course she'd eaten more than she usually did; she could feel the waistband of her jeans digging into her stomach.

Even more irritating—Karl had been excused, on the grounds of being an ex-athlete, and therefore . . . what? Too nutrition-conscious? Anneke had no idea; she only knew that this was one hell of a way to run a honeymoon. She looked longingly across the room, where her new husband was deep in conversation—football-related conversation, she assumed jealously—with a tall, gray-haired African American man who looked like, and might well be, a former basketball player.

And of course there was the endless talk about food—restaurants, chefs, menus, diets, past meals, future meals. And all the while, there was Lindsay Summers, watching and listening and scribbling constantly in her notebook.

"The sausages are his own recipe, aren't they?" Blair Falcone, ignoring both his wife and Lindsay Summers, spoke across the table to Noelle Greene. Noelle was a large woman with a beautiful face and a mass of improbably colored hair shading from deep auburn to maroon.

"Yes. He has them made at a place up in Napa," Noelle replied. "But I think Cody's real signature dish is going to be the Cotswold Fusilli—makes you rethink everything you ever believed about macaroni and cheese." Noelle wore a tight, low-cut crimson tee under a crisp white cotton shirt unbuttoned and tied at the waist; when she leaned forward, the white shirt gaped open and her impressive breasts strained against the fabric of the T-shirt.

"Macaroni and cheese?" Elisa Falcone tilted her sleek dark head, gold earrings gleaming. "Oh, I don't think so, dear. I mean, simplicity is all very well, but what puts Cody in such a special category is his ability to blend complex flavors into entirely new combinations."

"Some of his Michigan cherry recipes are going to become standards," George McMartin said. "Five years from now you'll be telling people you were eating Cody Jarrett's food before he was famous." George, stocky and middle-aged with a closely cropped salt-and-pepper beard, wore a pristine white V-neck sweater over a navy blue silk turtleneck with a small block-M pin at the neck. He looked like a banker; what he was, was a restaurant critic and food writer so famous even Anneke had heard of him. "In fact," he went on, "I've nominated Cody for Rising Star Chef in this year's culinary competition. Believe me, Nouvelle Midwest is going to be the hottest food trend in the country."

"Really?" Blair appeared deeply satisfied.

"Dear, I told you that last week." Elisa shook her head with an air of patience. "Oh, look, Christa Collier finally got here." She waved across the room, bracelets clinking.

"Do you often eat more than you should at the Maize and Blue?" Lindsay Summers's voice was snappish; she was having trouble controlling the conversation, and she didn't like it. Anneke noted that "more than you usually eat for breakfast" had now become "more than you should." Not only was Lindsay Summers annoying, she was a lousy researcher.

"I didn't eat 'more than I should.' I ate the wrong things, that's all." Mimi Rojas, plump and darkly pretty in a navy blue shirt, heavy silver earrings, and round wire-rimmed glasses, sounded defensive. Lindsay Summers had the ability to make everyone feel defensive. "I wanted to taste Cody's food, that's all, and the buffet gave me a chance to sample a lot of different things. I'll go back to my normal diet tomorrow."

"I see." Lindsay made a note, then put down her pen as a waiter appeared and set down a plate containing two thick slabs of sourdough toast in front of her. Lindsay nodded to him and shoved the glass to one side.

"Normal?" Jeremy Blake glared at Mimi. "How can you call a diet of pure fat normal?" Jeremy was probably in his early thirties, although the buzz-cut hair and gold hoop earring made him appear younger. He propped his elbows on the table, displaying the kind of defined musculature that Anneke seemed to recall was referred to as "ripped." Jeremy wore a chest-hugging navy blue tee that said BLAKE'S FITNESS—FOR LIFE. It looked as if it had been painted on; his bulbous chest muscles—"pecs"?—expanded and contracted as he spoke. Anneke, half-fascinated, half-repelled, could hardly tear her eyes away from them.

"Lay off, Jeremy." Mimi returned his glare. "You don't tell me how to eat, and I don't tell you how to dress, remember?"

"This is advertising, not fashion." Jeremy waved a hand at his T-shirt. "Besides, clothes won't clog your arteries."

"Neither will the Cornwell Diet, if you do it right," Mimi snapped. Anneke thought their exchange sounded almost perfunctory, as though they'd been having the same argument for a long time.

"So you think you'd have eaten less if you'd ordered from a menu instead of going to a buffet?" Lindsay spoke loudly to Mimi.

"I don't know. Maybe." Mimi shrugged. "It's not a big deal."

"Actually, I think it's the sitting around for so long that's the real problem." Jeremy reached into his pocket and withdrew a small cellophane bag containing half a dozen assorted pills, which he proceeded to pop into his mouth one by one as he spoke, interspersed with little sips of orange juice. "You sit around, and you nibble, you watch some of the game and you nibble some more, y'know?" He tossed the now-empty bag on the table, where Anneke could make out the words BLAKE'S ENERGY MIXTURE. "I mean, it's okay for special occasions, as long as you take the right supplements. You can't get all the nutrients you need from food anyway."

"Maybe not," Mimi said waspishly, "but you can screw up your body just as much with weird New-Age concoctions as you can with a high-protein diet."

"There's nothing weird about Blake's Energy Mixture," Jeremy retorted.

"So you consider watching football a special occasion?" Lindsay asked Jeremy. "Is that why you gave yourself permission to eat more than you should have?"

"I guess." Of them all, Jeremy seemed the least annoyed by Lindsay's questions. "I mean, I know eggs and croissants are high-fat, but at least Cody's doing low-fat sausage. And he's cutting the fat content in a lot of his other dishes, too. That's one of the things—"

"As long as it doesn't affect the taste," George McMartin interrupted. "I mean, it's one thing to focus on foods that are naturally low-fat, but trying to force a naturally rich food into low-fat mode is just a recipe for disaster." He held up a tiny croissant. "This is delicious, but just imagine what it would taste like if it was filled with that slimy fat-free cream cheese."

"So you eat things here that you know are bad for you just because they taste good?" Lindsay turned her attention to George.

"I didn't say that at all." He glared at her. "I merely refuse to eat things that taste like horse droppings simply because some self-styled expert has declared it the health miracle *du jour*."

A roar filled the room, and Anneke spun around to the television screen in time to see a Michigan player, knees pumping, break out of the pack and charge downfield. He did a juke step around an oncoming linebacker; cut toward the sideline; did a pinpoint swivel to avoid the desperate grab of the Penn State cornerback; and he was in the clear at last, rocketing the last fifteen yards and into the end zone with the ball held triumphantly aloft just as the game clock ticked down to the end of the first half.

"Did you see the move Truesdale put on that linebacker?" Jeremy Blake shouted over the uproar. He was on his feet; so were most of the other people in the room.

"My God, is he fast, or is he fast?" Noelle crowed.

"I think they clocked him at four-three-something for the forty," Anneke said, searching the room for Karl. She spotted him finally and gave him an excited thumbs-up before sitting back down in her chair.

"Now, darlin', come on." Richard Killian was hovering behind Lindsay, apparently oblivious to the excitement in Ann Arbor. His customary charm was cranked up to Overkill, but it seemed to be having no effect whatsoever on Lindsay, and Richard was beginning to sound nervous—which he damn well should be, Anneke reasoned, since she was going to murder him before the morning was over.

"I assume you're aware of the connection between saturated fats and heart disease." Lindsay spoke over her shoulder, without bothering to face him. If she'd even noticed the touchdown she gave no sign of it. "Not to mention the surgeon general's declaration of obesity as a public health crisis. And the Maize and Blue menu is absolutely loaded with high-fat foods."

"Well, yes, but . . ." Richard dithered, casting an anxious

glance at the young woman on Lindsay's right. Like Lindsay, she had a notebook in front of her, but there the similarity ended. Barbara . . . Williams, wasn't it? . . . was the kind of woman people forgot about. Medium height, pudgy body, medium brown hair, round, colorless face devoid of makeup; everything about her seemed to fade into the background. Only, on this occasion, her notebook gave her presence—Barbara Williams was writing an article about Lindsay's research for the food section of the local newspaper. No wonder Richard was worried. It occurred to Anneke that he might have usefully applied some of his charm in her direction, but then, Richard never even noticed women who looked like Barbara Williams.

"So the purpose of your research is to prove that food shouldn't taste good?" Noelle Greene looked at Lindsay innocently.

"The purpose of my research is to determine the triggers that cause people to eat badly." Lindsay glanced at Noelle and looked away, as though Noelle's size was a personal offense.

"Yes, but didn't you just suggest that taste was one of those triggers?" Noelle grinned, clearly enjoying herself.

"We don't know what the triggers are," Lindsay replied severely. "I don't argue ahead of my data." Like hell you don't, Anneke snorted to herself.

"There's nothing unhealthy about Cody's Nouvelle Midwest cuisine," Richard protested. He flicked another glance at Barbara Williams, writing something in her notebook. Lindsay ignored him.

"Nouvelle Midwest?" The phrase, repeated for the second time, dragged Anneke's attention away from the TV screen, where other Big Ten scores were being shown.

"Think gourmet comfort food." It was George McMartin who replied. "Sausages and scrambled eggs, just like Mom used to make. Only instead of greasy kielbasa, you get delicate caraway-seasoned sausage, and instead of fried onions, you get the lighter flavor of leeks." He bit a miniature doughnut in half, chewed, swallowed, then examined the remaining half of the pastry carefully. "Of course, if you're only going to be in town for a week or so, you'll want to sample a number of different cuisines. The tapas at Mustafa's are worth a trip to San Francisco all by themselves."

"Oh, tapas." Noelle Greene fluttered impossibly long eyelashes, dismissing tapas. "For a honeymoon? Dessert at Schilling's. Not only do they do the most absolutely gorgeous constructions, but it is only the best chocolate in the whole city." She kissed the crimson-enameled tips of her fingers and waggled them at Anneke. "I promise you, it's better than sex."

Noelle's laughter was infectious. Anneke held out both hands, palms down. "Hmm." She turned over her left hand. "Chocolate." She turned over the right hand. "Sex." She spread both hands and shook her head. "Sorry, not a choice I want to make. Guess I'll hold out for both."

"Hey, whatever works." Noelle laughed again. "In fact . . . George, what's the name of that erotic bakery?"

"The one that does the penis-shaped cakes?" George put a hand to his beard and shook his head. "Utterly tasteless. You're better off putting first-rate chocolate on the real thing. In fact, if you want some very fine erotic chocolate, Callista Chocolate makes a fudge sauce that's absolute nirvana—dark and bitter with the perfect level of sweetness. And it's the right consistency, too—spreads evenly, but it's thick enough so it doesn't drip off onto the sheets."

Good Lord, he seemed to be serious. Anneke blinked. *Was* he serious? And what was the name of that chocolate sauce again? Maybe all this talk about food wasn't completely useless after all.

# TWO

Food and sex. It was all about appetites, wasn't it? And if people couldn't control their appetites, they were no better than animals. Lindsay Summers's glance fell on Noelle Greene and she quickly averted her eyes. She couldn't stand to look at the woman. The thick arms, the broad hips, those breasts . . . She could at least have the decency to cover herself up, instead of flaunting that obscene body. As if she were proud of her own lack of self-control. And there was Blair Falcone leaning toward her, smiling, just as if he didn't find her repulsive. Ridiculous—no man could be attracted to that mountain of flesh.

You'd think that educating them would work, but it didn't. Just look at the people here if you doubted it. It was exactly the kind of group she'd wanted, exactly what she needed to prove her hypothesis. All of them well-educated, all of them upper-middle-class, and still they stuffed themselves with food they knew would kill them. All of them had food issues they refused to confront.

A waiter arrived finally, and Lindsay accepted her measured six ounces of tomato juice. You wouldn't think a restaurant—even one as sickly unhealthy as the Maize and Blue—would have so much trouble providing a simple glass of unsalted tomato juice. She checked her list of questions. She needed to record their attitudes toward healthy versus unhealthy food. She wanted good, strong anecdotal evidence that they knew how toxic the Maize and Blue was, yet continued to stuff themselves with its poisons. Richard Killian was no better than a drug pusher, yet nobody even tried to stop him. She reached for her tomato juice and took a sip. It tasted bitter, she thought; it was unsalted, wasn't it? Grimacing, she drank the glass off in three long swallows.

"How would you rate the health quality of the food here?" she asked, knowing what their answers would be.

"Probably pretty poor." Jeremy Blake's cheerful disregard grated on her nerves. You'd think someone who ran a chain of so-called "health clubs" would be more concerned with his own health. But even Jeremy could never control his appetites; worse, he didn't even seem to care. He really believed that if you pumped iron and popped enough of his ridiculous pills, you could eat anything you wanted. He even believed that all that inflated musculature—steroid-induced, she'd bet—was healthier than the correct thinness.

"Nonsense," George McMartin said. "It's perfectly fine as long as you don't overeat." Lindsay shuddered as he patted his disgusting paunch. George McMartin would be as much The Enemy as Richard Killian; Lindsay's research would be a threat to his whole way of life, even his career. Because her results would drive the campaign for legislation to control American eating habits.

That was the whole point of her research. Just as there were laws to control drugs, and alcohol, and smoking, there had to be laws to control food. You couldn't actually ban unhealthy foods, unfortunately, at least not right away. But you could at least control them, the same way you controlled other self-destructive behaviors. You could use taxes, and child protection laws, and restaurant regulations. You could legislate restrictions, and encourage the use of harassment and shame tactics, and . . .

"Ah, Miss Summers, you're being too hard on people." Richard Killian really thought that charm would work on her, Lindsay thought contemptuously. "You don't really want to . . ." Whatever else he was about to say was lost in the raucous uproar from the rest of the dining room.

"Oh, good, they're going to show a replay of Truesdale's run." Anneke Haagen spun around toward the big TV screen and leaned forward expectantly. Funny, Lindsay thought, she doesn't look like a football fanatic. She tried to focus on the screen, where gigantic mesomorphs pummeled each other; oversized, overfed, utterly repulsive. And here was a room full of presumably intelligent people watching other people exercise instead of exercising themselves. Exercise, too, would figure in the new legislation. She and Griff would . . .

. . . What had she been thinking about? She felt a sharp pain in her stomach, and a sudden vertigo. She gripped the edge of the table, gritting her teeth against the wave of nausea that threatened to overcome her.

"Wow. Did you see Jackson throw that block?" Anneke pumped her fist in the air, grinning widely.

Lindsay felt her stomach heave; she tried to say something, but discovered she couldn't talk. . . .

# THREE

There were doctors in the house, of course—three of them, in fact—but none of them could do anything except pronounce Lindsay Summers dead. The paramedics, arriving in a blaze of sirens, concurred. Anneke, along with the others who'd been at her table, stood with her back to the wall, trying to keep out of the way. All of them appeared shocked and horrified; all of them seemed even more shocked when a contingent of police arrived to take control of the restaurant.

Anneke was less shocked by their arrival. She'd seen Karl swiftly cross the room to stand next to the table while medical personnel did their futile best, preventing anyone from touching anything but Lindsay herself. And she'd seen him make a call on his cell phone. Now, as uniforms and plainclothes personnel fanned out across the room, she moved over to stand next to him.

"You the one who made the call?" The man who approached was in his thirties, with a face of sharp planes and angles, alert and intense. He spoke quickly and jerkily, his brown eyes darting from point to point. He wore a black jacket over a dark red silk shirt buttoned but tieless, a black brush cut, and a diamond stud in one ear.

"Yes." Karl took out his wallet and flipped it open to display his police shield. "Karl Genesko, Ann Arbor PD." He indicated Anneke. "This is my wife, Anneke Haagen."

"Inspector Peter Braxton." He didn't offer to shake hands, but it seemed more preoccupation than rudeness. "Ann Arbor. You in town on business or pleasure?"

"Honeymoon, as a matter of fact."

"Honeymoon." Braxton looked momentarily surprised, and Anneke sighed inwardly. It was a word most people associated with dewy-eyed innocents, not two fifty-somethings. It was also a word that made a fine litmus test for maturity; if you sniggered, you were due a refresher course in how to be an adult.

Braxton passed. "You were at the table when she crashed?" he asked Karl.

"No, although Anneke was. But as soon as I saw the woman start to convulse I went over there, and when the doctor started working on her I stayed there to keep an eye on things."

"Why?" Braxton asked. "Force of habit, or was there a reason you suspected something?"

"I didn't suspect anything before the event, no. But as soon as I saw her go down . . ." Karl spread his hands. "It looked wrong."

"Yeah." Braxton nodded to show he understood, professional to professional. An Asian American woman with closely cropped hair and three gold studs in her right ear approached and whispered something to him. "Okay," he said to her. "Hold the staff and the ones who were at her table. Get names and addresses of all the others and clear them out."

"Okay, chief."

"And will you stop calling me chief?" He glanced at Karl with a look of sardonic amusement. "Boy, it's hard to get good help these days. Okay," he went on without pausing, "what can you tell me?"

"About the woman's death, very little," Karl replied. "I was across the room talking to some people."

"Back up a little." Braxton held up a hand. "How'd you happen to be here in the first place? Just looking for a place to watch this football game?"

"Yes and no." Karl paused, considering. "We met Richard Killian—the owner of the Maize and Blue—in Ann Arbor a year or so ago. He called us at our hotel on Wednesday and invited us here as his guests. A wedding present, he said. In fact, we'd been planning to come here this morning anyway to watch the game, so we accepted.".

"You're both such football fans, then?" He looked from Anneke to Karl. "You look like you played football some," he suggested. Anneke stifled a grin.

"I played for Michigan, and then for the Pittsburgh Steelers," Karl said. Braxton nodded, unimpressed.

"How'd Killian know you were in town? And which hotel you were at?"

"I've no idea." Karl shook his head. Braxton turned to Anneke, and she shook hers as well.

"He knew you were a cop, I assume." Braxton cocked his head, and Karl nodded. "Did he say anything to suggest why he might have wanted a cop here today?"

"No, nothing at all."

"Okay. What happened when you got over to this woman's table?" Braxton abandoned the question of Richard for the moment.

"She was already convulsing. There were three doctors in the room, but it was the woman out there who took charge." He pointed through the wide, open double doors to an outdoor patio, where two or three people sat clustered at a table.

"The gray-haired one smoking the cigarette? She's the doctor?" Braxton peered out at her. "Did she hesitate, or did she jump right in?"

"No." Karl seemed to answer a question Braxton hadn't quite asked. "She was apparently the one they decided was best qualified—although what she is, is a gynecologist. The other two were a dermatologist and an oncologist."

"And while she was working on the victim, what were the other people at the table doing?"

"They all stood up and moved well away from the table. No one took anything away, at least from the time I got there, although of course they could have pocketed something earlier. And none of them left the room between her collapse and your arrival."

"So, at least from the time the woman went down, the table was undisturbed." Braxton pursed his lips. "Well, it helps a little." Not the most gracious thank-you in the world, Anneke thought, but Karl only nodded.

"Damn little," he agreed.

"Okay then." Braxton gave a sharp little nod. "So what can you tell me about Lindsay Summers?"

"Not a thing. Sorry." Karl spread his hands. "Except for Richard Killian, I've never met any of these people until today."

Braxton raised an eyebrow. "How about you?" he asked Anneke.

"All I know about her is what she told us this morning." Anneke thought for a moment. "She was a graduate student in public health at Michigan, doing research for a study on . . . I think she called it 'eating triggers.' Those of us at the table were her subjects. Other than that, I don't know anything about her."

"You never knew her in Ann Arbor?" Braxton's tone was half-quizzical, half-suspicious.

Anneke sighed; she'd had this conversation before. "Inspector, Ann Arbor isn't a quaint little college town. It's a city of nearly a hundred and fifty thousand people, with a University enrollment of around forty thousand. In fact, Ann Arbor's about the same size as Berkeley—just cleaner and prettier."

"So how come you were one of her subjects?" Braxton looked at Karl. "And how come you weren't?"

"Just lucky, I guess." Anneke made a face. "All I know is that when we got here, Richard directed us to this table and introduced us to her. She asked us a few questions, then told Karl she couldn't use him because he was a former athlete. By the time I realized what I'd gotten myself into, it was too late to back out."

"So Richard Killian was the one who put you at the victim's table." Braxton seized on the salient point, glancing over at Richard. "All right, let's see what we've got." He made a beckoning motion, and the Asian woman broke off her conversation with one of the uniforms and came forward. "Marcy, I want to talk to everyone who was at the table with the Summers woman. Would you get them all together at a table? Oh, and get Killian there, too. Wait—first, would you ask that doctor to come in to talk to me?"

"You got it, chief." She trotted away, and Braxton turned back to Karl. "I'd like you there, too, if you don't mind."

"Of course." It was phrased as a polite invitation, but it didn't sound optional. Anneke was suddenly aware that Karl's status as a cop didn't erase his status as a suspect. Or hers. She decided that strychnine was probably going to be too good for Richard Killian.

"You wanted to see me?" The doctor was a small, stocky woman with short salt-and-pepper hair chopped off in a functional bob. She shoved a pack of cigarettes into the pocket of her blue Michigan windbreaker and held out her right hand to Braxton. "Sarah Feingold, M.D."

"Inspector Peter Braxton, SFPD." He shook her hand, cocking his head at her. "You're a doctor and you smoke?"

"Right." She nodded, her bright eyes on Braxton's face. "You're gay, aren't you?"

"Yes." Braxton returned her gaze. "Is that a problem?"

"Hell, no." Dr. Feingold waved a hand airily. "I just figured, as long as we were discussing each other's personal habits, we oughta share."

Braxton opened his mouth to say something, closed it, then tried again. "What can you tell me about the death?" he asked finally.

"Not much," Dr. Feingold said. "She was already convulsing when I got there. Whatever it was, it was fast-acting. I'd say it was some sort of alkaloid, but of course your people will tell you more specifically."

"All right. Thanks." Braxton turned away and the doctor stumped back outside.

# FOUR

"I'm sure you want to get this over with as quickly as possible." Braxton stood next to a round table identical to the one at
which Lindsay Summers had died; Sergeant Marcy Liu sat in
one of the chairs. The suspects—Anneke couldn't think of a
more polite way to put it—stood around the perimeter, looking
annoyed or anxious or interested. "Now," Braxton directed,
"Sergeant Liu is sitting in for Lindsay Summers. Would the
rest of you please take the same seats you had before? Mr. Killian, if you and Mr. Genesko would just stand over here?"
Richard nodded jerkily. There were beads of sweat at his hair-
line, and deep lines at his mouth; he looked positively middle-
age—which of course he was, Anneke realized in some surprise.

There was a certain amount of milling as they sorted themselves out. Anneke found herself directly across the table from
Marcy Liu, as she had been from Lindsay Summers. To her
right, Blair and Elisa Falcone sat next to each other in expen-
sively dressed silence, each in their own isolated bubble.
George McMartin, to Elisa's right, appeared sunk in gloom, or
possibly dyspepsia.

To Anneke's left, Jeremy Blake and Mimi Rojas sat close together, their hands touching. Anneke hadn't realized before that they were a couple, but now she saw Mimi grip Jeremy's fingers in her own, and saw him respond by taking both her hands in a comforting squeeze, the muscles in his forearms rippling. Beyond them, Noelle Greene looked alert and interested rather than nervous; her eyes flicked occasionally to Barbara Williams on her left, next to Sergeant Liu.

So Lindsay had been flanked by George on her left and the reporter on her right. The most likely suspects, then? Not necessarily; Anneke tried to visualize the moments leading up to Lindsay's death and realized she'd been more interested in the game than in her tablemates.

"Inspector?" Richard's voice cracked on the word. He cleared his throat before continuing. "I think . . . that is . . ." He pointed to Barbara Williams. "She's a reporter."

"Oh?" Braxton turned to the woman. "Is that true, Ms. Williams?"

"Yeah." Barbara looked up from her notebook, her lank brownish hair screening her face. Richard stared at her as if she were a bad lot of hamburger, all his famous charm gone.

"This is bad enough without her peeking and prying into our private business," he said to Braxton.

"He's right, Inspector." Somewhat to Anneke's surprise, it was Mimi who spoke up. "If you're going to question us, it should be in private."

"Yes, of course." Braxton nodded. "But this is just preliminary, and to get an idea of how it happened." He held up a hand to stem Mimi's protest. "You can hold anything confidential for later. Just now, I'd simply like all of you to identify yourselves for the record."

"All right." Oddly, it was Mimi who spoke. "Let's just do it. Our identities will be public information anyway." She glanced at the others before continuing. "Mercedes Rojas," she said to Braxton. "Attorney with Garcia and Rosenberg." Anneke looked at her in surprise; Mimi's round young face didn't look anything like her mental image of a lawyer.

"Jeremy Blake." Jeremy's voice cracked slightly. "I own Blake's Fitness health clubs."

"George McMartin. Food writer." George clipped off the words; his left hand twitched at his clipped beard and he kept his eyes fixed on the table.

"Blair Falcone, of Falcone Venture Capital, Incorporated." Blair's voice was pleasant and conversational; he gazed directly at Braxton, man to man.

"Elisa Falcone. Inspector, will this take long?" she asked impatiently.

"I'll try to move things along as quickly as possible, Ms. Falcone." Braxton's words were polite but perfunctory; his eyes moved from her down the table.

"Noelle Greene. Vice president with Connor Finch investment bank." This time Anneke was truly startled. It must have showed in her face, because Noelle grinned across the table at her. "It's a very *big* investment bank," she said, extending both arms out to the sides and doing a burlesque shoulder roll that set her huge breasts quivering under the scarlet tee.

Even Braxton smiled. "All right. Thank you." He surveyed the table. "Now, I understand—" he flicked a glance at Anneke "—that Ann Arbor is a fair-sized town, but as a matter of form, I want to ask all of you if you'd ever met Lindsay Summers before this morning." There were general head-shakings. Braxton nodded as though he'd expected it, which he presumably had.

"All right," he went on. "Let's try this—how did you all happen to be here this morning?"

"Because of Richard's letter." Mimi seemed to have appointed herself spokeswoman.

"Richard's letter?" Braxton turned to face Richard. "What letter?"

"Just a note." Richard took a step backward, waving his hands in the air. "When Ms. Summers asked me if she could interview people here, and that there'd be a reporter along, I thought . . ." His eyes flicked to Barbara Williams.

So that's what this was all about—Richard playing absolutely true to form. Anneke would have laughed if the circumstances hadn't been so grim. Richard had thought Lindsay could be a publicity coup, and he'd papered the house with all the minor celebrities he could dredge up. He hadn't invited Karl because he was a cop; he'd invited him because he was an ex-football player. Too bad he hadn't bothered to find out the direction of Lindsay's reseach.

"I see." Anneke thought with some relief that Braxton actually did see. He returned his attention to the people at the table. "Did all of you receive invitations from Mr. Killian?"

"I didn't." Barbara Williams spoke without looking up; her voice sounded rusty with disuse.

"You're the reporter," Braxton said. "What paper are you with?"

"Freelance. I was doing this for the *Bay Guardian*. Right kind of story for them. Poisoning of America, that kind of thing." She ignored the outraged look on Richard's face.

"If you weren't invited, how did you happen to be here?" Braxton asked.

"Got interested in the diet wars, thought there might be a story in it. Saw Lindsay's name on a report to a Congressional committee, found out about her research." Barbara looked up for the first time. "When I wrote to her, she told me she was going to be in San Francisco and invited me to the restaurant to write about it."

"Diet wars?" Braxton was momentarily diverted.

"Right. See that?" Barbara jerked her head toward the outdoor patio. Anneke looked through the doors, but all she saw was Sarah Feingold, sitting by herself quietly smoking a cigarette. "Remember when the surgeon general declared smoking a national health emergency? Well, the tobacco wars are pretty much over, and the troops in the front lines have run out of enemies. So a couple of years ago, the surgeon general declared obesity the next national health crisis." She shrugged without looking at Braxton. "So now they're working on food-control legislation. Gonna get us all to look like Lindsay Summers." Her voice was flat and matter-of-fact.

"So you came here with her." Braxton returned to the main issue. "Were you with her the entire time she was here?"

"Yeah. Well, except for when I went to the buffet, and once to the john."

"You and she didn't go to the buffet together?"

Babara snickered, an unpleasant sound. "Are you kidding? Lindsay didn't go near the buffet."

"Didn't she eat anything at all?"

"He sent her some stuff from the kitchen." She indicated Richard, who backed up another step, directing a poisonous look at Barbara.

"She asked for some things that weren't on the buffet," he said defensively. "I just provided what she asked for."

"And that was . . . ?"

"Two pieces of unbuttered sourdough toast and six ounces of unsalted tomato juice with a wedge of lemon." Richard wrinkled his nose in unconscious distaste. "We had to send out for the tomato juice, so she didn't get it until I think just before halftime."

"And were those the only things she ate or drank?" Braxton's question, addressed to the group at large, elicited shrugs all around.

"Who brought her the juice and toast?"

"One of the waiters." Richard looked around as though expecting the waiter to pop out of the ground. "Probably Jase." Braxton made a slight head motion toward Marcy Liu, who rose from her seat and disappeared into the kitchen.

"Did Lindsay leave the table at all after her food was

brought to her?" Braxton returned to his questioning. No one replied. "Did anyone else touch her plate or glass—say, to move it aside?" Still no one replied.

"We weren't all sitting down the whole time, Inspector," Anneke said. "People got up and moved around—to the buffet for more food, to the bathroom, that kind of thing."

"But there were always several other people at the table, I assume." Braxton sounded gloomy, and no wonder, Anneke thought; if Lindsay Summers had been poisoned, there didn't seem to be any window of opportunity for anyone to do it. Except in the kitchen before her food was brought out, of course. She glanced at Richard, whose face indicated he'd reached the same conclusion.

"Truesdale's run," she said suddenly.

"I beg your pardon?" Braxton turned toward her.

"Cary Truesdale, the Michigan running back," she explained. "When he broke that forty-three-yard run at the end of the half, everyone was watching the TV screen." She flicked her eyes to the now-blank screen, wondered how the game had come out, and caught herself guiltily.

"That's true," Jeremy Blake agreed. "You could have run a herd of elephants across the table and no one would have noticed. Even the people who aren't particularly football fans turned to look, because there was such an uproar."

"In fact, I imagine that happened several times," Anneke said. "I know everyone turned around when Wade Furlong threw that touchdown pass in the first quarter. And again on that sixty-five-yard kickoff return. Well, maybe not everyone," she corrected herself.

"Did you all turn around to watch?" Braxton directed the question to the group at large.

"I know I did," George McMartin replied. "And I'm not even much of a football fan. It's an automatic reaction, I think, isn't it? When everyone in a group starts shouting, you turn around to see what the excitement's about."

"That last run—how long before Lindsay Summers collapsed did that one occur?" There were blank looks all around.

"Only minutes," Anneke said. "I was watching the halftime report because I wanted to see the Ohio State score. I'm pretty sure they were just reporting the Virginia Tech game when I heard . . ." She stopped, and Braxton nodded. "So I think if you get a tape of the game, you can time it exactly."

"You're sure of that." Braxton made it half question, half statement.

"Pretty well positive." Even under his questioning gaze, she refused to admit that her first thought when she saw Lindsay facedown on the table had been: Dammit, now I'll never get to see the rest of the game.

He took them through it again, with no further information forthcoming. Finally, he shrugged. "All right. Sergeant, will you please take Ms. Williams into the back and wait there with her? Ms. Williams, I'll be along shortly to ask you a few questions, and then you'll be free to go."

Barbara started to protest, then shrugged and stood, her expression sullen. "All right. I can find out anything I want to know later."

"Just stay away from the Maize and Blue," Richard warned her.

"It's a public place. I can come here if I want." She threw the last words over her shoulder as Marcy Liu took her by the elbow. Richard curled his lip at her.

"Ugly." Richard said the one word aloud to no one in particular, loud enough for Barbara to hear.

When Barbara and the sergeant had disappeared into a back room, Braxton turned back to the group. "Now, let me repeat a question I asked earlier. Did any of you know Lindsay Summers before today?" There was silence. And then there was the sound of throat-clearing.

"I did." Jeremy Blake looked directly at Braxton. "In fact, she was my ex-wife."

There were startled looks from the others. "She . . ." Mimi bit off whatever she was going to say.

Braxton's face remained neutral. "I see. How long ago was that?"

"More than ten years ago." Jeremy spread his hands. "Look, Lindsay and I were married for about a minute and a half, back when we were undergraduates. It was probably the most ridiculous pairing in the history of matrimony, and both of us realized it almost immediately. We got a quick divorce, went our separate ways, and haven't—hadn't—seen each other since." He looked directly at Braxton. "That's all there was to it."

Braxton started to speak, then stopped as Marcy Liu approached the table with a muscular, dark-haired young man in tow.

"Inspector, this is Jason Blethridge," she said. "He was the waiter who delivered the juice and toast."

Jason Blethridge was young and buffed and good-looking and apparently scared out of his wits. "All I did was take the stuff straight from the kitchen to the table." Blethridge's voice was a bleat of fear.

"Take it easy, son," Braxton soothed. "No one's accusing you of anything. Just tell us what you did."

"Like I said, I just took the glass of tomato juice from the kitchen, and put it on a tray and carried it right to the table. I didn't stop or nothing."

"Did you speak to anyone on your way?"

"No, honestly. I did just like I was told."

Braxton looked at him severely, and the boy shivered with fear but remained silent. After a moment, Braxton nodded and said: "All right. If you think of anything else, Jason, you'll let us know." It wasn't a question. Jason gulped and nodded and scuttled away.

Braxton returned his attention to Jeremy. "Did you know your ex-wife would be here today?"

Jeremy sighed. "Yes. It was in Richard's letter."

"So everyone at this table knew Lindsay Summers would be here." Braxton looked at Richard. "Was her presence publicized otherwise?"

"No." Richard shook his head agitatedly. "I didn't tell anyone else. Well, except Cody, I wanted him to know so he'd be on top of his game, you know?"

"So the kitchen knew also." Braxton was silent for several seconds. "All right, let's move on. If you'll all wait here, I'll get to you as expeditiously as possible."

He left them there staring at each other. Anneke glanced at the blank eye of the big television screen and wondered guiltily if she could suggest turning on SportsCenter.

# FIVE

"Well, other than that, Mrs. Lincoln, how did you enjoy the play?" Anneke grimaced at her own words. "Forget I said that, okay?" she said to Karl, at the wheel of the rented Ford Explorer. It was the kind of black humor that never seemed offensive on the Internet, but sounded ugly and unfeeling spoken aloud.

Still, the Internet approach at least had the virtue of honesty. She'd known Lindsay Summers for little more than an hour, and what she had known of her she'd disliked.

But what difference did that make? Couldn't she even have the common decency to feel horror and pity for a young life cut short? Apparently not; Anneke examined her real feelings with all the brutal candor she could muster, and discovered that her overriding emotion was . . . resentment.

She resented Lindsay Summers for spoiling her perfect honeymoon. Could I possibly be so hideously, unspeakably selfish? she asked herself. And at the same time every bit as unspeakably guilty for her own selfishness. Damn the girl—even dead, Lindsay Summers managed to guilt-trip people.

"Oh, shit." She leaned back against the passenger seat and looked out the window. To her right, a grove of silvery-barked trees drifted past. They seemed slightly blurred, and she saw that the fog was drifting in. "Where are we?" she asked. "Aren't we going back to the hotel?"

"Golden Gate Park." Karl answered her first question. "There's a place here I thought you'd enjoy." He steered the car into a narrow road bordered by overhanging trees, up a small incline, and emerged into pale, filtered light by the side of a small lake. In its center, a tree-covered island rose steeply above the sun-sparkled water.

Anneke got out of the car and stood for a moment on the narrow path, listening. She knew they couldn't be more than a hundred yards from city streets, but all she heard was lapping water and bird sound. Seagulls wheeled and squawked overhead; a few people sat on benches facing the lake; two small Asian children tossed chunks of bread to a quacking mass of mallards; a pair of elderly women strolled by, conversing quietly.

Anneke hadn't known the knot in her back was there until she felt it loosen. She spotted a small stone bridge on her right and grabbed Karl by the hand. "Let's go across to the island."

They strolled along the narrow path encircling the island, listening to the silence and the cry of seagulls and the skittering sound of an occasional squirrel. Then suddenly there was a waterfall, and across from it a small pagoda where they sat for a few minutes in the white noise of falling water.

"Look." Anneke pointed to a set of narrow wooden steps alongside the waterfall. "Does it go all the way to the top?"

"Let's find out." Karl stood up and led the way across damp broken paving stones. The steps barely qualified for the name, being little more than chunks of wood edging layers of earth, and when Anneke looked upward dubiously the steps seemed to disappear into the fog. She felt like Jack peering up at his beanstalk.

"Well?" Karl asked.

"I'm game if you are." He raised an eyebrow at her, and she grinned. "For the steps, I mean."

She took a tight grasp on the iron bar that served as a banister, and for a while they climbed into the fog. When they reached the second switchback landing, they could no longer see the lake and the waterfall was close enough to touch, its silvery flow disappearing through the fog and falling out of sight somewhere below them. She stepped off the landing into a tangle of trees and shrubbery, feeling it close around her until even the sound of the waterfall was muffled.

"We could be the only people in the world." She found herself whispering into the heavy silence.

"In that case, shouldn't we think about the future of the human race?" His arms closed around her from behind, and his mouth traced the line of her neck beneath her ear. She felt his warm breath on her skin and was amazed at the sudden spike of desire she felt. She turned inside the circle of his arms and pressed her body against his, and his hands moved under her shirt.

"How fast can we get back to the hotel?" she whispered.

"Not fast enough." He was grinning down at her, his hands making circles on her skin. She shivered. "Unless you're afraid someone will see us?"

She laughed at the challenge in his voice. "Afraid? Hell, you're the one who's the celebrity, Lieutenant." She found the buckle of his belt and slipped it open. "If we get busted, it'll be your name in the papers." The element of danger made her bolder instead of more cautious. She laughed again, louder this time, and he bent down and covered her mouth with his.

When they got back to the hotel there were three messages waiting for them, all from Richard. Anneke thanked the hotel operator and replaced the telephone receiver with a purposeful thump. "I'm going to shower and change clothes," she announced. "Then we're going to have an early—and light—dinner, and then we're going to the theater. But first . . ." She moved to the side of the bed.

"First?" Karl raised an eyebrow, grinning.

"First," she said, picking up the television remote, "we're going to turn on ESPN and find out the score of the damn game."

"Mmff?" Anneke felt herself dragged upward through a cloud of whipped cream, floating through a waterfall of chocolate syrup on her way to consciousness. She groped for the telephone and mumbled something into it.

"Anneke? Thank God. Listen, it's Richard. Please, I need you. You and Karl. Anneke, they think I killed her. Me or Cody. They think her juice was poisoned in the kitchen, but it wasn't, I swear to you. Please, you don't think I killed her, do you? Anneke?"

"Of course not, Richard." She shook her head to clear away whipped-cream cobwebs and glanced at the clock. Seven-thirty in the morning was a hell of a time to call people on their honeymoon.

"Thank God," Richard repeated fervently. "Look, everyone's going to be here at nine. You've got to help me."

"Richard, I—"

"Please, Anneke, they're going to destroy me. Even if they can't pin it on me—and they can't, I didn't do it, I swear—this'll destroy me. Just the rumors alone, the suspicion . . . You don't know this town. Please. You have to have breakfast anyway. Just come and talk to people, see if you can . . ."

"Richard, we have—"

"Please. Nine o'clock. Everyone else will be here waiting for you. Anneke, I'll be grateful forever. Thank you. Thank you."

"Richard—" She was talking to the dial tone. "Damn damn damn. *Shit*." She slammed down the receiver.

"I take it that was Richard?" Karl, propped on one elbow next to her, raised an eyebrow.

"Lieutenant, your powers of deduction never cease to amaze me."

"Oh, that was just a small sample. Let me expand. Richard is convinced the police think he poisoned Lindsay Summers, and he wants you, or more likely, us, to investigate. What's more, being raised on bad television and antique mystery novels, he's gathered all the suspects together and invited you to interrogate them en masse."

"Gee, I don't know how you do it, Nero."

"Oh, we have our ways. What's more, I further deduce that he hung up before you had a chance to refuse."

"Which doesn't mean we have to let ourselves be dragooned into this," she insisted.

"Of course not. At least," he said, reaching for her, "not for a little while, anyway."

# SIX

Most urban business districts feel abandoned on Sunday mornings; San Francisco felt . . . surreal. Skyscrapers disappeared into the fog above like dream towers, their truncated shapes suggesting hidden wonders just out of reach. In the pearl gray light, the cable cars gliding down California Street had a mysterious Flying-Dutchman quality, a manifestation out of time. The Bay Bridge in the distance was a wraith just barely sensed on the horizon.

The fairytale ambience disappeared with a thud once they reached the Maize and Blue, where Richard hurried them into a private dining room, chattering with nerves.

"Before anyone says a word, there's something you need to know." Karl gathered their attention. "This morning I called Inspector Braxton of the San Francisco PD. He agreed to let me interfere in his case—" he emphasized the word *his* "—so long as I report directly to him, fully and completely, every single thing I hear, see, infer, or deduce. Is that clear to everyone?" He paused. There were a few mutterings, but no overt objection from the eight people sitting at the round table in a private dining room.

Braxton, in fact, had been more amused than offended. "Hell, if you want to play Sherlock Holmes, it's all right with me." Listening on the extension, Anneke had heard the sardonic tone of his voice. "And I suppose there's always the chance that if you get them talking, one of them'll drop something. Your people have pretty good things to say about you, by the way."

"That's good to hear," Karl replied. "Did they have anything for you on the Summers woman's background?"

"Nothing relevant so far, but they're checking some more. Oh, and one more thing." He chuckled. "Wes Kramer said to ask you if the Viagra's working."

"So that's where it came from." Karl laughed aloud. "I should have guessed. If you talk to him again, please tell him his medication got into my suitcase somehow, and that I hope his girlfriend doesn't mind cold showers until we get back."

"Got it." Anneke could hear the grin in Braxton's voice. "I'll expect to hear from you as soon as the dog-and-pony show's over."

"Of course. No problem in the world. We want to cooperate with the police." Richard Killian spoke jerkily. Anneke thought he'd have agreed to self-immolation—or even a Big Mac—if Karl would get him out of this mess.

They were eating again, of course. This time the buffet was simpler—bagels with cream cheese and smoked salmon or smoked whitefish; light and crisp Danish pastries; strawberries dredged in confectioner's sugar; an assortment of tiny muffins. Anneke had resolutely settled on a single bagel with a thin layer of cream cheese, then at the last minute added a nearly translucent slice of smoked salmon. It was so thin, how fattening could it be? Now she took a bite and made a face. The smoked salmon was delicious, but the bagel was thick and soft and puffy, a kind of bready doughnut. If this thing showed up at Zingerman's, she decided, the only thing they'd use it for would be scrubbing tables.

"We've told the San Francisco police everything we could, you know," Elisa Falcone said. This morning she wore a charcoal gray cashmere sweater and matching tailored pants with a collection of gold chains at her neck. "But we do want to help Cody, of course." She patted the hand of the young man in the chair next to her. Anneke blinked; Cody Jarrett looked more like a high school student than a chef. A mildly punk high school student, with a splash of bright blue down one side of his blond hair, and two gold hoops in his left ear. Without the starched, impeccably white chef's jacket, he'd have looked like a kid on his way to a video arcade.

"I'm sure you did," Karl said to her. "And I'll tell you up front that I think this is going to be an exercise in futility. So if you'd all prefer not to waste your Sunday morning this way, I absolutely wouldn't blame you."

"No, we have to do something," Richard insisted. "Have you seen this?" He waved a newspaper at them.

"Oh, newspapers." Noelle Greene, resplendent in yards of dark red silk, flapped a hand holding a chocolate muffin. "Nobody pays any attention to the newspapers in San Francisco."

"Maybe not," George McMartin said, "but when people see the words 'restaurant' and 'poisoning' in the same sentence, they tend to draw unfortunate conclusions."

"Exactly." Richard dropped the paper on the table, and Anneke picked it up and read the story quickly while the others chattered and commiserated.

The coverage of the death itself was fairly straightforward, including the phrase "the police are treating Summers's death as a homicide." Still, the headline—WOMAN POISONED AT SF RESTAURANT—was the sort of thing calculated to send diners elsewhere. There were sketchy details about Lindsay Summers. Besides what she already knew, Anneke learned that Lindsay had been twenty-eight years old, unmarried, and originally from Chicago.

There was a sidebar about the Maize and Blue, and especially about Cody Jarrett, the twenty-five-year-old "wunderkind chef" who was bringing a "new sensibility to classic American cuisine." Cody and Richard, it seemed, were "reinventing Americana for the new millennium," "unashamed to revel in old-fashioned pleasures reinterpreted for our times." Sports and food, apparently, were so old they were new again. The story was bylined Frank Romano, but at the bottom were the words: "Food critic George McMartin also contributed to this report."

"I think we ought to go ahead." George took a bite of bagel and smoked salmon. "The faster this gets settled, the better. Cody, where did you get this salmon?"

"Coupla guys in Vancouver. They smoke their own salmon right off the boat." Cody grinned. "I grabbed up half their stock last month, right out from under Goldman's broker."

"Very delicate." George broke off a minuscule morsel of salmon and rolled it around in his mouth. "Perhaps a tad more salt?"

"That would make it more robust," Jeremy agreed.

"That might be fine for a bagel topping," Elisa said, "but in a salad it would overpower the greens. And you might lose that lovely silky texture."

"People, could we focus please?" Mimi Rojas interrupted. "We'll do whatever we can to get this solved, Lieutenant," she said to Karl.

"Are you serving as the attorney for everyone here?" he asked.

"For the moment." Mimi used a forefinger to settle her glasses more firmly on her nose. "Michigan Law, class of 'ninety-five. I'm Richard's attorney."

"All right then." Karl regarded them all for a moment before directing his attention to Richard. "The group at Lindsay Summers's table wasn't random or self-selected, was it?"

"N-no." Richard looked sheepish. "It was . . . Okay, look, here's what happened." The words came out in a rush. "I got this letter from the Summers girl saying that she was doing research on food choices—that's exactly the phrase she used—and could she come by and interview people here. She went on and on about how San Francisco was such a great food city, and how she wanted an educated sample, and that there'd even be a reporter with her." He spread his hands. "So of course I said yes. How did I know she was out to do a hatchet job?"

"You might have asked a more probing question than, 'How soon can you get here'," Blair Falcone said acidly.

"That's not fair," Richard said. "Besides, you thought it was a great idea, too."

"Let's not waste time with recriminations." Jeremy Blake interrupted the incipient argument. "We got mousetrapped, that's all."

"And anyway," Richard went on, "it's not like I just turned her loose here. I made sure she talked to people who'd say the right things, didn't I?"

Karl held up a hand. "Exactly why did you select these particular people?"

"Because I wanted her to talk to people who could be trusted. And everyone here has a stake in the Maize and Blue's reputation."

"How so? Are you all investors?" Karl asked.

"Not exactly." It was Mimi who answered. "At least, not yet." She darted a glance at Blair Falcone, who took a bite of muffin and chewed thoughtfully for a moment.

"All right," he said finally. "It's not a deep, dark secret, I suppose." He paused. "Here's the thing, Lieutenant. Cody

Jarrett's a hot property here in San Francisco, but so far he's primarily a local phenomenon. We believe that he's got national potential—that Nouvelle Midwest can be the next big food trend. Our intention is a carefully managed expansion into selected markets, all featuring Cody's food. But since we're still working out the details, we'd rather our plans not become publicly known until we're ready to announce."

"How would the expansion work?" Karl asked. "Would you simply license his name and his recipes to use in other restaurants?"

"No." Blair shook his head. "For one thing, Cody's under contract to the Maize and Blue for another two years, so Cody and Richard are a package deal. Besides, the Maize and Blue concept is a sound one. We may expand it to include Fighting Irish or Halls of Ivy sports bars, something like that, but the general theme of college nostalgia is highly marketable, and Cody's food plays directly to it."

Anneke, who'd been typing notes on her laptop, looked up from the keyboard. "What about a Stanford or Cal bar? I'd think that would give you a larger local clientele."

"No, you're missing the point." Blair shook his head. "This is about nostalgia, not reality. The farther you get from an experience, the rosier it looks. Sort of like the old joke—How can I miss you if you won't go away?"

"I see your point." Anneke nodded. "I suppose a Maize and Blue would be redundant in Ann Arbor, wouldn't it?"

"What exactly is your role in this?" Karl asked Blair. "Will you be managing the operation?"

"Good heavens, no. I'm strictly venture capital. I doubt that I could tell a chanterelle from a morel."

"Oh, that reminds me," Elisa said. "Cody, are you going to be doing that morel quiche this month? Coco Linehan asked about it specifically."

"Probably not." Cody shook his head. "I can only get them

dried this time of year, and they just don't have the same flavor."

"The Pagan Grotto does a garlicky morel steak sauce that's out of this world," Mimi said.

"I thought it was too garlicky," Blair contradicted.

"Well, that's typical of Benito, isn't it?" Elisa cocked her head. "So heavy-handed."

"Will one of you be managing the operation?" Karl wrenched the conversation back on track. "Or will you be hiring from outside?"

"I'm the chief operating officer." Jeremy Blake flexed his biceps; he didn't seem conscious of doing it. "I won't have anything to do with the actual food side of it, of course—that's Cody's job—but beyond that, operating a chain of specialized restaurants isn't all that different from operating a chain of specialized health clubs. Maintain quality, never lose sight of your target market, and don't try to expand too far or too fast." He recited the last sentence like a mantra. "And locally, at least, my reputation as a health-and-fitness expert can be useful, too."

"What about you, Ms. Greene?" Karl turned to Noelle. "What's your role in this?"

"You mean besides being their best customer?" Noelle's booming laugh produced general smiles. "I'm a vice president at Connor Finch, the investment bank. We're going to be involved in the financing. If this little problem goes away, that is."

"And you, Mr. McMartin?"

"Now that's a little harder to explain." George McMartin stared upward in thought before continuing. "Lieutenant, I have a, ah, certain reputation in the world of food. And my, ah, influence seems to count for something. Now, mind you, I'm very sensitive to the ethical question involved, and I have every intention of disclosing my, ah, interest in the Maize and Blue venture."

"In other words," Karl deconstructed George's words, "you will be providing publicity?"

"Oh, not publicity per se," George said hurriedly. "Just, shall we say, adding credibility to Cody's perfectly deserved reputation."

"In fact, publicity's just a matter of getting noticed by the right people," Elisa Falcone said shrewdly, patting the young chef's hand again. Cody, who was scribbling on a lined pad, didn't seem to notice. "Politicians, socialites, actors, sports figures—the trick is to attract the names who attract the media. Like yourself." She smiled at Karl.

"I'm long out of the celebrity category," he said.

"Oh, don't sell yourself short, Lieutenant. After all, your name was in the *Chronicle* last week."

"It was?"

"Didn't you see it?" She laughed a tinkling laugh. "In the sports section. They mentioned that you were at a Forty-Niners practice."

"So that's how you knew we were in town." Karl looked at Richard, who shrugged and grinned uneasily. "And I imagine you just called hotels until you found us. Never mind." He turned back to Elisa. "So your role is to make Cody Jarrett trendy."

"Exactly!" She clapped her hands.

"The thing is," Noelle said, "not only is there no possible motive for any of us to have killed that girl, but as a group we'd have every motive to prevent it—at least, the way it happened. Having someone poisoned at your restaurant isn't exactly the way to endear it to the movers and shakers."

"And except for Jeremy, none of us had ever even heard of her before yesterday." Mimi directed a sharp look at Jeremy before biting into a slice of smoked salmon rolled around a thick log of cream cheese.

"And I told you I hadn't laid eyes on her for over ten years,"

Jeremy said plaintively. He eyed Mimi's salmon-and-cream-cheese log. She stared a warning back at him. "I'm sorry," he burst out, "but I can't stand seeing you kill yourself with that stuff. How could you fall for that charlatan Cornwell?"

"I'll overlook the slander because you obviously don't know what you're talking about. What I will remind you of is that a year ago I weighed one hundred seventy pounds, my blood pressure was two hundred over ninety, and I could hardly drag myself out of bed in the morning. Craig Cornwell's way of eating just about saved my life."

"It's ridiculous and dangerous, and you know it," Jeremy said hotly. "Do you know what all that fat is doing to your heart? And your arteries? Not to mention that you're guaranteed to gain it all back because you won't be able to keep denying yourself the foods you crave."

"Denying myself! I eat bacon and eggs for breakfast. I eat filet mignon, or chicken in cream sauce, or salmon with all the butter I want. I have cream in my coffee. What's more, I can eat as much as I want and I never have to feel hungry. Can you say the same thing?"

"Sure I can. The difference is, I fill up with healthy foods, not artery-clogging—"

"Oy! Knock it off!" Noelle's big voice overrode them both. "We're all tired of hearing you argue about this. If you two want to fight the diet wars, do it on your own time, all right?"

"Yes, but she—"

"I'm sick and tired of—"

"When we're done here, you can take it to the kitchen and go three rounds with rusty paring knives for all I care, but for the moment, do you think you could you possibly focus on our business and not your diet fetishes?" Noelle sounded legitimately angry. There were murmurs of agreement around the table.

"Sorry." Jeremy grinned sheepishly. "It's just . . . I worry about you," he said to Mimi.

"Well, you'll have to get over it," Mimi said unforgivingly. "It's not flattering and it's not charming and it's not something I want to come home to every night."

"I know, I know." Jeremy sighed. "Let's have coffee this afternoon and I'll work on it, okay? At least we can agree on Peet's."

"With real cream?" Mimi's lips twitched, in what could have been a half smile. "Now," she said briskly, "where were we?"

# SEVEN

"I believe you were talking about motive." Karl answered Mimi's question. "Ms. Rojas, you said that nobody here had ever heard of Lindsay Summers until yesterday. In fact, though, you have no way of knowing that."

"I suppose I don't," Mimi replied reluctantly.

"But that's silly, Lieutenant," Elisa Falcone said. "What connection could there possibly be between us and some random student?"

"I think the connection is fairly obvious." Noelle Greene waved an arm to encompass the maize-and-blue-filled room. Pennants and banners hung from the ceiling. A mural of the Diag covered the rear wall. The other walls were nearly filled with photographs of Michigan sports events and signed pictures of University of Michigan celebrities, athletes and playwrights and politicians and actors.

"Oh, well, I suppose." Elisa shrugged. "I'm not a Michigan alumnus myself. But in any case, that was back in college."

"Let me ask you something." Karl spoke to the group generally. "How did you all happen to get together in the first place?"

"Actually, through Michigan activities, one way and another." Jeremy Blake nodded his understanding. "Either through the San Francisco alumni club, or right here watching football or basketball games, things like that. Networking is one of the things alumni groups are for, after all."

"Which of you has been back to Ann Arbor in, say, the last two years?" Karl asked. Hands went up slowly, but in the end, all of them were raised except Cody Jarrett's and Elisa Falcone's.

"In fact, Lieutenant, I've never set foot in Ann Arbor in my life." Elisa sounded like she was bragging.

"I was there once with some friends when I was in high school," Cody said, "but I never had anything to do with the University."

"So all but two of you have been to Ann Arbor recently," Karl said.

"All right, point taken." Mimi looked at him. "But it's a hell of a big university. Why would any of us have crossed paths with some random grad student in public health?"

"I have no idea," Karl replied. "But since she'd never been to San Francisco before, it seems the likeliest place to start. Let me ask you all specifically—when did you last visit Ann Arbor, and for what purpose?"

"I was there just last month, for a board meeting," George offered. "I'm on the Board in Control of Student Publications, so I go there half a dozen times a year."

"How long were you there?" Karl asked.

"Just overnight." George shrugged. "Flew in, attended the meeting, stayed at the Campus Inn, flew out the next day." He turned to his left, passing the question to Blair.

"July, for a business school convocation," Blair said. "I spent most of my time with faculty and administrators, mostly talking about fund-raising."

"Not since last November." Richard squirmed as eyes turned to him. "I went back for homecoming, that's all. Just a football weekend." He sounded oddly defensive.

"In fact, I was there just last week," Noelle answered. "I was researching a company in Troy that's looking for expansion capital, so I stayed in Ann Arbor." She grinned. "I also spent an evening at the casino over in Windsor, so you can probably confirm my visit through customs records."

"I was there last month, but only for a quick visit." Jeremy glanced at Mimi out of the corner of his eye. "I was at a friend's wedding in Flint, but I drove down to Ann Arbor one afternoon just to wander around the place, have a bagel at Zingerman's, you know."

"And I haven't been back for more than a year," Mimi said. "Summer before last, for one of the law school's continuing ed classes." She twisted in her chair. "Look, this isn't getting us anywhere. Sure, all of us have Ann Arbor connections, but that's a given anyway."

"Besides," George said suddenly, "are we so sure it had to be one of us? What if someone sneaked into the kitchen and poisoned her juice before it came out?"

"The trouble with that scenario," Karl pointed out, "is that it had to be someone who knew she'd be here. And for that matter, knew it was her juice. This was a premeditated crime—people don't carry deadly poison around with them for no reason." He turned to Richard. "Who did you tell about Lindsay's visit?"

"Just the people here," he replied gloomily. "I thought about sending out a press release, but since there was going to be a reporter here anyway, I decided not to. I sent direct invitations to some other people—" he glanced at Anneke and quickly looked away "—but I didn't mention Lindsay."

"Still, we don't know who Lindsay might have told," George insisted. "Maybe a former boyfriend, for instance. Anyone could have sneaked into the kitchen," he repeated stubbornly.

"Not in my kitchen, they didn't." Cody Jarrett spoke in a matter-of-fact tone just this side of arrogance.

"How can you be so sure, Mr. Jarrett?" Karl asked.

"Take a look." Cody stood up and adjusted his white jacket.

"Oh, we believe you, Cody." Elisa glared at George.

"He still oughta see for himself," Cody said.

"That's not a bad idea," Karl agreed. "Why don't you show us how a restaurant kitchen operates?" He stood up and glanced briefly at Anneke, who left her doughy bagel behind without regret and followed the two men through a pair of swinging doors and into chaos. She had an impression of white, and chrome, and steam, and thumps, and metallic banging sounds, and deep, rich aromas. As far as she was concerned, six terrorists in Day-Glo ski masks could have charged into the kitchen and no one would have noticed.

There were about twenty people racketing from range to countertop to chopping block and back again; she kept losing track because none of them remained in one place long enough to be counted accurately. All of them wore white; the effect was a lot like watching the negative of a Jackie Chan movie.

But of course Jackie Chan movies weren't really chaotic whirls of action, she reminded herself. In fact, they were carefully choreographed and perfectly controlled. She looked more closely at the activity in front of her, and saw patterns of movement begin to emerge.

Cody seemed unfazed by the frantic activity. "See? It's all organized around six stations, and everyone has an assigned location. Anyone who didn't belong here would be spotted immediately."

"How can you be so sure?" Anneke asked. "They're all so frantic I wouldn't think they'd notice."

"They're not frantic," Cody contradicted her. "They know exactly what they're doing. That's the whole point. They'd notice an outsider because anyone out of place would interrupt the work flow. Everyone knows where they're supposed to be and who else is supposed to be there with them. A stranger would stand out like an artichoke in a cheesecake. The Summers chick sure did."

"Lindsay Summers was here in the kitchen?"

"Sure. Richard brought her in. She must've poked around for ten minutes or so annoying people. I thought Miguel was gonna deck her."

"Who is Miguel?"

"The pastry chef. She wanted to know what was in the galette, and of course he wouldn't tell her, and she accused him of exploiting fat addicts, or something like that." He plucked a strawberry from a basket on the counter and bit into it. His face darkened, and the blue streak in his hair seemed to bristle.

"Lena, are these from Hampton?"

"Yes." A young Asian woman stopped whisking something in a copper bowl. "Something wrong?"

"Yeah, they're woody. Didn't you check the shipment when it got here?"

"Just a quick look." Her voice was matter-of-fact, but she regarded Cody from under her eyelids in a gesture just this side of flirtatious. "Hampton's always been totally reliable."

"Well, not this time. Tell them that if there's ever another batch like this we'll buy from Kalajian." Cody was clearly oblivious to the woman's signals. "Meanwhile, don't use these whole. Cut them up and macerate them in lime juice and sugar. No, brown sugar." He cocked his head, staring at the ceiling for several seconds. "And I think I'll add allspice, but let me do that. We can use it in strawberry crepes, and maybe with some pound cake." He trotted to a small desk and scribbled away on a yellow pad. "Gotta change the dinner menu," he said to Karl when he was done.

"Tricky, doing it on the fly like that, isn't it?"

"Not really." Cody shrugged. "Just working with what you've got, that's all."

"But don't you have to test recipes before you use them?" Anneke asked curiously.

"If it's complicated, maybe. But most of the time I already know what it's supposed to taste like. I test it to see if it's right."

"So you start out with a taste in your mind, and work with the ingredients to replicate it?"

"Sure."

"Like a musician's perfect pitch."

"Yeah, I guess." Cody seemed struck by the notion. "Right." He smiled and nodded. The smile made him look about sixteen.

"Is it always this busy?" Karl asked.

"Well, Saturdays and Sundays are more complex than the rest of the week, because we open at nine A.M. for the football crowds." He moved from the desk to one of the cooktops and peered into a huge stainless steel stockpot. "We do a special weekend menu—brunch until two P.M., then a series of small plates for snacking, kind of like midwestern tapas, and then we do a dinner menu from five o'clock on. So we're on the clock from the time we get here, cooking one set of dishes while preparing for the later ones." He stirred the ingredients of the stockpot with a wooden spoon, raised the spoon, and sniffed at it delicately.

Karl made a motion to indicate the white-coated staff. "Are these the same people who were here yesterday morning?"

"Mostly." Cody replaced the wooden spoon in the stockpot and took two steps to the oven. "I think the weekend vegetable chef is off today—his son's sick. Otherwise, this is the full weekend staff. But the police already questioned all of them, and they swore no one set foot in the kitchen who wasn't supposed to." He peered through the window in the oven door.

"And if there's any connection between Lindsay Summers

and anyone in your kitchen, they'll have a lot better luck finding it than we will." Karl spoke almost to himself. "All right," he said to Cody. "Thank you."

They returned to the dining room. "I think," Karl announced, "that, at least for the moment, we should proceed on the assumption that no outsider got into the kitchen."

"Of course not," Elisa said firmly.

"Which means it pretty well has to be one of us." Mimi Rojas's tone was grim. "So what do we do now?"

"I have to get back to the kitchen." Cody remained standing, bouncing on the balls of his feet. "Have to get ready for the crowds."

"That's right." Richard checked his watch. "The Forty-Niner game starts in a couple of hours."

Anneke looked at her own wristwatch and calculated driving times. She glanced at Karl anxiously. He nodded in her direction but kept his attention on Cody.

"A couple of questions before you leave, Mr. Jarrett. Where did you work before coming here?"

"I didn't." Cody shrugged. "Richard hired me right out of CCA."

"That's the California Culinary Academy here in San Francisco," Richard amplified.

"Isn't that rather unusual?" Karl raised an eyebrow. "To pluck someone right out of school for a job this big?"

"Yes and no," Richard replied. "I was looking for something different, someone who wasn't locked into the same old same old, you know? I mean, the last thing this city needs is another fusion-California-French-Asian-whatnot. Cody didn't have any previous restaurant experience, but he had his own vision. And of course he had experience in CCA's own restaurants." On his own ground talking about his own field, Richard seemed more self-assured. "The only concern was whether he was too young to manage a staff, and that's never been a problem."

"Besides," Elisa Falcone interjected, "it wasn't that big until Cody got here."

"I suppose that's true." Richard smiled amiably. "I won't deny that Cody's the one who made the Maize and Blue hot."

"How did you come across him in the first place? Was that also through alumni networking?"

"I recommended him," George McMartin volunteered. "I met him when I did a piece on CCA for *USA Today*."

"And you yourself have no connection to Michigan?" Karl asked Cody.

"Nope. Wisconsin, until I came out here four years ago." Cody bounced in impatience. "Look, if I don't get back to the kitchen, that duck confit is going to taste like canned hash." He turned and left without waiting for dismissal.

"We're not really getting anywhere, are we." Blair Falcone made it a statement rather than a question.

"And if the motive has its roots in Ann Arbor," George McMartin pointed out, "there really isn't anything we can do here anyway." He shoved his chair back from the table slightly, as if preparing to leave.

"Ann Arbor." Richard's eyes widened. "Look, what if . . ."

Anneke had a sudden premonition about what he was about to say. But before he could go on, there was a knock on the dining room door, and a voice said: "Mr. Killian? Can I talk to you?"

The nondescript woman standing in the doorway looked familiar, but it took Anneke a second to recognize her. Barbara Williams, the reporter who'd been with Lindsay Summers.

"I'm sorry, but this is a private function." Richard spoke sharply; his eyes flicked over the woman's round, flat face and the sagging brown skirt she wore, and dismissed her. He stood up and went toward the door. "We have nothing to say to the press at this time." He tried to close the door, but Barbara held her ground.

"Mr. Killian, I'm going to do a story about Cody Jarrett for the *Chron*. You can use all the good publicity you can get." She rattled off the words quickly, squeezing them against Richard's attempt to eject her.

"No, sorry." Richard shook his head. "No interviews right now."

"You've got everyone here." She craned her neck to see into the room. "Are you talking about the murder? Do you think it was one of you people?"

"Sorry, but you'll have to leave now."

"But all I—"

"Ms., uh, sorry, no comment. That's all."

"But—" She was still talking as Richard shoved the door closed against her by pure force. He wiped his hand over his face. "My God, that's all we need."

"Better warn Cody," Jeremy Blake said.

"And the rest of the kitchen staff." George McMartin looked as worried as Richard. "That woman smells like trouble."

"I'll call the *Chron*," Elisa Falcone offered. "They don't usually make trouble for local businesses, especially ones that attract tourists. And the last thing anyone wants is bad press for the restaurant trade."

"I thought she was writing for some other publication." Anneke tried to recall Barbara's statement yesterday. *"The Guardian?"*

"That's right, she did say that, didn't she?" Mimi pondered. "If she's passing herself off as a *Chron* reporter, we'd better talk to both papers. Let them handle her." She sighed. "What now?" she looked at Karl expectantly.

"I'm afraid we have to leave," he said, to Anneke's relief.

"But we haven't come up with anything," Richard protested.

"Richard, I simply don't see anything I can do." Karl held out his hands, palms up. "The San Francisco police will handle it. Trust me, they have no intention of railroading anyone."

"I know, but what if they never . . . Look," Richard said. "If this is really connected to Ann Arbor somehow, what about having someone investigate at that end?"

"In fact, Inspector Braxton is already in touch with the Ann Arbor police."

"Sure, but all they'll do is maybe a background check on Summers, stuff like that. They won't actively investigate, will they?" There was a pleading look on his face. "What about . . ."

Anneke sighed. She already knew what he was going to ask.

# EIGHT

"Is there a Zoe Kaplan around?" The freshman trainee yelled her name out across the *Michigan Daily* city room, interrupting Zoe's search for the perfect word to describe Michigan's star wide receiver. She'd reluctantly discarded "asshole" and was contemplating "schmuck," or possibly "dickhead."

"Over here," she called, temporarily putting aside fantasies of journalistic revenge. "Who is it?"

"Guy named Richard Killian."

"Who? You're kidding." Zoe scooted her chair from the row of computer terminals to the sports desk and reached for the phone, pausing only briefly before punching in the line and picking up the receiver. "Hello?"

"Zoe! Beautiful girl, thank heaven you're there. Darlin', tell me you haven't lost your gift for investigating."

"Hello, Richard." Zoe grinned into the receiver. Richard was a hound, but at least when he put the moves on you, he did it with a little class. Unlike a certain wide receiver she could name. Although, when they'd met last year during an NCAA investigation, Richard hadn't bothered to mention that he was married. "How's your wife?" she asked sweetly.

"Rich, Republican, and remarried," he said.

"Oops. Sorry, Richard."

"Ah, well." He sighed dramatically. "Zoe, I need you."

"Now, Richard, I'm sure once the word gets out that you're available there'll be thousands of beautiful San Francisco girls lining up at your door." Zoe laughed at herself; even though she knew he was game-playing, she could feel the warmth of his charm creeping down the phone line.

"Ah, but darlin', none of them will have your eyes, those beautiful copper-colored eyes that see into a man's soul."

Zoe burst out laughing. "God, Richard, you must want something awfully bad to bring out the heavy artillery." As she said it, she realized it was true. "What's going on?"

"Do you happen to know a woman—a grad student—named Lindsay Summers?"

Zoe thought for a minute. "No. Should I?"

"Then it hasn't made the Ann Arbor papers yet?"

"What hasn't? I haven't seen this morning's paper yet. Come on, Richard," she said impatiently, "what's going on?"

She could hear Richard take a deep breath. "Lindsay Summers was murdered yesterday in the Maize and Blue."

"Yikes." Zoe realized she could have said something more solemn. "And she was a Michigan student? What happened?"

She listened while he recounted the events of Saturday morning, scribbling notes on a sheet of copy paper from force of habit. It wouldn't be her story, of course—she already had two sports stories due for tomorrow's *Daily*—but she'd turn it over to someone on the city side. She was just about to interrupt Richard's account when she heard him say the names "Karl and Anneke."

"You must be joking." Zoe blinked. "They were there?"

"They're here right now," Richard said. "But you see, that's the problem. They're *here*, but we need someone in Ann Arbor."

So that was it. Zoe put down her pencil and leaned back in her chair. "Let me talk to Anneke."

"Right. Just a minute." Zoe heard muttering in the background, then:

"Hello, Zoe." Anneke's voice sounded half-amused, half-resigned.

"Sheesh, is this your idea of a romantic honeymoon?"

"Right. And after this we're going to spend a couple of days field-stripping a Jeep."

"So what's going on? Are you two really investigating?"

"Absolutely not."

"Liar," Zoe said cheerfully. "So what do you want me to do?"

"Don't ask me. I'm just a passenger on this bus."

"Well then, why don't you let me talk to the driver?"

"Gladly. Hang on."

"Hello, Zoe." Genesko's deep voice rumbled through the receiver.

"Hi, Lieutenant. Boy, you really know how to throw a honeymoon."

"So it seems." He paused. "I'm not officially involved in this case, of course."

"But?" Zoe knew a "but" when she didn't hear one.

"The Ann Arbor connection feels too strong to ignore." He spoke slowly, measuring his words. "At the same time, it's so amorphous that there doesn't seem to be a handle on it. The AAPD will investigate, of course, but . . ."

"But it's not their case, so they can't afford to spend hours of manpower on it." Zoe nodded at the phone. "Well, amorphous is my middle name." She picked up her pencil again and grabbed a clean sheet of copy paper. "Okay, what do you want me to do? And what's on and off the record?"

When she finally hung up, after fending off Richard's protestations of undying devotion, she had a list of eight names, a couple of brief notes about each, and a pretty good story that some city side reporter would get the credit for. She also had no idea where to start, especially since it was Sunday and the public health school would be closed.

Well, start with Lindsay Summers herself, she decided after a moment. Her housemates, if she had any, ought to be home. But first she'd better get back to her computer terminal and finish ripping a new asshole for a certain wide receiver.

Lindsay Summers had lived in one of the anonymous cardboard-and-aluminum buildings that erupted, like fungus, on various blocks near campus. The living room was a square white box floored with stained, worn carpet of that peculiar green only rapacious landlords seem able to find. A row of cheap kitchen appliances sulked behind a peeling Formica counter, where Zoe sat next to Lindsay's housemate on a wobbly bar stool.

"I just didn't know her that well," Jill Sainsbury said for the third time. Jill was tall and dark-skinned and muscular, athletic-looking in the way only a real athlete could manage. Her Michigan tee was baggy and faded, but the Lycra shorts that strained over her thickly muscled thighs were bright and new, and she could have fed a small third-world country for the price of the Nikes on her long feet.

"You didn't run together, I assume?" Zoe asked. Jill Sainsbury was a Runner, capital R. She already held the NCAA record for the 400 meters, and everyone who understood women's track expected her to hold a lot more before she was through. Zoe, who'd never covered track, hadn't met her before, but at least Jill had recognized her name from *Daily* bylines.

"Good Lord, no." Jill looked at Zoe as though she were

insane. "Lindsay was lucky if she could do two miles without collapsing. No big surprise, the way she starved herself."

"So I assume you didn't do meals together either."

"Meals?" Jill snorted. "Lindsay didn't eat 'meals.' She ate, I don't know, stuff. One cup of raw vegetables, three ounces of steamed fish, two and a half strawberries, things like that. Everything measured and weighed and calculated like a freaking science experiment." As though the conversation was making her hungry, Jill reached a muscular arm across the counter and snatched a handful of pretzels.

"If you had so little in common, how'd you come to be housemates?" Zoe was frankly curious. In her experience, jocks roomed with jocks, and sadly, blacks roomed with blacks.

"I was Leanna Jordan's roommate." Jill's direct gaze challenged Zoe, who nodded with what she hoped was a matter-of-fact air. Leanna Jordan was—had been—a ranking volleyball player until she'd been caught shoplifting. Not the usual student nonsense of lifting a six-pack, either. Leanna Jordan had been stopped at the door of a local jewelry store with a twenty-thousand-dollar diamond bracelet stuffed casually in the pocket of her Michigan warmup jacket.

"Tough," Zoe said. "So you needed a roommate fast, and Lindsay Summers showed up?"

"Right." Jill relaxed fractionally, as though Zoe had passed some sort of test. "She was the best of the lot who answered my ad. In fact, when she said she was doing food research, I thought it might be interesting."

"And it wasn't." Zoe made it a statement of fact.

"Shit, no." Jill popped a handful of pretzels into her mouth. "The chick was obsessed with food. I think she was trying to find out how little people could eat and still survive, you know?" She shoved the bowl of pretzels across the table and Zoe took one and munched on it for a minute.

"Was she bulimic, do you think?"

"I don't think so." Jill shook her head. "I never heard her

hurl, anyway. And I don't think she really qualified as anorexic, either, at least not as I understand it." Most women athletes, Zoe knew, had an unfortunate familiarity with the whole range of eating disorders. "I mean, she wasn't scary thin, and she wasn't trying to get any thinner." She cocked her head. "I think," she said slowly, "that she hated food, like it was some kind of punishment. Something she knew she had to endure, but she wanted to make it as painless as possible. Kind of the way some people feel about exercise, you know?"

Zoe, who did know because she was one of those people, nodded sagely.

"The worst of it was," Jill went on, "she thought everyone else should feel exactly the way she did. You know she was working with that Healthy Food thing?"

"The what?"

"I think it's called the Healthy Food Initiative. It's a campus group that's lobbying the U to improve their food service."

"That doesn't sound so bad." Zoe had endured her share of Jell-O salads and other repulsive dorm offerings.

"Depends on what you call improvement. And how you go about doing it," Jill said. "Believe me, you wouldn't want dorm meals à la Lindsay Summers."

"Was she heading this group?"

"I don't think so. She just mentioned that she was writing some proposals for them and I think helping them set up some research thingie." Jill took a swig from a plastic bottle of water. "I've gotta admit, every time she started talking about it I tuned her out."

"Did she try to get you to eat her way?"

"Only once." Jill scowled so fiercely that Zoe didn't pursue the issue. Instead she asked:

"How come Lindsay needed a place to live so late in the semester?"

"She said she'd been planning on someplace else, but it fell through."

"Oh?" Zoe's interest quickened. "Did she say what it was?"

"Not exactly." Jill cocked her head in thought. "She said something about some guy, but she didn't go into details. She was kind of secretive about it, you know? If I had to guess, I'd guess it was a guy who was married and didn't come through like she'd hoped."

"She didn't give you any idea who he was?"

"Nope." Jill shrugged. "Remember, she was only here for a month. And the truth is, we didn't really talk all that much. Between classes, and practice, and workouts, I don't have a lot of time for just hanging, you know?"

"When you did talk, what did you talk about?" The more Zoe heard about Lindsay Summers, the more curious she became.

"That's easy," Jill replied promptly. "Food. I told you, Lindsay was obsessed with it. She wasn't just interested in campus food, you know. She was out to prove that the government needed to control what everyone ate."

"So she talked about her research?"

"A little. I've gotta admit I tuned her out most of the time. If I ate the way she did, I couldn't break fifteen seconds for the hundred." Jill laughed at the notion. Zoe, whose short legs were the bane of her life, wondered if she herself could even break twenty. "Anyway," Jill went on, "when she was home, she spent most of her time at her computer."

"I suppose she wasn't home that much anyway," Zoe said.

"Well, I'm not either, so I don't really know. But I know she spent a lot of time at Carr's office."

"Carr?"

"Griffith Carr, the congressman. He was going to introduce some sort of law based on Lindsay's research. At least, that's what Lindsay said."

"No shit." Zoe scribbled the name Carr in her notebook and scrawled a circle around it. "That'd be a real coup for a grad student. So her stuff must've been pretty good?"

"Beats me." Jill shrugged. "If you want to take a look, it's probably all on her computer." She jerked her head toward a closed door behind her.

"If it's okay, sure. It'd help to be able to include her work." Zoe kept to the fiction that she was doing a profile of a murder victim.

"I don't see why not." Jill stood up, towering over Zoe even with the added height of the bar stool she sat on. "The police have already been here, and her parents are coming tomorrow to take her stuff away." She put her Nike-clad foot on the bar stool and leaned forward, touching her forehead to her ankle. "I want to do some stretching before practice. You go ahead, if that's all right."

"Sure," Zoe said again, feeling a familiar bubble of excitement and trying to keep it out of her voice. "No reason to waste any more of your time."

# NINE

Candlestick Park is a big concrete bowl out on a spit of land extending into the Bay, as windy and uncomfortable as its mythology advertised. Anneke sat with Karl on the end of the 49ers' bench, surrounded by and occasionally bumped into by large, sweaty, dirt-smeared men who ignored her as though she were invisible. Here at ground level, it was harder to follow the action than it was from up in the stands; you couldn't see the plays unfold, and there always seemed to be someone in the way. (Although, she noted, Karl didn't seem to be having any trouble.)

So why was she enjoying it so much? She concluded finally that while you could see less, you could feel more. The raw and often violent emotion seemed to ripple down the bench and surround her. As the first half neared its end, an Atlanta receiver catapulted into her, courtesy of a bone-jarring hit by a 49er safety. When she caught her breath, she realized she had blood on the sleeve of her camel's-hair jacket.

It was, she thought—except for the small matter of murder—the best honeymoon she could imagine.

"Want to come into the clubhouse?" Mike McCauley asked Karl. "I wouldn't mind having you talk to the boys." McCauley, the 49ers' linebacker coach, was a short, stocky redhead who'd been a third-stringer during Karl's playing days at Michigan.

"Thanks, Mike, but I think I'll stay here with Anneke."

"Don't be silly." She stood up quickly. "Glad to have you take him off my hands for a while, Mike."

"Wearing you out, is he?" McCauley winked at her.

"Oh, I think I can just about keep up with him." She grinned at him. "But maybe I'd better go carb up just to be sure."

She made her way up into the stands, weaving through red-and-gold-clad hordes until she fetched up finally at a food concourse. She passed on the toxic-looking hot dogs and limp pizza slices, along with the overcooked burgers, sloppy barbecue plates, and a truly evil-looking concoction labeled nachos. So this is where bad food sets up camp in San Francisco, she thought. But as she turned to leave she spotted a booth displaying a small stack of paper-wrapped bundles under a printed sign that read CODY JARRETT'S AUTHENTIC MICHIGAN PASTIES.

"I'll have one of those, and a Diet Coke." She had worked her way finally to the head of the line and pointed to the stack of pasties behind the counter.

"Six dollars." The stocky woman in a satin 49er jacket handed her a small pasty and a dripping paper cup.

Anneke blanched at the price. "Have you been carrying these long?" she asked.

"Don't know, sorry." The woman looked past Anneke's shoulder. "Next?"

Anneke backed out of the concourse and wound her way downward to ground level, where she sat on a concrete bench, unwrapped her prize, and took an experimental bite. Well, it had been nuked, so of course the pastry was inevitably both soggy and tough, but the filling was marvelous, rich and peppery with an undertone of something she couldn't identify but that made her mouth water. She wolfed down the rest of the small pasty and wished she'd bought two of them, but when she turned back to the food concourse, the crowds were even thicker. Besides, the second half was about to start, and she figured she had just enough time to stand in one more line. With a hungry sigh, she headed for a bathroom.

Back on the sideline, she handed Karl the pasty wrapper. "It looks like they're already starting to spin off Cody's cooking," she said. "I wonder how it works—does Richard own the rights? Are they splitting the profits? For that matter, we don't even know what sort of deal they've made for this chain operation."

"There isn't anything to suggest that it matters, you know."

"Hey, you got one of Cody's pasties." An offensive lineman loomed over them. "Aren't they great?"

"You know Cody Jarrett?" Anneke asked.

"Sure." The lineman nodded massively. "My wife and I eat at his place a couple of times a month. Ever taste his trout in Madeira-cherry glaze? Those tart Michigan cherries really make it zing."

"No, but I'll try it." Anneke kept from laughing through sheer force of will. Was *everyone* in San Francisco a budding gourmet?

"You're stereotyping, you know." Karl grinned at her as the lineman lumbered away.

"I suppose I am. It's just not the sort of conversation you'd expect to have with a three-hundred-pound jock."

"Athletes have to be more aware of food than civilians," he pointed out. "Our bodies are our working tools, remember."

"That's true, isn't it." She noted the inclusive pronoun; here on a football field, Karl thought of himself as a football player still. She wondered how much he missed it, and knew the answer would always be: A lot. "I don't have to pay much attention to what I eat, but they do. Kind of like having enough free RAM on a computer."

"And not just enough, but the right—*duck*!"

The right duck? Before she could figure out what he meant, his hand flashed in front of her face and a fast-moving football caromed off it at just about the point her nose would have been. She flinched and ducked—so obvious once you knew the context—and tried to make herself smaller as a 49er wide receiver and a Falcon cornerback barrelled into her line of vision and rolled to the ground at her feet, followed immediately by a 49er running back, another Falcon player, and a zebra-striped referee throwing a yellow penalty flag.

"Late hit?" she asked breathlessly when the players had sorted themselves out and returned to the field without even a glance in their direction.

"Right. You okay?"

"I'm fine. Thank God you've still got those linebacker reflexes."

"More than you know." He smiled, and Anneke saw something behind his eyes that made her throat tighten. "I damn near tackled the guy."

The 49ers won late, which meant few people left before the final gun, which meant the brutal postgame traffic was even more brutal. Karl steered the rented Explorer down side alleys and onto Third Street, avoiding the jammed freeway in favor of the equally jammed, but at least shorter, surface route back to the city. Anneke felt tired and grimy and wanted nothing more than to go back to the hotel, shower, and put her feet up for a while. Unfortunately, that wasn't one of her choices.

"What time did you tell Braxton we'd be there?" she asked as they waited at an interminable red light.

"I just told him we'd come to his office after the game." Karl steered around a long line of cars turning left, and found a clear half block before the traffic closed in around them again. "It shouldn't take too long. We don't really have anything to tell him."

"No." Anneke leaned back against the seat. "Are you going to tell him about Zoe?"

"I don't think so. Time enough for that if she turns up anything."

"She would be a little hard to explain, wouldn't she?"

"Oh, you can never explain Zoe." Karl grinned. "You can only hope to contain her."

The building was bigger and more imposing, but Peter Braxton's office looked like every other cop's office Anneke had ever seen—cramped, overcrowded, and hopelessly cluttered. Braxton greeted them from behind his desk and motioned to a pair of metal chairs.

"Got it solved yet?" he asked when they were seated.

"Of course." Karl waved a hand. "All I had to do was point a finger at the culprit, and he broke down and confessed."

"Just like on television." Braxton propped his elbows on the desktop. "So?"

"Like I said—an exercise in futility." Karl spread his hands. "We went over the same ground you did—no outsiders in the kitchen, no one except Jeremy Blake admitted knowing her before today, everyone had opportunity, no one had motive. In fact, they were all at some pains to point out how much damage the murder had done to the restaurant."

"Yes." Braxton rolled a pencil between his fingers. "There is that."

"Do you know what the financial arrangement was between them?" Karl asked.

"They were still ironing it out." Braxton dropped the pencil and picked up a pen. "At least, that's what they told me." He tapped the pen on the desk, leaving a trail of ink dots on a computer printout. "I did get the impression they weren't talking about equal shares."

"Still, since nothing's been signed yet, if any of the parties didn't like the terms, they could always pull out of the deal," Karl said. "Couldn't they?" He and Braxton looked at each other for a moment, until Braxton nodded.

"All but Cody. He was contractually tied up."

"To Richard, or to the Maize and Blue?"

"To the restaurant." Braxton doodled a series of unconnected curves. "His contract is with M and B, Incorporated. If there's no Maize and Blue, the contract is void." He dropped the pen and tapped his fingers on a brass paperweight. "Pretty far-fetched. And there's no evidence that he was being screwed—in fact, Rojas said they were rewriting his contract to make sure he was satisfied with it. Nobody wants an unhappy celebrity chef."

"Does he really qualify as a celebrity chef?"

"Oh, absolutely," Braxton said. "In this town, food celebrities are as famous as movie celebrities. And the gossip, if anything, is even worse. Even the rumor that Cody was discontented would hurt the Maize and Blue."

"Have there been any such rumors?" Karl asked.

"Not that I've heard." Braxton shook his head. "Remember, this is all pretty new. Killian hired him right out of CCA and gave him a totally free hand. That's pretty heady stuff for a kid his age." He paused. "I think Killian was as surprised as anyone else when he broke out of the pack the way he did."

"Who did he replace as chef?"

"Nobody in particular." Braxton shuffled papers, then shoved them aside. "The thing is, until Cody got there the Maize and Blue was just your average sports bar. It's Cody these people are investing in, not Killian."

"Even considering his success, isn't Cody a little young for experienced investors to be gambling on?"

"Probably." Braxton shrugged. "But investing in a hot new chef is a lot sexier than investing in IBM. It's kind of a yuppie thing."

"You do have to wonder if Cody resented all these other people getting rich off his creativity," Karl mused.

"If he is, there's no sign of it." Braxton teetered his chair onto its back legs. "Besides, he's going to get just as rich. And killing a random patron is a hell of a convoluted way to break a contract."

"Which means . . ." Karl let the sentence die off.

"Yeah." Braxton made a face. "The Ann Arbor connection. Shit, I hate cases that hang on motive." He brought his chair down onto its front legs with a thud. "Look, as long as you're here, what about doing liaison with the AAPD? I know, I know." He glanced at Anneke for the first time. "You're on your honeymoon. But if you go home with this thing still open, you'll be stuck with it anyway, won't you?"

"We can log in to the AAPD from the hotel." Anneke spoke immediately, knowing Karl wanted to agree and not wanting him to have to ask. The look of surprise on Braxton's face was either comical or insulting or both. As if he'd just heard a dog quote Shakespeare.

"Anneke's a computer consultant with the AAPD." Karl was grinning widely. "We may want to access their files if we're going to work on this."

"Sounds good." Braxton turned to Anneke and nodded quickly, accepting her new status without objection. "Just let me know if you need anything from our end, and we'll set you up."

"Not at the moment." This time it was Karl who replied. He checked his watch. "It's too late back home to do anything now. Why don't I call the department tomorrow morning, and get back to you after I talk to them?"

"Good." Braxton shoved his chair back and stood up. "I've got a dinner date myself, and he doesn't like to be kept waiting. We're going to this new Thai place in the Castro—Thai Me Up. Have you tried it?"

"No." Karl shook his head, and Anneke sighed. She didn't think she could stand one more conversation about food.

# TEN

"Are you sure you don't want to just call out for pizza?" Anneke heard the plaintive note in her voice and laughed at herself.

"Not a chance. You'll love Clair de Lune—even if it is trendy." He laughed with her, putting an arm around her shoulders. "Are you warm enough?"

"More or less. But I'm beginning to understand why everyone in San Francisco wears leather." Outside the Ritz-Carlton, near the top of Nob Hill, the fog had settled around them once again, and a chill wind ripped down California Street. Anneke pulled the belt of her leather coat more tightly around her waist and peered uphill. "There it is," she said, pointing to the square silhouette looming at the top of the hill.

The cable car clanked and rattled to a stop at Stockton, and they sat on the outside bench and shivered as it clanked and rattled its way down toward the Embarcadero. The necklace of lights on the Bay Bridge shimmered through the fog and reflected off the water, and Anneke knew it was beautiful and didn't really care. She seemed to be pretty much ooh'd-and-aah'd out, suffering from scenery overload.

"I wonder who got stuck with the Summers investigation," she mused.

"Probably Wes." Karl tightened his arm around her shoulders, and she huddled against him, using him as a windbreak. "You are cold, aren't you?"

" 'Dress for fall,' you said." She laughed up at him, burrowing into his chest. "You didn't mention that it would be fall in Siberia."

They got off the cable car at the end of the line, and walked two freezing, windy blocks to an elegant old brick building with decorated cornices. Anneke all but fell into the warmth of the restaurant, reluctant even to remove her coat until she'd thawed out.

"Lieutenant Genesko! What a nice surprise!" Elisa Falcone cut off their approach to the maître d'. "Won't you join us? Just Blair and I, and Stacey and Barkley Malinov—Malintech Software, you know." She waved a red-silk-clad arm in the general direction of the dining room. "Joseph, will you set two more places at our table?" She put her hand familiarly on the maître d's arm.

Anneke and Karl shared a moment of silent telepathy and inward smiles. "Thank you," Karl said to Elisa. "We'd like that."

"Lovely." Elisa nodded to Joseph, who led them through the dining room with a subdued flourish. "Blair, look who I found. Stacey, Barkley, I'd like you to meet Karl and Anneke Genesko." Blair Falcone stood up when they reached the table; the others didn't.

"It's Anneke Haagen, actually," she corrected Elisa.

"Of course. Karl is the Pittsburgh Steelers linebacker who was written up in the *Chron*." Anneke noted that the brief mention in the sports pages had been significantly upgraded.

"And he's also a police lieutenant." She beamed as though she were somehow personally responsible for Karl's dual career.

"Hi." Barkley Malinov looked up from his menu and waved a hand. He looked about sixteen, was probably twenty-three, and wore a tuxedo jacket with wide satin lapels, a white T-shirt, and a blue-white diamond stud in his left ear that Anneke estimated at around one and a half carats. His brown hair was shaved to the scalp from neck to earlobe, with a long, straight fringe that flopped over one eye.

"Hi." Stacey Malinov looked even younger than her husband, a big-eyed waif of a girl almost lost in an oversized tuxedo shirt hanging loose over black satin pants. Its starched collar rose nearly to her ears; inside the vee of the shirt's open neckline, a huge gold-and-topaz pendant hung from a heavy gold chain. Compared to the Malinov children, the four adults—Anneke suddenly thought of herself that way—seemed overdressed, overaccessorized, almost tacky in their carefully tailored suits and silks.

"Malintech's officially pre-IPO," Elisa chattered as they were seated and busboys rearranged the table. "Isn't it exciting? You've heard of Netcredit, of course—that's Malintech's. It's going to revolutionize Internet shopping, isn't it?" She beamed at Barkley, who had returned to studying the menu.

"Only if we can get at least five percent market penetration before going IPO," Stacey warned. "We need a synergy of consumer acceptance and market availability. That's why the contract with greatfood dot com is so important." She gave Blair a meaningful look that caused Anneke to rearrange her first opinion of the girl.

"We're talking to their people Wednesday," Blair reassured her.

"Yes, of course." Elisa smiled amiably. "Did you know that Lieutenant Genesko has three Super Bowl rings?"

"Is that a lot?" Barkley looked up from his menu with curiosity. Anneke stifled a giggle.

"Barkley, the most any player in the whole NFL ever got is five," Elisa said with exaggerated patience.

"Oh. Cool." Barkley returned to his menu.

Elisa rolled her eyes. "Would you pour the wine, Blair? And then I think we'll be ready to order." She set down the menu with authority. "Karl, if you like crab cakes, Marquez is the only chef in town who uses real Chesapeake Bay crab."

"That sounds very good," Karl agreed amicably.

"It all does." Anneke looked at Elisa over her menu. "The menu certainly is different from Cody's, isn't it?" she offered.

"Heavens, yes." Elisa's mouth curved in a gentle smile. "Marquez is in the true classic mode. Cody is more . . . earthy, I think is a good description." She contemplated the word for a moment, and seemed to find it good. "Yes, definitely earthy. Wouldn't you agree, dear?"

"Agree to what?" Blair looked up from his menu.

"That Cody's cuisine might be described as earthy."

"Earthy? I don't think so. It sounds too ordinary. Anyway, they'll have marketing people to do that sort of thing."

"I didn't mean—oh, never mind. Oh look, there's Tallie and that awful husband of hers." Elisa waved and smiled across the room, then altered the smile for the arriving waiter. "Oh, good. Are we all ready? Why don't we start with Marquez's wonderful pâté," she said to the waiter. "Bring a terrine of it for us to share, please. And then I'll have the petrale with artichoke risotto. Oh, and would you ask Marquez if there's any orange-glazed asparagus tonight?" She handed her menu to the waiter. "Anneke, what would you like?"

Anneke ordered scallops in wine sauce; Stacey selected filet mignon; Karl and Blair both opted for the crab cakes.

"I want shrimp," Barkley said.

"The prawns in pomegranate sauce?" the waiter asked, pencil poised over his pad.

"No." Barkley shook his head. "Just shrimp—no, okay,

make it prawns, with some of that chili sauce. Lots of extra horseradish, too."

"A prawn cocktail, you mean?"

"I guess. Maybe three of them? And a baked potato with sour cream. Oh, and some of that asparagus with the orange stuff."

The waiter wrote down the order gravely. Elisa made an impressively complicated moue of amused condescension, catching the waiter's eye to ensure he understood.

"I think I like the food at the Maize and Blue better myself," Stacey said when the waiter had left. "You still going ahead with the chain project even after that murder?"

"Yes, of course," Blair replied. "By the time we're ready to move, it'll all have blown over."

"Hey, that's right, you were there when that girl was killed, weren't you?" Barkley showed interest in something besides food for the first time.

"Yes, I'm afraid we were." Elisa shuddered.

"Weird. I've never seen anyone dead. Was it really gross?"

"Barkley!" Stacey glared at him.

"What? Oh, sorry." Barkley shrugged. "It's just interesting. I mean, isn't it?" he appealed to no one in particular.

"In a way, I suppose it is." Anneke ignored Elisa's look of delicate distaste. "It was awful, of course, but it's human nature to be curious, isn't it? Especially when you're personally involved."

"I'd hardly say we were 'personally involved,' " Elisa said, rather more sharply than she'd spoken before. "We didn't even know the girl."

"But you're involved with Cody Jarrett, and with, what's his name, Killian? The guy who owns the Maize and Blue." Stacey looked thoughtful. "I'm surprised you haven't backed off," she said to Blair. "At least until you know neither of them have their asses in a sling."

"That's not an issue, I assure you." Blair spoke smoothly,

reaching for the terrine that the waiter had set on the table. He spread pâté on a square of toast. "Please, everyone, have some pâté."

"You've already committed the capital, haven't you?" Stacey said suddenly. "How much do you stand to lose if it goes under?"

"Stacey, that's a question you never, ever ask a venture capitalist." Blair chuckled. "It's as impolite as asking a woman her weight."

"It isn't impolite if your survival depends on it," Stacey retorted. "If you're all going up in a hot-air balloon together, you damn well have a right to know how much the other passengers weigh."

"Point taken." Blair sighed. "Your funding's already in place, Stacey, so don't worry about it."

"It's my job to worry about it." Stacey smeared pâté on toast and handed it to Barkley, who was scribbling on a scrap of paper. He wolfed it down without looking up. "I know we've got ten percent in escrow, but even so . . ." Stacey let the sentence die off, but her eyes were fixed on Blair.

"It's a shame this happened just when you had everything finalized," Anneke said, putting sympathy into her voice.

"Well, it can't be helped." Blair raked a hand through his hair, a gesture more disturbed than his calm face indicated. "And I really can't imagine that it will cause any problems."

"Of course not," Elisa said. "After all, it's not as though Cody had anything to do with it."

"You sure?" Stacey asked bluntly.

"Of course I'm sure," Elisa snapped. "I'm very close to Cody, you know. Once I helped him get noticed by the right people, it put him on the threshhold of a great career. And I don't intend to let anything get in his way."

"It's so nice of you to help him," Anneke said earnestly. "He must be very grateful to you."

"Oh, he deserves it." Elisa waved the compliment away.

"He's so bright, and so talented, that it's a privilege to open doors for him." She winced and rubbed at her right arm.

"Are you hurt?" Anneke asked.

"Not really." Elisa let the arm hang loosely from her shoulder, wiggling her fingers. "I think I overworked it this morning."

"Oh? What kind of work do you do?"

"No, I meant working out." Elisa smiled at the notion of work. "I always do at *least* an hour a day, of course, but after Cody's wonderful brunch yesterday I did an extra session."

"Do you go to one of Jeremy's clubs?"

"Well, no." Elisa sounded more amused than apologetic. "Jeremy's clubs are very good, of course, but not quite . . . private enough." For private, read: exclusive, Anneke thought. "I go to a private club on Nob Hill. In fact," she turned to Karl, "if you'd like a place to work out while you're here, I'd be glad to arrange a guest card for you."

"Thank you." Karl didn't actually say yes or no, a fact which Anneke thought Elisa noted.

"So you don't use his supplements either?" Anneke probed.

"Oh, heavens." Elisa's laugh tinkled across the table. "Poor Jeremy, he's such a fanatic about his roots and berries. Just as Mimi's a fanatic about her Cornwell sugar-free routine. They're all so obsessed with their diets."

"I suppose most people are, these days."

"Well, but they miss out on so much," Elisa protested. "I'd much rather just skip breakfast and lunch, so when we go out to dinner I can enjoy myself and not worry about calories."

Anneke opened her mouth to point out that this was exactly opposite the recommended approach to eating, then closed it again. Elisa hadn't asked for diet advice, and God knows, there was enough of it going around.

Stacey Malinov wasn't so forbearing. In fact, she giggled. "Boy, would you never survive as a programmer. If we didn't keep the doughnut box full we'd have a company-wide walk-out on our hands."

Anneke, who also operated an office full of young programmers, laughed with her. "Doughnuts, Coke, and pizza—the programmer's three food groups."

"Lately it's been Cracker Jacks." Stacey grinned, then peered at Elisa. "How do you get a day's work done without energy food?"

"I manage, I assure you." There was a frosty tone to her voice, although whether she was offended by criticism of her diet, or the notion that she worked at all, was unclear.

"Jeremy and Mimi do make an unlikely couple," Anneke suggested. It was time to start mining for gossip, the only reason they were sharing the Falcones' table in the first place.

"My dear, you can't imagine." Elisa spread her hands. "They spend half their time arguing about diets, and vitamins, and sugar versus fat." She smiled and sighed. "So dreary."

"Still, I suppose they get along well otherwise."

"Ye-es." Elisa sounded mildly dubious. "I can't say that they display much passion, but they seem comfortable with each other."

"It doesn't sound very exciting." Anneke glanced sideways at Karl, and saw the ghost of a grin on his face.

"Well, they're both extremely *ambitious*, of course. And they both have to deal with family issues. Mimi is the first one in her family even to go to college, let alone law school, and I think she feels a lot of pressure to live up to their expectations. Whereas with Jeremy it's rather the other way around." She paused.

"What do you mean?"

"Jeremy's father is some sort of medical researcher, Princeton I think. And his mother is a botany professor. He's mentioned that he used some of her work to develop those little pills of his. But both of them were . . . shall we say, disappointed . . . when their only son decided to make a career out of exercising."

"So being a successful entrepreneur is a way of proving his

worth." Anneke nodded. "Yes, I can see that. I wonder if it worked."

"If what worked?"

"Proving himself to his parents. Are they suitably impressed with his accomplishments?"

"Heavens, they certainly should be," Elisa said. "He's become quite a little celebrity here in The City." Anneke could hear the capital letters, and the mildly waspish tone.

"What about Noelle?" There was no segue, but Anneke was pretty sure Elisa wouldn't notice.

"Oh, I *like* Noelle." Elisa spoke with the condescending tone that thin people often use toward fat people. "I don't know her all that well, of course—Blair's the one who works closely with her."

"She must be pretty good at her job." Anneke directed the question toward both Falcones.

"She's brilliant," Blair said. "She can massage financials better than anyone I've ever seen." What on earth did that mean? Anneke wondered. And why did Blair sound slightly defensive?

"Poor thing." Elisa shook her head. "It's so nice that she has a promising career." Blair shot his wife a look that Anneke couldn't quite interpret before reaching for the terrine of pâté. Elisa didn't seem to notice. "By the way," she said to him, "I arranged a membership for Cody at my club. He's such a real celebrity now that he needs the privacy. And I hope you've noticed how well he handles it. Which is why," she insisted, "that you absolutely must use him in your pro-motional campaign."

"I told you, that's a decision for the marketing agency." Blair spoke as though this were an old argument. "Oh, good. Our food's here." He sounded more relieved than expectant.

# ELEVEN

"Okay, first question—do you think Elisa is sleeping with Cody?"

"What do you think?" Karl passed the question back to her. He was stretched out on the Ritz-Carlton's king-size bed, his hands clasped behind his neck.

"I think . . . Put it this way. If you put a gun to my head and forced me to say yes or no, I'd say no. But without the gun, I'd have to say I'm not sure. What I'm damn sure of is that she'd like to be." Anneke, sitting at the small desk across the room, plugged her laptop into the phone's data port and opened an Internet connection.

"So you think her sponsorship of Cody is purely disinterested philanthropy?"

"Riiight." She drawled out the word sarcastically. "About as disinterested as the gun lobby's contributions to Bush's presidential campaign." She opened Eudora and began downloading e-mail. "I think it has a lot to do with the celebrity-chef syndrome in San Francisco."

"Cody as a form of social climbing, you mean." Karl nodded.

"Yes. She's made Cody her protégé. So if he becomes trendy, so does Elisa." She sorted her e-mail, deleting spam and forwarding business messages to her office. "I may be wrong, but I have a feeling Elisa Falcone isn't a born socialite—at least, not born into the San Francisco elite. I think she's working her way up the social ladder." She wrinkled her nose. "Honestly, what a way to spend your time."

"She does seem to work awfully hard at it, doesn't she?" He unclasped his hands and sat up. "What's more, if I'm her idea of a celebrity catch, she's not very good at it, either."

"Oh, I don't know." Anneke turned in her chair and examined him solemnly. He had changed into silk pajamas and robe, and looked good enough to . . . Uh-uh. Good grief, San Francisco was really getting to her.

"What are you grinning at?" he asked.

"Never mind." She laughed. "Let's just say *I* think you're a celebrity."

"Ah, but you have the football smarts to appreciate defense." He sighed dramatically. "And even you'd pass me up in a minute if you could get Steve Young."

"Oh, well, that's a special case." She laughed before turning to another thought. "Do you think Mimi and Jeremy are as casual about their relationship as they seem?"

"You mean, could Mimi have been jealous of Lindsay?" He interpreted her question correctly. "There's no way to tell, is there? It's almost impossible to deconstruct a relationship from the outside."

"Mimi denied knowing that Lindsay was Jeremy's ex-wife, but of course that doesn't prove anything."

"No. But if the marriage really was as short, and as long ago as Jeremy said, there doesn't seem to be any reason for Mimi to be concerned in any case." He made a face. "I hate cases that involve relationships."

"Speaking of which, it occurred to me . . ." She hesitated, recognizing the incongruity of the idea. "Is it possible that there's something between Blair and Noelle?"

"You picked up on that, too, did you?" He nodded slowly. "I had the same thought."

"But they're such an unlikely couple." She found herself protesting her own suggestion.

"Not necessarily. Buttoned-down types like Blair Falcone are often attracted to free spirits."

"Can you imagine Elisa's shock if she found out it was true?" The thought shouldn't have amused her, but it did. She realized that she didn't like Elisa Falcone—a lot.

She turned back to the laptop. "Oh, good. There's an e-mail from Zoe." There were, in fact, two of them, one with an attached file that even zipped was nearly six megs. While it downloaded at painful modem speed, she brought up AltaVista and typed "cody jarrett" into the search window.

"What have you got?" Karl pulled over a chair and sat down to look over her shoulder.

"I thought I'd do some trolling, just to see what I can find. That looks like the Maize and Blue's home site." She clicked on the link to *mandbsf.com*. It was a clean, simple page, dark blue text on a pale yellow background with a photograph of the restaurant's interior at the center. She clicked on a link labeled "menu"—because Saturday had been a buffet, she hadn't seen it—and examined it curiously.

She was surprised at the number of fish dishes, and at the varieties of fruit used in sauces and side dishes. There was Lake Superior whitefish in a tart blueberry sauce; brook trout in a merlot-cherry reduction; grilled coho salmon with an almond-peach risotto. There was linguine with morels, and venison with a wild cherry glaze. And of course there were several varieties of pasties, along with the famous Cotswold Fusilli. Desserts included maple-nut baked apple, fresh peach mousse, and a chocolate-cherry concoction that made Anneke want to jump out of her chair and drive right down to get one.

"You know, I've always thought of Michigan food as kielbasa and fried potatoes," she said, "but these are all Michigan ingredients, aren't they?" She read aloud from the screen: " 'Strip steak with garlic mashed potatoes and a fresh peach-blueberry garnish.' So why is it when a Michigan menu says fruit on the side, it's always a canned peach half?"

"Because you eat too many meals at campus lunch counters," he said, laughing. "There's plenty of good food in Michigan. You just have to be motivated to find it."

"Yes, but even little corner cafés here use fresh fruit. And that spongy bread you get in the midwest doesn't even seem to exist here." She returned to the Maize and Blue's home page and read the promotional text at the bottom. "Join us for Michigan football games and other Big Ten action," it read. "Nibble on Cody Jarrett's Trail Mix while you watch, or you can buy bags of this unique and delicious dried cherry-blueberry-pecan combination to enjoy at home."

"So they're retailing more of Cody's food," she noted. "Pasties, trail mix—I wonder who owns the rights to Cody's recipes?"

"I imagine it was negotiated as part of the agreement with Blair's firm."

"Yes." Anneke gnawed on her lower lip. "But who owned them before? Cody or Richard?" When he shrugged without answering, she returned to AltaVista and scanned the list of hits, spotting George McMartin's name near the top. It was a restaurant review in the *Chronicle* headed: CODY JARRETT SCORES A TOUCHDOWN AT THE MAIZE AND BLUE. She read it through, reading choice passages aloud to Karl:

" 'Jarrett exhibits a masterful command of textural contrast . . . ', ' . . . napped in an unctuous Hollandaise sauce . . . ' What on earth is an 'unctuous' sauce? ' . . . turnip gratin almost indecently rich for such a humble vegetable . . . ' Good grief," she said finally, "do foodies really talk that way?"

"Pretension sells." Karl chuckled. "You should read wine reviews."

"No, I shouldn't." She shuddered, returned to AltaVista and scanned the hits. "He made *Food Lovers* magazine," she noted, clicking on the link.

In a column headlined "Newcomers," the magazine asked: "Is San Francisco's Cody Jarrett the New Wunderkind?" They went on to answer, roughly: Not yet. "His repertoire is still far from flawless," the writer noted waspishly, "and he often overreaches himself. His charred duck with a burgundy-anchovy glaze, for instance, is a strange hybrid of discordant flavors. And Jarrett hasn't truly begun to master the art of presentation. Still, for a chef of his tender years, Cody Jarrett is one to watch."

There were other reviews, especially in San Francisco media. One writer called Nouvelle Midwest "the American cuisine for the next millennium." On the other hand, a Los Angeles magazine noted that "San Francisco has a tendency to believe itself the center of the culinary world" and called Cody's menu "an immature hodgepodge, decently executed but basically timid and conventional despite its gloss." And a brief mention in a Chicago newspaper's food supplement referred to the "culinary debate over Nouvelle Midwest" as "a bicoastal battle that completely ignores the realities of the heartland it misrepresents."

She was about to log off when she spotted an odd header in the AltaVista list: "Nouvelle Assault on America's Health." Clicking on the link took her to the Web site of Scientists for a Healthy America, where Nouvelle Midwest was included on their list of health outrages *du jour*.

". . . just another high-fat food scam . . .", ". . . the quaint notion that if it was good enough for our ancestors it's good enough for us overlooks the fact that the average life expectancy one hundred years ago was only . . ." Anneke read the blurb aloud to Karl. "Good grief, Cody's becoming famous enough to attack. No wonder Richard is desperate to cash in while he has the chance."

"Cody might be just as desperate," Karl pointed out. "The combination of Cody's celebrity and the Maize-and-Blue concept makes an attractive package for expansion, but only *as* a package."

"That's true. Cody is this year's celebrity, but next year the whole bubble could burst." The material from Zoe had finally downloaded, and Anneke logged off and opened the message with the attached file.

It was brief and to the point. "I'm at Lindsay's computer in her apartment," Zoe wrote, "but I don't have time to plow through her stuff, so I figured it'd be quicker to just bundle up everything that looks like it might be useful and e-mail it to you. More later."

"How on earth did she get into Lindsay's computer?" Anneke threw up her hands and laughed. "Leave it to Zoe." She opened the second message.

"Talked to Lindsay's roommate this afternoon," she wrote, "who turns out to be Jill Sainsbury. Here are my notes. I'll get to the public health school and Congressman Carr's office tomorrow when things are open. You guys sure have a weird idea of a romantic honeymoon. Tell Richard he owes me."

Underneath the message was the heading: INTERVIEW: JILL SAINSBURY, followed by Zoe's admirably complete report. When they'd read through to the end, Anneke scrolled up and pointed to the paragraph about the man in Lindsay's life. "I wonder. Could the man in question by any chance be the congressman?"

"It's a thought," Karl said. "But if he's the one she'd just ended a relationship with, would she go on working for him?"

"That depends." Anneke thought it over. "She might if she

was the one who broke it off. And even if it went the other way, remember how critical he was to her academic work. And besides, there's no suggestion that she was particularly upset over the breakup." She thought for a moment. "Or she could have just refused to believe him."

"He is married, of course," Karl pointed out. "A public mess of that sort would be political suicide."

"True. Okay, try it this way. Suppose Carr tells her he's going to leave his wife, but not until after the next election? So she decides to move in with Jill Sainsbury just until after the election, when she thinks he'll actually separate from his wife. Which," she added, "he may or may not have had any real intention of doing."

"I think you're reaching." Karl shook his head. "You could devise a dozen scenarios just as likely."

"But not as logically satisfying." She laughed at his expression. "I know, I know—the human need to impose a logical pattern on discrete phenomena. Still, it's worth checking, isn't it?"

"Oh, of course. The man, or men, need to be found no matter who they are."

"Oh, all right." She clicked on the file Zoe had attached to her e-mail, while Karl picked up the TV remote and turned on the evening news. The file was named, economically, "lindsay1.zip." Anneke unzipped it and examined the list of folders. She was just about to open the one labeled "Personal" when she heard the words "Ann Arbor." She swiveled to face the TV.

". . . about the health crisis that was the central focus of the murdered woman's work." The newscaster was female, dark-haired, and dark-skinned. She spoke in the professionally mournful tone that TV news people use to manipulate sorrow from their viewers.

The cameras cut to a head shot of Griffith Carr, D-Mich., sitting at a desk with a map of Michigan behind him. He was nearly bald, with only a close-cropped fringe of light brown hair, and a thin, ascetic face that was deeply tanned and deeply lined; he looked more like the professor he'd been than the politican he was.

"The tragedy of Lindsay Summers's murder isn't only about a young life cut short, but about the loss of a brilliant mind and a dedicated spirit," Griffith Carr said. "Lindsay Summers was committed to nurturing the health and well-being of all the people. Luckily for all of us, the bulk of her research was completed. And I can think of no better memorial to her spirit than to turn her ideals into reality."

The camera cut back to the anchor desk. "Carr will hold a news conference at noon tomorrow on the steps of City Hall here in San Francisco," the dark-haired woman announced, "to unveil the bill he plans to introduce in the next session of Congress."

The camera cut to the male anchor, a middle-aged Asian man. "Next, Jim Reid reports on the latest wave of SUV vandalism in the Mission."

Karl punched the mute button on the remote. "Interesting. This will give Carr's bill a good deal more publicity than it would have had otherwise."

"What's more, it's *national* publicity." Anneke wrinkled her nose. "Announcing a major piece of legislation at City Hall in San Francisco is a lot more newsworthy than announcing it from an Ann Arbor office. It gets him major exposure in the biggest state in the country." She turned back to her laptop and looked once more at the list of files from Lindsay's computer, focusing on a folder labeled "Dissertation." "You know," she said slowly, "I thought Lindsay's research was being done for Carr's office, to produce data for his bill." She turned to face Karl. "But if that's true, how come Carr has his legislation already prepared?"

He stood up and came around behind her, putting his hands on her shoulders and leaning forward to look at the screen.

"An interesting question," he said, "but probably irrelevant."
He ran his hands along her arms, sending pleasant shivers
through her.

"There's something odd here, but I'm damned if I know
what it is." She felt his hand on the nape of her neck, tracing
the lace edging of her robe. "Well, whatever it is," she said, "I
think it can wait until morning."

# TWELVE

They ate croissants filled with scrambled eggs and brie at Roxanne's on Powell Street, reading the morning paper and watching the cable cars go by. Griffith Carr's announcement had kept Lindsay Summers's murder on the front page, but there was nothing new from the police. Anneke was more interested in a sidebar article headlined: FIRST TOBACCO, NEXT FAT? After a long disquisition on whether obesity was or was not a "disease," the article went on:

> The idea of a "fat tax" isn't new. One vocal proponent is pediatrician Melvin DiQuesta, whose show on public television continues to hammer away at his central theme: that the federal government take a militant attitude toward what he calls "toxic" foods. DiQuesta, who likens his proposals to those that have been used against tobacco, has urged the government to use heavy taxation to make so-called "unhealthy foods" less attractive, especially to children. He also has demanded that the FDA regulate food advertising

aimed at children. His most controversial proposal would ban tie-in advertising between children's movies and toys, and fast-food restaurants.

DiQuesta seems unfazed by objections to government interference with individual rights. "The same objections were raised over the issue of tobacco restrictions," he said. "But sometimes the greater good of society is more important than individual freedom."

"When did this happen?" Anneke asked.

"When did what happen?" Karl looked up from the sports section.

"When did the public health establishment grab control of our lives?" She waved the newspaper at him.

"When they discovered they could get away with it." Karl shrugged. "It started with automobile seat-belt laws, actually."

"Yes, but that was . . ."

"Different?" He cocked his head.

"It isn't different, is it?" she conceded. "Seat-belt laws, motorcycle helmet laws, anti-smoking laws, anti-food laws—they're all the same thing."

"What they have in common is that they're all risky behaviors, and governments dislike risk-takers. They rattle the bars."

"That's one reason for sports, isn't it?" she asked. "Give people the illusion of risk-taking, carefully controlled and sequestered." She made a face, started to pursue the subject, then stopped. "So Carr's speaking at noon. I suppose we ought to go?"

"Not if you don't want to," Karl said.

"You know perfectly well I do." She grinned at him. "Besides, isn't San Francisco's City Hall supposed to be some sort of architectural masterpiece? We wouldn't want to miss it, would we?"

They finished breakfast and climbed the two blocks back uphill to the Ritz-Carlton, where Karl checked in with Wes

Kramer in Ann Arbor while Anneke returned to the files Zoe had e-mailed her.

There were four folders, labeled "Personal," "Initiative," "Legislation," and "Dissertation," each of them with a welter of subfolders attached.

The first thing she did was run a global search for the names of each of the suspects, unsurprised at the negative return. She started then with the Personal folder, where she found a file labeled "Calendar," but it was disappointingly sparse. Lindsay had apparently deleted each entry when it was completed, so only future appointments were listed. In the 9 A.M. slot for Saturday, a notation read only: "SF: M&B;" and in the noon slot for Tuesday, "LA: Martini's." That was tomorrow, Anneke realized, and wondered if anyone at Martini's, whatever it was, would be waiting for Lindsay to arrive.

There were few other appointments listed—classes, one meeting with someone whose initials were P W, and another with G C. Probably Griffith Carr, Anneke reasoned, but the minor deduction gave her no further information. She closed the file with a sigh, wondering whether Lindsay Summers's life really was as sterile as it implied, or if she simply didn't use her calendar for personal activities.

She browsed through the rest of the material for a while, examining the short file named "Address Book," and another in the Dissertation folder called "Notes."

"Primitive peoples eat to survive, and thus instinctively eat healthy diets," Lindsay had written. Anneke snorted under her breath; she wasn't an expert in the field by any means, but she knew damn well that was bad anthropology. Most primitive peoples had lived feast-or-famine existences; to them, food was a joy and a sacrament.

Another entry read: "The connection between food and spectator sports in American culture is that both are self-indulgent—eating for pleasure, and watching other people doing physical activities one should do oneself."

She browsed a bit further, not sure whether to be angry or saddened. It was clear Lindsay viewed food as The Enemy; in her mind, the only correct attitude toward food was for fuel. Never mind food as celebration; Lindsay would probably replace the Thanksgiving turkey with the Thanksgiving . . . what? Head of lettuce? Stair climb? It occurred to her to wonder just what Lindsay did do for fun. It also occurred to her how much of any celebration—in every culture she could think of—revolved around feasting. Around food.

She sighed and returned to Lindsay's files, but there was so much material she didn't know how to approach it methodically. She was still trying to figure out how to proceed when she saw Karl hang up the phone.

"Anything?" she asked him.

"Not really. They're faxing her University records to Braxton, and their interview notes with her roommate and a few other people who knew her, but my guess is they'll have less than Zoe got. Speaking of which, we need to give her material to Braxton."

"I know." Anneke looked down at the laptop, gnawing her lip. "There's so much of it I don't know where to start. I guess the easiest thing to do is just to dump it all onto floppies and drop them off at his office."

"All right." He stood up. "Let's do that now. Then we'll have time for some sightseeing before Carr's speech."

"Good." Anneke tried to sound enthusiastic, but in fact she was more interested in investigating a murder than in Yet Another museum or Victorian house or panoramic view. She wondered if there was something wrong with her, but then she looked at Karl's face and realized she didn't much care if there was. He was grinning widely.

"I thought you might like the displays at Gump's," he suggested innocently. "And there's a gallery on Sutter called Compositions which carries some of the best art glass in the world."

"Even better." She returned his grin. Shopping was something she hadn't OD'd on yet. And probably never would, she concluded, laughing at herself. "And if we just happen to pass the Galleria, or Wilkes Bashford, it would be a shame not to drop in, wouldn't it?"

# THIRTEEN

Monday morning's *Daily* front-paged Griffith Carr's proposed legislation and his trip to San Francisco. Zoe read the story over breakfast in the East Quad dining room, eating bacon and eggs with a side of jelly doughnut and wondering if she should be looking over her shoulder for the food police.

She'd been planning to hit Carr's office this morning, but if he was going to be in San Francisco . . . Well, there was still his staff. It might even be a plus; maybe they'd talk more freely with the boss gone. She licked the last of the jelly off her fingers and grabbed her backpack.

Her first reaction to her first sight of a congressional office was surprise. She'd expected it to be more showy, designed to impress. Instead, it looked like every faculty office she'd ever seen, overcrowded and roughly furnished and spilling over with papers and reading material of every description.

The woman behind the battered wooden desk shared the same less-than-glossy appearance. She wasn't a small woman, but there was something birdlike about her, the effect of brown hair and brown-rimmed glasses and a pilled brown cardigan that all accentuated her resemblance to a large, middle-aged sparrow. The nameplate in front of her read GLORIA MCGYVER, ADMINISTRATIVE ASSISTANT. Zoe categorized her instantly as one of those people who make a profession out of being overburdened.

"Yes? Can I help you?" She sighed the sigh of the overworked and underappreciated.

"I'm Zoe Kaplan. *Michigan Daily*." Under the woman's annoyed gaze, Zoe felt the urge to apologize for living. "I'm sorry to intrude, but I'm following up on Lindsay Summers's death. If I could ask you some questions?"

"Zoe Kaplan." Gloria McGyver looked at her. "But you're a sportswriter, aren't you?"

"Mostly." Zoe looked at her in surprise. "I'm surprised you've heard of me."

"It's my job to know the district media." The woman sounded offended. "You've also covered a couple of murders, and you're a friend of Lieutenant Karl Genesko, I believe." She proffered this information with a tight-lipped smile, as though scoring a point.

"Right." Zoe opened her mouth, closed it, then made a snap decision. "Actually, that's why I'm here. Lieutenant Genesko is in San Francisco—in fact, he was at the restaurant when Lindsay died. He's working with the San Francisco police, and he asked me to collect background information on Lindsay. This isn't for publication, I promise you."

"Oh?" McGyver glared suspicion. "And of course I can call Lieutenant Genesko to confirm that?"

"Absolutely," Zoe replied at once. "He's staying at the Ritz-Carlton Hotel. You should be able to reach him there. Or I can give you his cell phone number. It's three oh nine, four—"

McGyver sighed impatiently. "Oh, very well. There isn't much I can tell you, really, but I can give you—" she checked a large, leather-bound calendar book on her desk and simultaneously waved at a chair next to the desk "—about fifteen minutes."

"Thank you." Zoe sat down and tried to keep her sigh of relief inaudible. "That's a beautiful calendar," she said, still trying to make points.

"It's Japanese." McGyver actually seemed pleased by the compliment. She pointed to a line of ideographs stamped in gold on the cover. "It says 'Golden Year.' "

"You read Japanese?"

"Yes. My master's degree was in history, specializing in American-Asian relations." McGyver preened. "In fact, I just returned from Tokyo yesterday. Congressman Carr is hoping to convince certain Japanese companies to locate plants in the district."

"Wow, cool." Zoe, who'd barely struggled through high school Spanish, didn't have to pretend to be impressed. She pulled a pad and a pen from her backpack and mentally rearranged her approach; like a lot of middle-aged women in Ann Arbor, there was more to Gloria McGyver than bifocals and an ugly sweater. Okay, start with a nice, open-ended question. "What kind of work was Lindsay doing for the congressman?"

"Lindsay didn't work for the congressman," McGyver snapped. "She was merely one of Congressman Carr's graduate assistants when he was a public health professor. When he took a sabbatical to run for Congress, he used some of her work to develop a position paper on food marketing and public health. It turned out to be a very popular campaign issue— at least, among the Ann Arbor part of his constituency." She made a face before picking up a piece of paper and handing it to Zoe. "This is a draft of the bill he's introducing."

Zoe took the paper and glanced at it, but didn't try to decipher the legalese. "And this is based on Lindsay's research?"

"Well, to a certain extent. But of course this is Congressman Carr's own field of expertise. Lindsay Summers was only providing confirmatory data. She wasn't actually preparing the legislation, regardless of her own . . ." McGyver clamped her lips shut.

"Lindsay was still just in the data-collection stage, wasn't she?" Zoe looked at the bill again. "So if this bill is already prepared, her work wasn't the real basis of it?"

"Exactly!" McGyver nodded her head rapidly, looking even more like a large sparrow.

"But—" Zoe stopped; she wasn't here to argue. "What exactly does the bill do?"

"Basically, it's a bill to tax unhealthy foods, and to use the revenue for nutrition education." McGyver picked up a pen and rolled it between her fingers. "It's modeled after the anti-tobacco legislation, of course, which gives it political legitimacy and a first step toward public acceptance."

"And Lindsay's research was going to be used to back it up?"

"More or less. Now, of course, we'll have to cobble together other data." McGyver sighed, more in aggravation than in sorrow, Zoe thought.

"Do you get stuck doing that, or is there other staff?" Zoe asked.

"Other staff? For a freshman congressman?" McGyver snorted. "There's an AA in Washington, but he mostly handles political matters. And the health committee staff works for the committee chairman, not for newcomers, no matter how important their work is." McGyver left no doubt whose work she considered more important.

"So you get stuck with it," Zoe commiserated. "You must think this is a pretty important issue."

"It's one of many important issues that we have to deal with," McGyver said repressively. "But it's also a very divisive issue, especially in this district. Which, by the way, is not composed entirely of perfectly correct Ann Arbor liberals. There are an awful lot of good Democratic voters in the Wayne County part of this district who don't want a batch of holier-than-thou academics telling them what they can and can't eat."

"So it's a risky issue." Zoe knew when she'd hit a nerve, and she wanted to follow up fast. "Was Lindsay the one pushing him to run with it?"

"Lindsay . . ." McGyver stopped. "Lindsay thought she knew how everyone else should run their lives. Especially how everyone else should eat." She looked up from the pen she still held in her fingers, and Zoe recognized a shrewd intelligence beneath the long-suffering personality. "Lindsay had some sort of personal vendetta with food," McGyver said at last.

"She must have been difficult to be around," Zoe probed. "Jeez, I'd be afraid to eat anything in front of someone like that."

"I don't allow other people to dictate how I live. And as I said, she didn't actually work here. In fact, I haven't—hadn't—seen her for several months."

"Really? Did she and the congressman have a falling out?"

"Not that I know of." Was there a flicker of triumph on McGyver's face? "Once the legislation was well in hand, there was no longer any need for Miss Summers's services."

"So there was no personal relationship between Lindsay and the congressman?"

"Congressman Carr is a married man with two children." McGyver snapped her lips shut angrily. "His wife is a lovely woman, and that sort of accusation is both vicious and slanderous. It would damage both his family life and his political career, and if we see it in print we will most certainly take action."

"I didn't mean it like that," Zoe backpedaled. "I just meant, sometimes people working together on an important project develop, you know, a kind of personal rapport. And sometimes, if it's a young woman working with an older man, the woman can read more into it than there really is, you know?"

"Yes, and it can be very difficult for those around them." To

Zoe's delight, McGyver bit. "And of course for a man like Congressman Carr, there's always the risk of an adolescent crush. Also, it wasn't lost on Miss Summers that he had a brilliant political career ahead of him."

It wasn't lost on Gloria McGyver, either, Zoe thought. Aloud, she said: "But if Lindsay hadn't been around the office for a while, you think she'd gotten over her crush?"

"I really don't know." McGyver seemed suddenly aware that she'd said more than she'd intended. She dropped her pen on the desk and placed her hands flat in front of her. "I believe I've told you everything I can about Miss Summers, so if you'll please excuse me, I have a great deal of work to do."

# FOURTEEN

She'd expected marble, and fluted columns, and pretentious statuary—the kind of ponderous dignity that normally characterizes public buildings in America. Instead, Anneke gazed in delight at the light and elegant confection of limestone and wrought iron that sprawled along Van Ness Avenue. Everywhere, from the high, elongated dome to the lampposts lining the sidewalk, brilliant gilt highlighted delicate details of doors and windows and fixtures. Under the bright noon sun, San Francisco's City Hall glittered and preened.

The people massed on the plaza at the rear entrance were another matter, neither delicate nor elegant. There seemed to be several hundred of them, a rainbow of bouncing, chattering, sign-waving humanity.

"Oh, good grief." Anneke and Karl stopped at the edge of the crowd to get their bearings. "I suppose we should have expected this."

"If you televise it, they will come." Karl pointed to the camera trucks lining the street.

"Who are they?" Anneke asked the question rhetorically,

scanning the crowd. It could have been any group at any protest in front of the Michigan Union, chanting and waving homemade picket signs. Except . . . well, not exactly. This crowd was more colorful than any Ann Arbor protest would have been, colorful in all the several meanings of the word.

The first thing she noted was the ethnic mix, Anglo and Asian and Latino and African American and other exotic faces all swirled together. Colorful in dress, too, splashes of bright hues drawing the eye from one cluster of protesters to another. And just as colorful in behavior, she thought. There was a group singing "Scarborough Fair" in surprisingly good voices; there was a ragged line of people holding hands and snaking along the walk, to what purpose she had no idea; there was even a juggler working the edge of the crowd, collecting contributions in a floppy yellow hat.

It was, she thought, half political protest, half street theater.

She read some of the picket signs aloud. " 'Meat is murder.' 'Government out of our refrigerators.' 'Die, Ally McBeal, die.' " She giggled. " 'Anglo hands off my quesadillas. Defend food diversity.' 'Fat isn't the problem, fatheads are.' 'Experiment with your own genes.' Good grief," she said again. "I didn't know there were so many different food causes."

"I didn't either, but when you think about it, it shouldn't surprise us. Food is so elemental that anything to do with it strikes a nerve."

"Oh, look." Anneke pointed to a group nearby, each of them holding a picket sign in one hand and a leash in the other. The signs read, variously, ANIMALS ARE PEOPLE TOO, VEGANS DO IT WITH CUCUMBERS, and SUPPORT THE FALK INITIATIVE. The leashes were attached to, variously, dogs, several placid cats, more than one ferret, and a large pale green lizard.

"Are you familiar with the Falk initiative?" A middle-aged woman in a long, dark red cotton dress approached Anneke cheerfully. The macaw on her shoulder bobbed and weaved. "If we can require life insurance companies to offer lower rates to vegetarians, it will mean official recognition that vegetarians live longer than people who eat dead animals." She waited for a response; when Karl merely took the pamphlet without comment she smiled and moved away.

A splash of color caught Anneke's eye, a couple of dozen people grouped together in brilliant plumage. It took her a minute to sort it out visually; they wore what seemed to be an assortment of ethnic costumes, Chinese robes next to Polynesian sarongs, Latin-American peasant skirts next to African dashikis and Indian saris and other clothing that she couldn't begin to identify. All of them carried signs with hand-lettered slogans: DIVERSITY BEGINS IN THE KITCHEN, and PROTECT ETHNIC FOOD CHOICES, and MAN DOES NOT LIVE BY BREAD ALONE, this last emblazoned with a group of Chinese characters and a picture of a bowl of rice.

There was a sudden clash of sound, and a huge dragon head appeared, its bright red-and-green body whipping behind it. The group chanted and applauded as the dragon danced and swayed.

Anneke clapped her hands with delight. "I don't know if it works, but this is certainly a lot more fun than your average protest."

The crowd moved then, pressing forward into a tighter group. The wrought-iron-clad City Hall doors opened and Griffith Carr emerged. There were shouts and catcalls; several groups began chanting, their competing messages drowning each other out; picket signs waggled. Television lights flashed on, and in their sudden glare Anneke caught a look of triumph, instantly shuttered, in Griffith Carr's pale blue eyes.

"Thank you all for coming." Carr's voice, amplified through the microphones, had the practiced timbre of the experienced lecturer. "This is an important moment—the moment in which we reclaim the right of the American people to make healthy food choices. This is the moment when we tell the multinational food corporations and their marketing manipulators that we will no longer allow them to get rich at the expense of the health of the American people." He paused, and small groups scattered throughout the crowd burst into applause. Scattered, or stationed? Anneke wondered.

"So that's where he's going." Karl spoke under his breath. "Clever."

"Three years ago," Carr went on, "the surgeon general of the United States declared obesity to be the number one public health crisis in the United States. Since that time, not only has there been no progress in controlling this crisis, but in fact corporate food interests have blatantly *increased* their hold over the minds of the American public."

"Oh, he is good, isn't he?" Anneke said. "Instead of blaming people for being fat, he's blaming corporations for manipulating them into it."

"Well, you don't dare demonize overweight people; that would be politically incorrect. By painting them as victims, you allow them to feel it isn't their fault and you come off as their defender instead of their attacker."

"Right. Poor things, they're not responsible for their actions, the devil made them do it."

"And of course, if the devil makes you do something, then that thing is by definition evil, isn't it? So hamburgers are the devil's work."

"It also reinforces the view that fat people are weak," she pursued the logic to its conclusion. "And from there, it's only a step to concluding that they need to be protected from themselves by a benevolent, all-knowing government." If they were giving out awards for manipulation, Anneke thought Griffith Carr could beat out the fast-food industry in a heartbeat.

Carr had finished his disquisition on the obesity crisis. His carefully modulated voice dropped. "Lindsay Summers died surrounded by the toxic substances some people choose to call Classic American Cuisine." He twisted the last word into something unspeakably disgusting. "She died trying to save lives, the lives of millions of people who have been manipulated into believing that high-fat, high-cholesterol, nutrient-deficient food will reconnect them to the heartland of our country."

"Good grief, he's making it sound like she was poisoned by the food at the Maize and Blue," Anneke said. "Isn't that slanderous?"

Karl shook his head. "He's being very careful."

"But why is he attacking the Maize and Blue?"

"My guess is because focusing on 'cuisine' puts the spotlight on upscale restaurants that most voters don't patronize anyway. If he starts talking about fast-food hamburgers and french fries, he's attacking something the majority of people care about."

"On Tuesday morning," Carr boomed through the microphone, "I will introduce legislation in the House of Representatives that will change all that." There were more cheers. "We're putting a bounty on fat and on the people who are profiting from . . ."

"Hit it, ladies!" The deep contralto voice boomed out across the crowd, followed immediately by the crashing sound of a full orchestra at maximum amp, coming through a sound system that made Griffith Carr's sound like a damp karaoke machine. Heads swiveled; so did television cameras, as a conga line of gorgeous women strutted across the sidewalk and stopped directly in front of the podium. They stood with their legs planted apart in classic diva pose, raised their right arms high over their heads and pumped their fists. The music rose higher; the women raised cordless microphones to their lips and belted out the song.

*If. They. Could.* See. *Me now, those skinny friends of mine,*

The words boomed out over the crowd.

*Eating steak and ice cream in a chorus line,*

There were ten of them, in full regalia—long, slinky gowns slit to the thigh, elbow-length gloves, glittery high heels. The lead singer, in the center of the line, was an African American well above six feet tall, her high-piled hair making her even taller; she was wearing a form-fitting strapless electric blue taffeta dress, with a feather boa flipped artfully around her shoulders. Another wore rhinestone-studded scarlet slit to the hip; the woman at one end of the line wore hot pink, with rhinestones wound throughout her amazing mass of waist-length blond-and-purple hair. They were absolutely gorgeous.

*I'll let those dismal geeks choke down their bran flakes,*
*'Cause meanwhile I'm blissed out on choc-o-late cakes.*

And they were fat. Not just pudgy, but frankly fat. Flesh billowed over the tops of their gowns, and wobbled under the tight silks and taffetas; breasts thrust forward, straining against fabric. And they danced. They high-stepped, they strutted, they twirled, they shook their impressive booty at the audience.

*All I can say is, hon, I'll stick with apple pies,*

Which was now frankly audience instead of protest crowd, cheering and applauding as the women swung their hips and belted out the song in rich, powerful voices.

*Tonight I'm having burgers and a side of fries.*

A movement at the podium caught Anneke's eye. Griffith Carr was leaning down and whispering something to one of the uniformed police standing at the edge of the platform. The policeman listened, then shook his head and shrugged. Anneke thought she saw the ghost of a grin on his face. Carr kept his face smoothly neutral as he straightened and rested his elbows on the podium. It wasn't bad, Anneke thought, but it wasn't good enough; when everyone else is delighted with something, the astute politician registers equal delight.

> *So am I having fun yet? Hey, you better believe it,*
> *And my friends should see me now.*

"My God!" Anneke pointed. "Isn't that Noelle Greene?"

Karl nodded. "Didn't you recognize her until now?"

"I guess I don't have the trained cop's eye, Lieutenant. Besides, you can see over the crowd a lot better than I can."

"Want me to put you up on my shoulders?" He grinned down at her.

"Gee, I guess I'll pass." Anneke craned to get a clearer look. Noelle wore a taffeta confection of dark red and gold, with a waterfall of golden daisies wound in her thick auburn hair. Her smile was equally brilliant as the women swung into a reprise of the final chorus.

> *So here's to Häagen-Dazs, Godiva, Niman-Schell,*
> *Along with Mrs. Fields, and Sara Lee as well,*
> *So am I having fun? You better believe it,*
> *And my friends should see me no-o-ow.*

As the music crescendoed and finally died away, the lead singer stepped forward, towering over the crowd. "Thank you, ladies and gentlemen," she crowed through the microphone. "We're glad you enjoyed the show." She wriggled her lush body suggestively, and the crowd cheered. "If you'd like to see more—don't be naughty, you know what I mean—several of us are performing tomorrow night at Boney's." She leaned forward, cleavage heaving, and grinned wickedly at the audience. "Y'all come by, hear?"

Give Carr credit, Anneke thought; at least he knew when he was licked. As the crowd roared its approval, the congressman smiled and applauded with the rest. "Thank you all for coming," he said as the crowds dispersed. "I'll be available for media questions in the press room."

"I want to talk to Noelle." Anneke grabbed Karl's arm and pressed forward against the tide of people and animals and picket signs, fetching up finally in front of the steps, where the performers were still surrounded by spectators and fans and friends. "Noelle, you were wonderful!"

"Thank you, thank you." Noelle laughed and curtsied, her face flushed with pleasure and exertion.

"Wasn't she terrific?" The tall African American threw a massive arm around her shoulders. "I keep telling her to give up that tacky bank job and let me make her a star."

"Roxanne's seen *Victor/Victoria* seventeen times," Noelle said obscurely.

"Honey, you'd put Julie Andrews to shame." Roxanne hugged her. "Now I've got to get out of this regalia and become Rocky again. This wig's itching to drive me crazy." She reached up and tugged at her high-piled hair, which came away in his hand to reveal a smooth, short brush cut. "Bye-bye, love." He gave her a kiss on the cheek and strode away.

"Noelle, we need to talk." Mimi's arrival gave Anneke a chance to stifle her surprise at the sudden gender transformation. Mimi wore a charcoal gray power suit, Dolce & Gabbana shoes, and a grim expression on her face. She waved a leather-bound notebook. "We have to prepare a response to that." She jerked her head at the now-empty podium.

"I know." Noelle nodded, instantly businesslike. "A diversion can only do so much."

"I've made reservations at Colette's," Mimi said. "George is going to meet us there."

"Good." Noelle paused and shared a glance with the other woman. "Why don't you two join us?" she said to Anneke and Karl.

"Thank you, we will," Karl replied.

"One o'clock, then." Mimi spoke abruptly, shot Noelle another glance, and turned and walked away.

# FIFTEEN

"If we issue a statement, it will only focus more attention on it." Mimi took a bite of her crab salad, swirling it to pick up more of the thick bleu-cheese dressing.

"Well then, what can we do?" George McMartin asked peevishly. His bacon-tomato-chicken club sandwich, with green chile mayonnaise, lay half-eaten on his plate.

"How about providing nutrition information on the menu?" Noelle dipped a forkful of ahi with red pepper sauce into a mound of garlic mashed potatoes. She still wore the red-and-gold taffeta with daisies in her hair. She should have looked ridiculous in a room full of business suits, Anneke thought, but she just looked glorious. A few people had turned and smiled at her entrance, but after that her dress went unremarked.

"No!" George slapped his hand on the table. "Next you'll be suggesting that we include one of those barbarous 'lite' menus."

"Besides, all that does is play into their hands," Mimi pointed out. "It's practically an admission that Cody's food is unhealthy."

"The truth is, there isn't much we can do." Noelle shrugged, her cleavage quivering. "Any response will just make it worse. I think we just need to keep a low profile until it blows over." The notion of keeping a low profile in scarlet taffeta made Anneke smile.

"What did you think of Carr?" Mimi directed the question to the group as a whole. "Do you think he seriously cares about this food issue, or is he just using it for political advancement?"

"Both," Noelle replied immediately. "He's a True Believer—one of those ectomorphs who actually believes he's thin out of personal effort." She took another bite of garlic mashed potatoes. "It's like Ann Richards said about George Bush—Carr was born on third base and he thinks he hit a triple." She laughed at her own joke; so did Anneke.

Mimi just looked even gloomier. "That's the worst kind, you know—an effective and ambitious ideologue."

"He certainly had no qualms about using Lindsay's death, did he?" George sounded querulous. "I kept waiting for him to say 'she would have wanted it that way.' "

"Unfortunately, he's smarter than that," Mimi said.

"She wouldn't have, you know," Anneke commented. "Wanted it that way, I mean. Lindsay wasn't about self-sacrifice."

"What do you think it was?" Noelle asked curiously.

"I think," Anneke said slowly, "that Lindsay was part of the Fear Generation. The one that's been so bludgeoned by warnings and terrors and conflicting threats that they're nearly paralyzed by it. I think Lindsay was one of those people, the young and scared ones, who thought she could live forever if she just did everything right."

"Well, right now Carr's the issue." Mimi wrenched the conversation back on track. "And he's perfectly capable of destroying us if this murder isn't solved fast." She looked at Karl. "Has there been any progress?"

"Probably not the kind you mean." He set down his roast

beef sandwich with horseradish mayonnaise. "This is the kind of case that takes time. But then you'd know that, being an attorney."

"Dammit, we don't have time." Mimi looked flustered by her own outburst. "Sorry. And I'm not that kind of attorney," she said, forcing a smile. "I do strictly corporate, not criminal."

"Is time an issue?" Anneke put down her fork and pushed aside her half-full dish. Determined to eat a light lunch, she'd followed Mimi's lead by ordering the crab salad, only to be served with a bowl the size of a young bathtub, the greens nearly hidden by mounds of crabmeat, hardboiled egg, avocado, and bacon.

"Only in that we can't proceed with this cloud hanging over us." Mimi's voice was too casual, Anneke decided. And wasn't that a meaningful glance between Noelle and George?

"How exactly does a project like this proceed?" Anneke matched Mimi's casual tone. "I mean, once you have the financial backing," she glanced at Noelle, "what's the next step?"

"There are a number of next steps that all happen together." It was Noelle who answered. "There's marketing, and contracts, and bidding, and real estate, and purchasing—once you green-light a project, everything else has to be coordinated within a very tight time frame."

"I see." Anneke didn't, quite, but a couple of thoughts occurred to her. "This murder couldn't have come at a worse time for you, could it?" There were nods of agreement. "But I suppose a newspaper article about Lindsay's research might have caused its own kind of firestorm, wouldn't it?"

"Not really," Mimi replied quickly. "Because she wasn't focusing that specifically on Cody and the Maize and Blue."

Oh, but she was, Anneke mused, thinking back over Lindsay's questions. It hadn't occurred to her before, but now she wondered if there might have been something personal in Lindsay's selection of the Maize and Blue as the site for her research. Or in the fact that a reporter had been present, surely an unusual circumstance for a series of research interviews.

"Ms. Rojas, are you planning a response to Congressman Carr's speech?"

The question took them all by surprise. Mimi's fork clattered against her plate as she spun around to face Barbara Williams. In the glitter of the upscale restaurant, the newcomer was a beige splotch against the darkly sophisticated background, her anonymous, colorless appearance far more out of place than Noelle's exaggerated finery.

"Excuse me, Ms. Williams." Mimi bit off the words. "This is a private gathering."

"Mr. McMartin, do you think the food at the Maize and Blue is unhealthy?" Barbara plowed ahead as though Mimi hadn't spoken. Anneke thought her face was curiously expressionless.

"Please leave, Ms. Williams." Mimi directed an unnecessary warning glance at George.

"Do you think the Maize and Blue will become a symbol for anti-fat activists?" Barbara aimed the question at the table generally.

"All right, that's enough," George snapped. He stood up and waved toward the front of the restaurant.

"Are you aware that a San Francisco public interest group plans to publish a nutritional analysis of the Maize and Blue's menu?" Barbara's voice was as expressionless as her face, but there was an unmistakable undercurrent of malice in the question.

"Is there a problem, Mr. McMartin?" The maître d', arriving in response to George's semaphore, cast a quelling glance at Barbara Williams.

"This woman is intruding on our lunch, Kenneth." George glared at Barbara. "Would you please ask her to leave?"

"Of course, Mr. McMartin." Kenneth, slim and suffocatingly elegant in buttoned-up black silk, inserted himself between Barbara and the table. "Please come with me, miss."

Barbara stiffened, then shrugged. "Oh, all right." She favored the group with a last glance, and this time the malice was overt. "You'll be sorry you wouldn't talk to me," she said.

When she had gone, stalking out with Kenneth close behind, there were general sighs of relief. Only Mimi still looked disturbed.

"Was she telling the truth about the public interest group?" Mimi asked. The question was rhetorical, answered with uneasy shrugs.

"I don't see how," Noelle said finally. "And even if it is true, a full-scale nutritional analysis would take months."

"Yes—if they're just starting now," Mimi responded. "But what if they planned it a long time ago?"

"But why would anyone do that?" George asked. "Why target the Maize and Blue?"

"Because of the expansion? These groups have always gone after chain restaurants." Noelle shrugged. "I don't know. We're probably just being paranoid. Odds are she was just yanking our chains to see if we'd say something she could print."

"That's another thing." Mimi looked even more worried. "I was going to mention this before. I called friends of mine at both the *Chron* and the *Bay Guardian*. Turns out no one at either paper ever heard of Barbara Williams."

There was a brief silence while they digested Mimi's revelation. Then Noelle offered: "She did say she was a freelance writer. Maybe she's doing it on spec."

"Maybe." Mimi sounded unconvinced. "But apparently she's never written anything for either of them before." She turned to Karl. "Did the police do a background check on her? Do they know anything about her?"

"I don't know." Karl shook his head. "I can ask, but . . ."

"But you probably can't tell us the answer," Noelle said.

"Well, at least we know she's not part of the media mainstream."

"That could be more bad news than good," George retorted. "For all we know, she could hammer us in a food magazine, or even some online thing like the Drudge Report."

Mimi sighed audibly. "Well, right now I don't see anything we can do about it except keep our mouths shut."

"I suppose," George said. "But I still wish we knew who the hell Barbara Williams *is*."

# SIXTEEN

Peter Braxton's desk was piled with a mass of paperwork that he shoved aside with apparent gratitude. He motioned Karl and Anneke to chairs and poured them each coffee without asking.

"Reports." He sat back down at his desk and pushed at a stack of papers. "More reports." He dumped another stack on top of the first. "Expense sheets. Departmental memos. Union minutes. Automobile usage statistics. This is what I became a cop for?"

"Well, we do get all the bad coffee we can drink." Karl picked up the white SFPD mug he'd accepted only out of politeness and took a cautious sip. Anneke did the same, then followed with a longer swallow. Either Peter Braxton brewed his own, or the San Francisco PD actually knew how to make coffee. She suspected the former.

"Right." Braxton sighed. "What've you got for me?" He didn't sound enthusiastic.

"Quite a lot, actually." Anneke set half a dozen floppies on his desk. "I don't know how useful any of it will be, of course."

"Why don't you dump it all into our system." Braxton pointed to a computer setup across from his desk. "There's a temp directory in my account that you can use."

"Fine." Anneke moved to the chair at the computer and began feeding disks into its drive.

"Was there anything useful from the AAPD?" Karl asked Braxton.

"Not really." Braxton sounded gloomy. "Not that they didn't do their job," he acknowledged, "but except for the ex-husband, they didn't come up with any connection between the Summers girl and any of the others. I don't suppose . . ." He glanced toward Anneke hopefully.

"Afraid not." Karl shook his head.

"And of course, there may not even be any personal connection with the murderer." Braxton sounded, if possible, even gloomier. "If she was seen as a threat to the Maize and Blue expansion project, for instance. Sex or money—the two elemental motives."

"If you're looking for sex, there's apparently a boyfriend." Anneke pulled the last disk out of the drive as she spoke.

Braxton burst out laughing. "Thanks, but I'm spoken for."

"Very funny." She laughed at him over her shoulder. "Still, you might want to upgrade—this one may be a congressman."

"Oh?" Braxton was suddenly alert.

"It's only a guess," she warned him. "Take a look at Zoe's interview notes."

"Zoe?"

"A friend of ours who's a local reporter." There didn't seem to be any more accurate way to explain Zoe. She clicked on the file and began printing it out. "She talked to Lindsay's roommate, and to Griffith Carr's administrative assistant. Here." She handed the printed pages to Braxton, who scanned them rapidly.

"Nothing but speculation. And anyway, Carr was in Washington when she was killed. It's the ex-husband who was right on the scene. Not to mention the ex's current squeeze." He dropped the pages onto his desktop and seemed to relapse into his earlier gloom. "I suppose it needs to be followed up. And Carr's going to be in here this afternoon anyway. You want to sit in?" he asked Karl.

"Sure." Karl nodded. "Was there anything that points to Jeremy Blake other than his relationship with the victim?"

"Nothing specific, no," Braxton admitted. "He was married to the Summers woman for only six months, there was a no-fault divorce, no alimony, and as far as we can tell, there hasn't been any contact between them since." He scrabbled among the piles of paper, unearthed a thick sheaf paper-clipped together, and riffled through it. "Graduated from Michigan in ninety-four with a business degree, got a job in San Francisco with Muscles—that's a West Coast chain of health clubs. He left them in ninety-eight to open his own club, and now he's got six of them around the Bay Area."

"Are they financially healthy?"

"As far as we know." Braxton shrugged. "No reason to assume they aren't. And no reason to assume it has anything to do with the murder anyway," he added peevishly.

"What about Mimi Rojas?"

Braxton turned pages. "Mercedes Rojas," he read aloud. "Born in Fresno. B.A. from Stanford, law degree from Michigan in nineteen ninety-seven." He looked up. "Blake had already left Ann Arbor by then," he noted. "She's an associate at Starks and Gonzalez. Says she and Blake met two years ago at some Michigan alumni function. They're a couple, but they're not living together. Also says she knew he'd been married and didn't think anything about it." He held out his hands, palms up. "Well, she would, wouldn't she?"

"But why *would* she care?" Anneke interjected. "I mean, so what if he'd been married? Besides," she added, "Mimi and Jeremy don't seem all that . . . I don't know, passionate about each other, do they?"

"You can't ever tell that from outside a relationship," Braxton argued. "Women can be very good at hiding their real feelings." There was no answer to that, and Anneke didn't try to give one. "Suppose Mimi thought there was still something between Jeremy and Lindsay?" Braxton said. Anneke didn't respond. There wasn't the slightest evidence for that, or he'd have said so.

"I assume the rest of your interrogations weren't any more useful?" Karl asked finally.

"You assume right." Braxton scrabbled around some more in the piles of paper and pulled out another thick sheaf. His face held a look of deep disgust. "See no evil, hear no evil, speak no evil." He tossed the papers to Karl, who skimmed them briefly, then went back and read one page more carefully.

"What's the Zero Café?" he asked.

"The place where that reporter works?" Braxton looked at him quizzically. "It's down in Mission Terrace. She said she works there part-time until she can support herself with her writing. Half the kids in this city support themselves working in cafés while they finish the Great American Novel, or the Great American Movie, or the Great American Computer Game."

"Have you seen anything that Barbara Williams has actually written?"

"No." Braxton leaned forward. "Why the interest?"

"Because she seems like some sort of wild card. Nobody's ever heard of her, including the newspapers she says she's writing for, and yet she keeps popping up everywhere we turn." He gestured at the report he'd put back on Braxton's desk. "And there's practically no personal background in your report."

Braxton picked up the report and glanced through it. "Born nineteen seventy-five in Baltimore. One year at Anne Arundel Community College. Shares an apartment on Guerrero with another girl and a guy. No priors here or back in Maryland." He looked at Karl. "You think she's hiding something?"

"I don't know." Karl spread his hands. "She just seems awfully . . . anonymous."

"It's San Francisco." Braxton sighed. "We get the drifters, and the dreamers, and the escapees, and the romantics. And the disenchanted and the angry, of course. Some of them even *do* write the novel or make the movie." He sighed again. "We'll check her out."

"It might be a good idea to have Ann Arbor check her out, too." Karl made a note to himself. "Sometimes it's the first stop for the kind of kids you're talking about."

"Good idea. If there's—" He stopped at the sound of a knock on the door. "That must be the congressman. Come in," he called.

"Inspector Braxton?" Griffith Carr entered the office and strode directly to Braxton's desk. He held out his hand. "Griffith Carr, Ann Arbor. You're in charge of the investigation into Lindsay's murder? What can you tell me so far? Have you made any progress?" Off the podium and without a prepared script, Griffith Carr talked too fast, the words tumbling out and tripping over each other. Braxton waited until he'd stopped, then waited another beat.

"Congressman." He inclined his head and accepted the handshake. "Please, sit down." Carr looked at the indicated chair almost with annoyance before finally perching on its front edge, leaning forward as though ready to spring to his feet at any second. Braxton motioned at Karl. "This is Lieutenant Karl Genesko, and Anneke Haagen, from the Ann Arbor Police Department." It was an odd—and calculated, Anneke thought—way of introducing them.

"Really." Carr looked momentarily startled. "I'm glad to see the Ann Arbor police putting so much effort into finding Lindsay's killer." He seemed to assume they'd been sent purposely to San Francisco, and Braxton didn't correct him. "What's the status of your investigation, Inspector?"

"In fact, we're hoping you can help." Braxton turned the question. "The more we know about Lindsay Summers, the faster we can solve this. And you were probably as close to her as anyone else." There wasn't the slightest trace of innuendo in his voice.

If it was bait, Carr didn't rise to it. "I suppose that's true," he agreed. "Lindsay was so focused on her work that perhaps she didn't spare enough time for personal relationships. But unfortunately I don't think I can tell you anything that will help."

"You were her academic advisor, is that right?" Braxton passed over Carr's denial.

"Yes." Carr nodded.

"Then you'd know why she selected the Maize and Blue for her research?"

"Well, not exactly." Carr moved in his chair. "We did feel that bars, especially sports bars, were an optimum target, but I don't know for a fact why she chose this particular one."

"Why were sports bars an optimum target?" Braxton asked.

"Because sports bars are perhaps the most pernicious example of toxic food in America." Carr's voice rose. "Think of the food choices at these places. Virtually everything on the menu is fried, or greasy, or fatty. Dripping cheeseburgers, potato skins oozing cheese and bacon, fried potatoes, fried onion rings, even fried *cheese*, for God's sake!" The very notion of fried cheese seemed to enrage him. "In fact, these bars are probably even worse than fast-food restaurants, because the servings are bigger and people tend to eat even more of it."

"But that doesn't really describe the kind of food the Maize and Blue serves," Braxton pointed out mildly. "Cody Jarrett does a much more sophisticated cuisine than the average sports bar."

"Sophisticated cuisine? Inspector, this Nouvelle Midwest scam is just a trendy way of pandering to people's worst appetites. Cholesterol-loaded scrambled eggs, fatty sausages, fried doughnuts, macaroni and cheese, and everything so loaded with eggs and butter and fatty meats it's amazing that anyone walks out of there alive." Carr seemed to hear his own intensity for the first time. "Sorry, Inspector." He smiled. "Didn't mean to get on my hobby horse."

"So Ms. Summers selected the Maize and Blue in order to discredit Nouvelle Midwest cuisine?" Braxton didn't respond to the smile.

"Not that I know of." Carr spread his hands. "At least, she never mentioned it to me. I'd never heard of Nouvelle Midwest until this happened. I think she just chose it because it was a sports bar in San Francisco. And the Michigan connection guaranteed an educated sample. You have to understand, Inspector, this wasn't just a fishing expedition." He spoke didactically. "There are required research parameters that have to be fulfilled, especially in the area of demographics. That means a variety of subjects differentiated by geographic area, and education, and income," he explained.

"Yes, I do know what demographic means." Braxton's mouth twitched. "How did she locate the Maize and Blue in the first place?" he went on. "Did she come out here in advance to search for sites?"

"No." Carr shook his head. "Mostly she got suggestions from people in Ann Arbor who'd been to the various cities she wanted to cover."

"Oh?" Braxton looked at him. "And who was it who suggested the Maize and Blue?"

"I have no idea," Carr replied.

"What about her personal life?" Braxton turned to another subject. "We understand she'd just broken up with her boyfriend?" He made it a question.

"Lindsay was very focused on her work," Carr didn't exactly answer the question. "I imagine most boys her age might find that hard to deal with." Anneke recalled that Lindsay Summers had been twenty-eight years old, hardly a kid, but didn't say anything.

"Was the boyfriend another student, then?"

"I have no idea." Carr shook his head. "I doubt that it was serious, whoever he was. Lindsay didn't really have much time for that sort of thing."

"So you don't know who this boyfriend was." Braxton waited until Carr shook his head again. "What about her other friends?"

"What do you mean?"

"Can you tell us who her close friends were?" Braxton let impatience creep into his voice. "Who she might have confided in?"

"Not really, no. As I said, I don't think Lindsay had much time for socializing. Her work was too important to her." For the first time, Anneke found herself feeling legitimately sorry for Lindsay Summers.

Braxton asked more questions about Lindsay's personal life, and Carr responded with more answers about her work. Either he didn't know anything about Lindsay on a personal level, or he was one of the better liars Anneke had ever seen. And Braxton had no leverage to use on him.

"Thank you, Congressman." Braxton capitulated finally. "Unless either of you has any questions?" he said to Karl and Anneke.

"Was Lindsay expecting to finish her dissertation this year?" Anneke asked.

"No." Carr looked startled by her question, although whether by the question itself or its source she couldn't tell. "She was still just at the data collection stage."

"But then how could she be far enough along for you to use her work as the basis for your legislation?"

"That's different." Carr looked momentarily annoyed. "Academic research operates under unique and sometimes arcane strictures that often have nothing to do with the real world." Carr stood up. "I have a plane to catch, Inspector. Please keep my office informed about your progress."

"Now what was that about?" Braxton asked when he was gone.

"I don't know." Anneke shook her head. "He seemed more disturbed by a question about Lindsay's research than about her personal life, didn't he?"

# SEVENTEEN

It took Zoe ten minutes wandering the halls of the public health school before she found the graduate student lounge. Along the way, she paused to read bulletin boards, not surprised to see Lindsay's name in a few places. Most of them were concerned with academic housekeeping. Lindsay was on a list of proseminar participants; she was on another list of research funding applicants; she was the subject of a congratulatory memo for an article in some academic journal Zoe had never heard of, with a title she didn't understand. But if there was any memorial service planned, Zoe saw no sign of it.

When she finally reached the grad lounge and stepped through the open door she saw three people sitting around a scarred Formica table. They looked up briefly when she arrived, then returned to their impassioned argument about—water?

"If you improved water quality, people wouldn't swill so much oversweetened crap." The speaker was a young woman in a denim shirt, plump and wholesome-looking, with light brown, flyaway hair and a scrubbed pink face. She picked up a plastic bottle of designer water and took a long drink.

"Oh, come on, Peg. As if people even care about water quality. Or the quality of anything they eat or drink, for that matter." The short, skinny guy next to her reached into a plastic bag, withdrew a carrot stick, and bit down savagely.

"Well, but that's part of our job, isn't it, Harry?" Peg insisted. "Educating them so they *will* care?"

"Hey, there's an idea." The woman leaning back in her chair seemed older than the other two, broad and muscular, with skin the color of shiny ebony and clever, humorous features. "How 'bout if we just *tell* people they should drink water instead of soda? And then maybe we could tell them they should eat more vegetables and fewer fried foods? Now why didn't anyone think of that before?" The words were sarcastic, but the woman's cheerful tone and good-humored expression made them amusing instead of offensive.

"All right, all right." Peg laughed and made a face. "I know it's not that simple. But that's one reason to improve water quality, isn't it? So people will *want* to drink more of it?"

"You're confusing quality with taste, honey. Unless you slop a pound of sugar into it, you still aren't going to be able to compete with the soda people." She looked at Zoe and winked. "How many glasses of water do you drink each day?" she asked.

"You mean, like, from the faucet?"

The woman roared with laughter. "There you have it. The American public has spoken."

"Oh, come on, Pauletta. Does she even know she's *supposed* to drink eight glasses of water a day?" Peg phrased the question for her friend, but directed it at Zoe.

"Well, but I get that much water from other drinks." Zoe suddenly felt defensive. "I mean, I drink lots of coffee, and soda, and juices sometimes."

This time all three of them broke up laughing. "You see?" Peg chortled. "She *doesn't* know."

"Know what?" Zoe tried to keep annoyance out of her voice.

"Honey, caffeine is a diuretic. Coffee and soda don't hydrate your body, they *de*hydrate it. Now," she said briskly, "were you looking for someone?"

"I've blown my cover as a public health student, right?" Zoe figured she might as well laugh at herself. "I'm Zoe Kaplan, from the *Daily*. I wanted to ask about Lindsay Summers." Both statements were perfectly true, she reflected; only the implied connection was off.

Their reactions were interesting. Peg looked uncomfortable, almost guilty; the man named Harry looked angry; Pauletta, for some reason, seemed wary. She straightened up and placed her hands on the table. "I'm Pauletta Woodson. What did you want to know?"

"Anything you can tell me," Zoe replied honestly. She waited, knowing at least one of them would break the silence and betting it would be Peg.

She was wrong. "Lindsay was brilliant." It was Harry who spoke. "She was a fruit loop, but she was brilliant and she could've done some great work if she'd had any sort of guidance. Instead, she got tangled up with God's Gift."

"That's not fair, Harry," Peg argued. "It wasn't Professor Carr's fault that Lindsay was such a pain in the ass." She flushed and looked at Zoe. "I shouldn't have said that. You're not going to print that, are you?"

"No, of course not," Zoe reassured her.

"And anyway, why not?" Even Harry's shrug looked angry. "That's maybe the kindest thing anyone's said about her. Look." He seemed anxious to talk. "Lindsay was a total wacko about food," he said to Zoe, "and it poisoned everything else in her life. She was a poster child for victims of controlling parents, you know? The kind of kid who tries to regain control over her own life by controlling her food intake? Only in Lindsay's case it spilled over into her relationships with other people, too. If controlling her own eating didn't make her feel more secure, maybe controlling other people's eating would. And if she could control the whole world, so much the better."

It was pop psychology at its worst, but Zoe thought there might be some truth in it. She also wondered why it made Harry so angry. Was he tapping in to his own family problems? Or had he maybe been in love with Lindsay? Could he be the missing boyfriend?

"Tough for her," Zoe said. The sympathy in her voice was real, although it was for Harry rather than Lindsay. "She must have been an awfully unhappy person."

"She was." Harry looked at her with surprised gratitude. "Most people didn't understand that."

"Harry, she wasn't any more unhappy than the rest of us, and a lot less than most." Pauletta spoke sharply. "She was arrogant, and demanding, and the most high-maintenance child I've ever seen. And you're not going to print that, either," she told Zoe.

"She wasn't like that at all once you got to know her," Harry retorted angrily.

"Yes, she was." This time it was Peg who seemed angry. "Lindsay wasn't just a control artist, she was a user."

"Oh, control artist." Harry fastened on the first accusation instead of the second. "Hell, we're all control addicts around this place." He waved an arm. "Why else would we be here if we didn't think we had all the answers to how people should live?"

"That's not true," Peg objected. "Making sure people have safe water to drink, and safe air to breathe, and safe food to eat isn't trying to control them."

"Yeah, but that's not all most of us are about." Pauletta unexpectedly sided with Harry. "Admit it, if you could force people to eat right, and exercise, and quit smoking, and all the things we know they should do, wouldn't you do it?"

"Not force." Peg shook her head stubbornly. "If we could *convince* people to live healthy lives we wouldn't have to force them."

Pauletta threw back her head and laughed. "In other words, you won't force them as long as they do it willingly."

"Besides," Peg went on, "I don't think Lindsay really cared about other people, she just wanted to get ahead. Look how she used Griff, sucking up to him to get on conference panels, and getting him to publicize that awful dissertation of hers."

"*She* used *him*?" Harry burst out. "It's *his* fault her dissertation is totally bogus. He took all her ideas, all her work, and he twisted it, and corrupted it, and turned it all into political hackwork for the glorification of the great and wonderful Griffith Carr." He jumped to his feet and grabbed at a stack of books on the table. "Oh, forget it," he shouted over his shoulder as he stamped out of the lounge.

"Poor Harry." Peg looked after him with an expression of sympathetic affection but not, Zoe thought, any deeper emotion.

"Did Lindsay know how he felt about her?" Zoe asked.

"If she did, she didn't bother to show it," Peg said bitterly. "After all, Griff could do so much more for her academic career."

Did Peg have a crush on Griffith Carr? "What's Carr like?" she asked lightly. "On his campaign posters he looks pretty hot."

"Hot? Griff?" Peg hooted with real amusement. "The guy's got all the sex appeal of a radish."

"Too bad." Zoe grinned, her mind racing. If not sex, what?

"He does have that whole committed, intense, ambitious thing going on," Pauletta said. "And that can be very attractive to a certain type of naive young girl who wants to change the world."

"I suppose that's an occupational hazard for a lot of faculty members. Kind of like psychiatrists," Zoe said. "And we all know they sometimes get offers they can't refuse."

"I suggest you be very careful about instigating false rumors, Miss Kaplan." Zoe whirled around; Gloria McGyver was standing in the doorway, with a look on her face that would have frozen Medusa herself in her tracks. "I would remind you that the laws of libel apply equally to slander."

"I was just . . ." Zoe found herself fluttering her hands, like a third-grader caught with the class gerbil in her pocket.

"I know perfectly well what you were 'just.'" McGyver sailed across the room to a bank of wooden cubbyholes, reached into one of them, and withdrew a messy collection of multicolored papers and envelopes. "And I'm warning you that gossip can be just as dangerous to the perpetrator as it is to the victim."

"I wasn't . . ." Whoa. Why was she letting this woman turn her into a blithering idiot? And anyway, what was McGyver doing here in the first place? Zoe pulled herself together and tried again. "Are you picking up Professor Carr's mail?"

"*Congressman* Carr's departmental mail goes to his own office." She thrust the mass of papers into the pocket of her brown wool coat and stalked out of the room. Zoe waited until she was gone before walking over to the bank of cubbyholes and peering at the one Gloria McGyver had just emptied. "She took Lindsay's mail," she said. "Should she have done that?"

"Probably." Pauletta waved a hand. "It's just the usual departmental junk. This week it's multiple memos about not putting our feet on the tables." She proceeded to demonstrate by leaning back and propping her size-ten Adidas on the wobbly coffee table.

"Yeah, I suppose." Zoe put aside the issue of departmental mail and turned to Peg. "McGyver seemed awfully worried about gossip. *Was* there any about Griff and any students?"

"Never," Peg replied sharply. "There's never been a single

rumor about him and a student. He was always too smart to risk that kind of trouble, until . . ." She didn't have to finish the sentence.

"Yeah, it is dangerous, isn't it?" The University regs prohibiting student-faculty sex had teeth in them, these days. Zoe wondered if maybe anyone—Peg?—had threatened to file a complaint against Carr, but decided probably not. It would be Carr who'd take the heat, not Lindsay. Still . . . "Still, I bet he had offers. They do say that power is an aphrodisiac."

"Power isn't an aphrodisiac, it's a lure, a mistress." Peg's scrubbed face suddenly twisted into something ugly. "And some people will do anything to get it, including pretending that it *is* sex appeal."

Bingo. Peg had been jealous of Lindsay, all right, but over academic, not sexual, favors. Zoe asked a question she already knew the answer to. "What exactly was her dissertation about?"

"Food choices—how and why people select the foods they eat."

"Sounds like a hot topic."

"Oh, it is." Peg laughed without humor. "Somebody should do research about it some day."

"They will, honey, they will." Pauletta took a sip from her bottle of water and set it down on the table with a thump. "There's always research money available for yuppie issues."

"What's your research interest?" Zoe asked out of curiousity.

"Well, my dissertation's about toxic waste dumping in African American neighborhoods," she replied, "but more broadly, I'm interested in public health issues that affect the black community. And believe me, honey, too much food is purely a white folks' issue." She laughed. "Ann Arbor yuppies sure are eating it up in this election, though."

"Yeah, that's pretty much Carr's major campaign focus, isn't it?" Zoe tried to recall recent election coverage; Griffith

Carr's campaign seemed to be mostly a series of statements concentrating on his public health expertise.

"Just about all of it." Pauletta nodded. "Oh, he says all the right liberal things about racism and unions and such, but he sure never sounds like he cares a whole lot." She leaned back and looked at Zoe shrewdly. "We haven't given you very much you can actually print, have we? Not much that wouldn't be libelous, anyway."

"No, I guess not." Zoe sighed with, she hoped, just the right amount of frustration. "Thanks anyway." She turned and left the way she'd come, uncomfortably aware of Pauletta Woodson's eyes following her.

# EIGHTEEN

There was still some afternoon remaining when they left the Hall of Justice. Anneke and Karl returned to the Ritz-Carlton, changed clothes, and drove out to the beach. While Karl set off for a run, Anneke strolled along the edge of the water, watching tiny darting birds racing before the tide and listening to the call of seagulls and the happy yapping of Frisbee-chasing dogs. By the time Karl returned, murder seemed very far away, and she sank into the car with a comfortable sigh, thinking of nothing more earthshaking than dinner somewhere by the water.

The car radio brought her back to earth with a thump. In the welter of traffic reports and local politics, she caught the words "Maize and Blue." She reached forward and turned up the volume.

". . . what they're calling a 'dine-in' in opposition to, quote, 'the tyranny of the low-fat paradigm.' "

The smooth voice of the professional newsreader was replaced by a sharply pitched female voice. "We've had low-fat eating shoved down our throats for more than a decade now, and yet year by year the American people get fatter instead of thinner. Their way doesn't work, and Craig Cornwell's way does, and we want to educate people to a way of eating they can actually live with."

"Dr. Cornwell," the newsreader returned, "is in the Bay Area speaking at a UCSF symposium, but the organizers of the dine-in haven't confirmed whether he'll be at the Maize and Blue this evening."

"Good God." Anneke shook her head in disbelief. "This is all Richard needs. Why the Maize and Blue, for heaven's sake?"

"Because it's in the news, and they can piggyback on its notoriety." Karl shrugged.

"I suppose we should . . . Damn. I really was looking forward to a nice, quiet—and *light*—dinner."

"We don't need to go at all, you know," Karl pointed out.

"No, but . . ." She wasn't sure what to put after the "but," only that there was a "but."

"Well, how about someplace for tapas and drinks, and then to the Maize and Blue afterward?"

"All right." She sighed. "What a mess. Poor Richard must be frantic."

But in fact, when they arrived at the Maize and Blue, it was Richard who seemed less frantic than anyone else. And God knew he'd have had good reason, given the crowds that filled the sidewalk.

There were—she did a quick estimate—maybe a hundred people in front of the restaurant, milling or marching, chanting or orating before the inevitable TV cameras. A line of resigned-looking uniformed cops stood between the demonstrators and the maize-and-blue door.

Nowadays, if you announce a demonstration, a dozen opposing or competing splinter groups will show up to jostle for TV time. Anneke recognized some of the same signs and placards she'd seen during the City Hall demonstration— ANIMALS ARE PEOPLE TOO, FAMILY FARMS = FAMILY VALUES— along with some new ones. BIKES, NOT DIETS, for instance, carried by an impossibly thin, stringy young man in neck-to-thigh Lycra perched on a seven-hundred-dollar mountain bike, surrounded by half a dozen similar bikers. An oldie but goodie, FAT IS A FEMINIST ISSUE in the hands of a plump, elderly woman. There was a small clutch of young people in blue surgical scrubs, sporting large red buttons that read PHYSICIANS FOR DIETARY SANITY and shoving pamphlets in people's faces.

And there was a darker, uglier tone to one segment of the crowd. A sign that read CORNWELL CONDONES MURDER was carried by a small, thin young girl—woman?—who shouted the slogan aloud, over and over, in a furious monotone. There was a sign with the words CORPORATE KILLERS over the logo of a famous fast-food chain. Another, bearing a picture of a bellowing cow, read EAT YOUR OWN CHILDREN, NOT OURS. They were only a small subgroup of the crowd, but they were tight-lipped and hostile and angry enough to make Anneke take a step away from them. She was relieved when Karl took her arm and steered her down the sidewalk away from the demonstrators.

"We'd better go in through the back," he said. He steered her around the side of the building and to the mouth of an alley, where three uniformed police blocked their way. He flipped open his wallet to display his shield. "Karl Genesko, Ann Arbor PD. I'm liaising with Inspector Braxton on the Summers case." One of the cops examined the shield and accompanying identification with painful thoroughness before stepping aside to let them through.

If it's this crazy out here, it must be a madhouse inside, she reasoned, but when she stepped through the back door Cody

Jarrett's kitchen seemed no more disorganized than it had . . . Good Lord, was it only one day ago?

"Anneke! Karl! Come in, come in!" Richard spotted them as they worked their way carefully past the salad station and the irritated glare of a large Asian man. Cody was right, she thought briefly; any outsider would have been spotted at once.

"Isn't this a hoot?" Richard beamed at them. "Mimi and Jeremy and some of the others are here. Come this way." He headed toward the swinging double doors without waiting for a response, and they followed him into the main dining room, where Anneke stopped for a minute, mildly stunned by the scene in front of her.

Every table was full, and the crowd around the bar was three deep. Harried servers whirled back and forth, loaded trays held high. And if the decibel level was any indication, everyone seemed to be enjoying themselves.

Richard led them to a table near the front door, where Mimi looked up anxiously at their approach.

"How's Cody doing?" she asked Richard.

"Fantastic." Richard beamed. "So far he's fired the dessert chef twice, quit once himself, and threatened to move to either Alaska or Cuba. I've never seen him play the temperamental chef before—it's an absolute revelation."

"Well, I suppose anyone would be unnerved to be surrounded by shouting protestors," Anneke said, sitting down across the table from Mimi.

"Oh, protestors." Richard waved a hand, dismissing protestors. "Cody doesn't care about that."

"Then what . . ."

"The menu." Elisa Falcone made a face. "All these people—" she waved a hand to encompass the jammed dining room "—and every one of them demanding off-menu food choices. It's too much, really it is." She glared at Mimi, who shrugged uneasily.

"*Au contraire*," Richard said, laughing. "The truth is,

Cody's having the time of his life—rewriting the menu, working out new combinations, inventing new recipes on the fly." He patted Elisa's shoulder, not seeming to notice that she drew away in annoyance. "Truly, he really is loving the sheer challenge of it."

And so was Richard, Anneke realized. Far from being frantic, he actually seemed to be enjoying the drama of it all. His face was flushed, his grin spread ear to ear, and he no longer looked tired or worried. Richard for once was in his element.

"Still, how can you expect a chef to function under these conditions?" Elisa was unappeased. "No bread, no potatoes or rice, no sugar—or even fruit!—for desserts. It's ridiculous."

"He's actually done very well, under the circumstances." George McMartin offered. "In fact, those cream cheese-caviar appetizers in lettuce rolls could become a permanent addition to the menu. And the shredded cabbage pancakes were actually more interesting than potato pancakes." He spooned something dark and chocolatey from a dessert dish in front of him and rolled it in his mouth thoughtfully.

"They're all insane, of course," Jeremy Blake muttered. He bit savagely into a breadstick. "If I ever get my hands on that quack Cornwell . . ."

"Oh, honestly," Elisa snapped. "Could we possibly have *one* occasion in which you two *didn't* fight the diet wars?"

"It's not—" Jeremy began.

"Yes, it is." It was George who interrupted. "Ever since you two got together, every conversation eventually devolves into the same damn argument."

"He's right." Mimi flushed with embarrassment. "We shouldn't . . ." She waved a hand in the air, and Jeremy captured it between his own.

"Hey, I'm sorry. You know." He didn't explain what she was supposed to know, and for a moment there was an awkward silence.

"How did you two happen to meet?" Anneke used the silence to probe for information.

"At one of Jeremy's health clubs." Mimi seemed grateful for the change of subject. "During one of my diet disasters, when I was trying to lose weight on a thousand calories of fruits and vegetables a day."

"Which you would have if—no, sorry." Jeremy grinned at her, looking suddenly like someone who cared. "I remember it was Cara English who brought you in. Another Michigan alum," he explained to Anneke. "I took one look at those great big eyes and that was it."

"I thought it was those great big other things," Mimi said.

"Well, that too." They both laughed, looking into each other's eyes, before Mimi colored and looked away. "Anyway, I still go to the club regularly, I just eat my own way now."

"Have you lost a lot of weight on the Cornwell diet?" Anneke asked.

"Seventeen pounds so far," she answered proudly. "Another thirty to go."

"Thirty!" Mimi was no sylph, but Anneke thought thirty pounds sounded extreme. "Do you really need to lose that much more?"

"Yep." Mimi nodded. "And now let's talk about something more interesting than my ongoing diet struggles." She turned to Karl. "What's happening outside?"

"Nothing very much," he replied. "Really just a lot of milling around."

"Well, we can't have that," Richard spoke up, smiling broadly. "I think it's time to do something for the poor wee folk out there."

"Richard . . ." Mimi's voice was heavy with warning.

"Not to worry, darlin'. I'm just going to provide a lovely treat for the poor dears, courtesy of the Maize and Blue." He held up a hand, and a young waiter scurried over. "Take the best care of these good people, Doug," he said, and then: "I'll just go and set things in motion."

"What on earth is he up to?" Anneke asked after they'd ordered drinks.

"I don't know." Mimi cast an uneasy glance toward the kitchen. "Oh, *Dios*," she said suddenly.

The swinging double doors flew open and Richard emerged, with a small parade of white-clad kitchen staff following behind. Each of them held aloft a huge tray of appetizer-sized morsels, beautifully arranged on beds of greens. In the center of each tray was a small Michigan pennant. The parade of servers swept to the front of the dining room, where Richard flung open the door and stepped out with a dramatic flourish. Anneke almost expected him to shout *"Voilà!"*

Instead, he stood still for a moment, and in that moment he was suddenly lit up by a blaze of television lights. He bowed and postured, sweeping the tray in front of him.

"Gentlemen and gentlewomen, welcome to the Maize and Blue!" There were shouts from the crowd outside, cheers mixed with boos and catcalls and shouted slogans. "No one," Richard proclaimed, "goes hungry here, no matter their beliefs or preferences or needs. For you good people who grace us with your presence at our door, we have food so pristinely vegan, yet so delicious, that I promise you'll dance with the joy of it!" This time the cheers definitely outnumbered the boos.

"Even for Richard, isn't this a little over the top?" Jeremy muttered.

"Maybe, but it's playing well," Mimi disagreed. They seemed to disagree on everything.

"I especially commend to you the mushrooms stuffed with hummus," Richard went on. He passed his tray to a white-coated server before continuing. "There's also a new specialty Cody's created just for you good people—the most absolutely sublime Michigan cherry fritters." This time the cheers were muffled through filled mouths; through the door, they could see the assembled demonstrators—most of them, anyway—throw themselves on the platters of food as the servers passed among them. "And for all of you, of course, packages of Cody Jarrett's signature trail mix to take home to your loved ones." He raised one arm like a conductor and waved it in the air. "Enjoy!" he shouted, whirled, and disappeared out of the glare of lights.

A burst of spontaneous applause erupted throughout the packed dining room. Richard reappeared, bowing and smiling. It was going to make a terrific TV sound bite, Anneke concluded.

"Wow." Noelle Greene appeared suddenly from the direction of the kitchen with Blair Falcone alongside her. He helped her off with her coat and pulled out her chair before seating himself across the table from her. Noelle, large and resplendent in yards of black silk over an emerald green slip dress, winked at him. "If that doesn't make tonight's news, nothing will."

"Yes, but this is hardly the kind of publicity we want." Elisa cast a severe look at Noelle. "Did you and Blair finish the financial prospectus?"

"Not yet." Noelle shook her head of cascading curls. "There are still a lot of numbers to crunch. We'll need to work nights for a while yet." She grinned at Blair, who smiled back.

Like hell numbers are what you're crunching, Anneke thought. She caught Noelle's eye, and was rewarded with a wink of her own. Elisa, oblivious, was gnawing her lower lip.

"There isn't going to be any problem with the financing, is there?" she asked.

"No, no," Blair answered her. "We just need to sort it all out." He reached for the bottle of wine in the middle of the table and poured some into a glass.

"Just one, Blair," Elisa warned him. He ignored her. He

ignored her most of the time, Anneke thought, or at least it seemed that way. Was theirs a marriage of convenience, she wondered? Elisa got wealth and position, Blair got—what? A social presence he couldn't manage on his own? Somehow that didn't seem like something he'd care about.

Well, what did he care about? Anneke wondered. She realized she hadn't paid much attention to him so far—for all his wealth and power, Blair Falcone managed a surprisingly low profile, at least in social settings. She looked at him now more closely, seeing his dark, rather closed face under crisp dark hair, the stocky body that even Armani tailoring couldn't make elegant, the heavy brows over eyes that remained fixed on his wineglass. His hands, large and square and unadorned except for a plain gold wedding band, rested on the table in front of him, utterly still. In fact, there was a stillness about Blair overall, a watchful quality even in repose. It occurred to Anneke that what Blair was, was that most unusual type of person, a true listener.

It also occurred to her that that was a quality that had a surprising level of sex appeal.

"When do you think it'll all be ready?" George asked.

"We're on schedule," Blair replied. "The contracts should be—" He stopped abruptly, stood up, and motioned toward the back of the room.

"Did you set this all up just for the publicity?" Barbara Williams seemed to pop up like a genie. Her face was as expressionless as ever, but her voice was accusing. George seemed to cower back in his chair; next to her, Anneke could feel rather than see Karl fix his attention on the newcomer. He didn't move, however, and neither did anyone else.

"Killian must've had the scene already prepared, didn't he?" Barbara went on. "And all this special food? Who's going to believe that even the great Cody Jarrett—" her voice dripped scorn "—could pull this off at a moment's notice?" When no one at the table replied, she raised her voice. "Don't think you can stonewall me and get away with it. I was there, remember? I—"

"Come with me, please, Ms. Williams." The rumbling baritone belonged to an enormous African American cop, so big he seemed to surround Barbara all by himself.

"This is a public place. I can—"

"No, you can't." The cop placed his hand on her arm. There were curious glances from nearby tables, but the policeman's voice was pitched so low that only the people in the immediate orbit could hear him.

"You can't—"

"Yes, I can," he interrupted her again. "I can escort you out, or I can arrest you." His hand tightened slightly on her arm. "Your choice."

"You'll be sorry." Barbara's gaze raked each of them in turn. "It's all going to come out, and there isn't a thing you can do about it." She allowed herself to be led toward the back door, where Richard stood, arms folded. She shot him a glare of such hatred as she passed that Richard took a step backward. Once again Anneke wondered exactly what Barbara's agenda was. She shared a glance with Karl; he'd also noted the silent exchange, but he only shook his head slightly.

"Did you read Walter Renaud's review of Down Home?" George asked.

"The place in Los Angeles that Disney's bankrolling?" Mimi shook her head. "What did he say?"

"Oh, he loved it. But then he would, wouldn't he?" George said bitchily. "It's L.A. They don't distinguish between quality and celebrity."

"They use *frozen* strawberries in their soufflés." Elisa shuddered delicately.

Anneke was suddenly fed up with food—eating it, talking about it, analyzing it, obsessing over it. She was fed up with these people, too, and completely and utterly sick of the Maize and Blue. She hadn't particularly wanted a traditional honeymoon, but this sure wasn't her alternative choice. She put her hand on Karl's knee under the table, and he glanced over at her and nodded.

"I think—" He started to rise, then stopped. There was a babble of noise as the front door was thrown open and a tall, silver-haired man strode into the dining room.

The room erupted. Diners stood and cheered, shouting and pounding on tables in paroxysms of excitement. The man smiled and waved as he progressed toward the bar, where he reached into a bowl, picked up a crisp bite of something, and popped it into his mouth. The assembled crowd roared its approval.

"What on earth—?" Anneke looked at Karl, but it was Mimi who responded.

"It's him!" Her dark eyes were wide and excited. "It's Craig Cornwell!"

# NINETEEN

Craig Cornwell had blue eyes, a tanned, cheerful face, and the lines and grooves that come with late middle age. Anneke guessed he was nearing sixty and carrying it with grace; he moved easily, like a man comfortable in his own skin.

And he wasn't thin, and neither was he fat. Anneke estimated him at around 180 pounds on an average-looking six-foot frame, with just the slightest hint of a paunch under his navy blue suit jacket. He was, in fact, a perfectly normal-looking man—if there was such a thing as normal, these days.

That much she noted before Cornwell was engulfed in an enthusiastic crowd, many of them waving books aloft, the whole scene lit by the TV camera crews that had followed Cornwell inside.

"Damn," Mimi muttered. "I wish I'd brought my book for him to sign."

"I wish I'd brought a gun," Jeremy said between gritted teeth.

"Dr. Cornwell, please?" A plump woman on the edge of the crowd was waving frantically, tears streaming down her face.

The TV crews, scenting drama, swiveled toward her as she worked her way through the cluster of people.

"Dr. Cornwell! I wanted . . . I just wanted to . . ." Her voice broke. "You saved my life," she said finally. The lights locked in on the tableau, Cornwell and the woman in high relief against the crowd.

Cornwell bent down slightly and took her hand. "I'm glad I could help," he said easily.

"I weighed three hundred and eighty pounds," the woman confided to him—and a few million TV voyeurs. "I was going to die. Now I weigh one sixty. It's a miracle." Tears continued to roll down her face as she gripped his hand.

"I'm so pleased for you." Cornwell smiled and disengaged his hand, patted her on the shoulder, turned toward the chubby man next to her, holding a book stiffly out in front of him. "Did you want me to sign that?" he asked, and took the book without waiting for a reply. He scribbled rapidly, returned it, and did the same for the woman behind him. The lights dimmed; book-signings apparently weren't the stuff of sound bites.

It was all very . . . practiced, Anneke thought. But then, to be fair, it would almost have to be. After all, he must deal with this every day. And there didn't seem to be anything phony or smarmy about him that she could see.

And frankly, she didn't give a damn. Craig Cornwell or no Craig Cornwell, she wanted to get out of here and spend some time with her new husband. She touched his arm and started to rise when a commotion arose outside.

". . . pernicious, life-threatening, and more cynically manipulative than even the fast-food lobby!"

"My God. It's *Danko*." Mimi made a sound like someone spitting out a bug.

"Danko?" Anneke couldn't help asking.

"Frau Doktor Melanie Danko." The name contained no sibilants, but Mimi contrived to hiss it anyway. "And *Sieg Heil* to you, too," she snarled.

"She's a TV doctor." Noelle came to Anneke's rescue, grinning. "Safe sex, safe eating, safe driving, safe drinking, safe living." She raised her wineglass high in the air. "To Melanie Danko, Queen of the Paranoiacs!" At the next table, a middle-aged couple laughed and threw Noelle a mock salute, the woman waving a forkful of steak.

". . . exploiting desperate people in order to sell books!" The woman's voice was sharp and clear and carried perfectly through the open door. The people in the dining room hissed and booed.

"How much is your TV contract, Danko?" a woman shouted from across the room.

"Dr. Cornwell!" The TV crew inside came back to life. A polished blonde in a navy blazer shoved a microphone at Cornwell. "What do you have to say about accusations that your diet is harmful?" she asked.

"I don't have to say anything," Cornwell replied. He gestured to the full restaurant. "There's a roomful of people here who are saying it for me." There were cheers all around. "And what they're saying is that low-fat eating doesn't work for huge numbers of people. Low-carb eating does."

". . . about a healthy lifestyle." Danko's voice rose again. "The people who insist a low-fat diet 'doesn't work' are the ones without the discipline to do it properly." More applause from outside, more jeers from inside.

"Look around you!" Danko's voice called. "Most of the people outside here are committed to a diet low in animal fats, and the result is that most of them are lean and fit and healthy. Can Doctor Cornwell say the same for his true believers inside?"

"How do you respond to that, Doctor?" the TV reporter asked Cornwell. The cameras swiveled across the dining room. Danko had a point, Anneke conceded. Most of the people in the dining room ranged from pudgy to plump to frankly fat.

Instead of answering the reporter directly, Cornwell spoke out to the dining room. "How many of you folks have tried low-fat diets?" he asked. A sea of hands were raised. "How many of you had any success with them?" Every hand went down, and laughter shot through the room. Cornwell turned back to the reporter. "The vast majority of those 'lean and fit' people outside are naturally thin," he said. "Go out there and interview them—I'll guarantee that you won't find more than a couple of them who've *ever* been overweight. Yet they're imposing their standards on a population that can't begin to achieve them." He seemed legitimately angry.

"The triumph of the ectomorphs," Noelle said. "People born with certain physical characteristics who've managed to make those characteristics a symbol of moral superiority."

"Dr. Cornwell and his ilk are manipulating people looking for a quick fix," Danko declared outside, "people who want results without having to exercise any self-discipline. We've become a culture seeking an easy answer instead of being willing to do the work."

"Oh, that's our really favorite criticism, isn't it?" Cornwell again directed his words to the assembled diners, who whooped with laughter. Apparently, Anneke concluded, this was something they were all familiar with. "Do you realize what that woman is saying?" he challenged the reporter. "She's saying that if there *is* an easy answer to weight and obesity problems, we *shouldn't use it*. In fact, she's saying we shouldn't even be looking for it, as if misery is some sort of moral imperative. But the people out there—her supporters—*aren't* miserable, because for them weight maintenance *isn't* a hardship and a challenge. Phooey." He threw back his head and laughed, and the dining room echoed his laughter like a congregation repeating a minister's hallelujah.

And that's what this was really about, Anneke realized suddenly. The diet war was a religious war, a conflict between competing cadres of true believers. A lot like the Mac-*vs*.-PC battles of the early computer days, in fact.

Well, in this particular conflict, she was Switzerland. She touched Karl's hand and made a slight motion with her head. There were a lot better ways to spend a honeymoon.

# TWENTY

"Hooray." Zoe jumped from her chair and followed the big flat Cottage Inn box down the wide center aisle of the *Daily* like a dog after a steak, her nose quivering at the scent of pepperoni and tomato sauce. "Hurry up, Gabriel, I'm starved."

"Jeez, Kaplan, take it easy." Sports editor Gabriel Marcus dropped the box on the sports desk. Zoe flipped it open, pulled a slice from the pizza, and shoved the end into her mouth.

"Mmm." She chewed blissfully for a moment. "I really needed that. And stop laughing at me," she said, making a face at him. "I didn't have any dinner, remember? And why didn't I have any dinner? Because you wanted that profile of Ward Regan for tonight's paper, that's why."

"Is it done?" Gabriel folded a piece of pizza and bit into it.

"Just about." Zoe wriggled back muscles stiff from an hour hunched over a keyboard. "Take a look."

Gabriel sat down at his terminal and punched keys; after a few minutes during which they both ate silently, he logged off and leaned back. "Good stuff. Thanks."

"Don't mention it." Zoe waved the crust of her second slice of pizza. "Bought and paid for. And don't ever say I'm not a cheap date." She grabbed a third piece of pizza, stretched again, and went back to her terminal. She read through the Regan profile, made a couple of changes, then closed the file and sat for a minute thinking, before reaching into her bookbag and withdrawing the list of names Anneke had sent her. She wasn't sure how far back the *Daily*'s online archives went, but it seemed like a reasonable place to start. Run each of the names through the search program and see what turns up, starting with Lindsay Summers. Not that she really expected . . . Bingo!

The article was headlined: REVIEW: "EATING FOR PLEASURE" CAN CAUSE REAL PAIN, and it was by-lined Lindsay Summers. But the best part was that the book's author was George McMartin, *Daily* alumnus and member of the board. Her eyes widened as she read the review, giggling at the choicer phrases.

> McMartin apparently finds pleasure in heart disease, diabetes, bone and joint disorders, and all the other ailments that are caused by obesity. . . .
>
> In fact, the whole approach of the book is pernicious, because encouraging people to eat purely for pleasure is encouraging them to commit suicide with knife and fork. . . .
>
> At a time when the American people need a dietary wake-up call, 'Eating for Pleasure' is an overdose of Nembutal.

Wow. Zoe'd read some bad reviews in her time, but this was something else. You'd think George McMartin had written the culinary equivalent of *Mein Kampf*. If this review wasn't a motive for murder, she'd never seen one.

She returned to her search, turning up bits and pieces of reference to the names on her list—Mercedes Rojas on a list of seminar speakers, Noelle Greene speaking at a Fat Acceptance rally, Richard's name in her own stories about last year's murder of an NCAA investigator, Summers again in a comment story about . . . Whoa. Zoe backed up and opened the story.

The headline read: NOT ALL AGREE ON FAT ACCEPTANCE MOVEMENT. There were quotes from a local doctor, and a psychologist, and an education professor. And finally, Summers, identified as "a public health researcher specializing in obesity issues."

"Instead of using laws to protect people who lack self-discipline," Summers was quoted, "we should be using the power of the law to prevent them from damaging themselves—and the whole society—even further. Medical care for obesity-related conditions costs Americans millions of dollars every year. I don't think it's appropriate to ask us to 'accept' that."

Wow. Hey, tell us what you really think, Zoe thought. She looked down the list again, and spotted a duplicate listing—hits on both Lindsay Summers and Noelle Greene. It was a letter to the editor, written by Greene:

"So now the public health establishment wants to criminalize fat people," Greene wrote.

> I can see it now. Chocolate smugglers! Black-market Twinkies! Dirty old men sidling up to school children and offering them a hit of hamburger!
>
> As for the famous "costs of obesity," you want to measure that against the cost of a government War on Fat? Figure it to be as expensive, and as effective, as the War on Drugs, or the War on Poverty before it. And think of the profits in those rehab programs! Especially when judges start issuing jail-or-rehab sentences.
>
> Bring it on, Summers and the rest of you food Nazis.

The rest of you—check your weight against the "official" recommendations before you decide how to vote.

Zoe was laughing out loud by the time she finished reading Greene's letter. She skimmed the rest of the file list, then dumped it all into a folder to e-mail to Anneke, pleased with what she'd found. There was more of Summers than she'd expected. In fact . . .

She looked around the city room. "Anybody seen Vanderlaan?" she called out.

"Library," a voice replied.

"Thanks." She got up and trotted down the corridor, stopping at the Coke machine on her way. When she poked her head in through the library door, she saw Eric Vanderlaan, the *Daily*'s arts editor, sitting at one of the long oak tables nearly buried in books and papers.

"Got a minute?" she asked.

"Not really." Vanderlaan looked up irritably, shoving wire-rimmed glasses higher on his long, pointed nose. Everything about him was pointed, long and skinny—pointy knees and elbows, pointy shoulder blades poking against a faded Metallica tee, ribs visible against the black fabric. "Why are all poets laureate such shitty writers?"

"Beats me." Vanderlaan was the only person in the world who'd actually put the "s" on poets instead of laureates. "Got a question," Zoe said quickly, before she lost his attention. "There was a review of a book last year by George McMartin—you know, the board member? It was written by a public health grad student, Lindsay Summers."

"Yeah," Vanderlaan said. "Great piece, wasn't it?"

"How'd she happen to write it?" Zoe kept her opinion of the great piece to herself. "Why her instead of someone on staff?"

"Wasn't that cool? Although my original idea was cooler yet." Vanderlaan leaned back in his chair. "The first person I asked to do the review was Griffith Carr. You know, the congressman. He turned me down, but he recommended this Summers chick."

"So you specifically went out looking for a public-health angle?"

"Right." Vanderlaan jumped up and paced to the window and back. "You ever read the book? Like, nothing matters to McMartin except his own personal appetites. Not health, not the environment, not the fact that most people on the planet go to bed hungry while he stuffs his belly. It really is a disgusting book."

"Did you hear from him after the review came out?"

"Nope." Vanderlaan sounded seriously disappointed. "In fact, I was hoping we would," he said defiantly. "I'd really like to've gotten a dialogue going. He was too chicken, I guess."

"Well, he's on the Board in Control," Zoe pointed out. "Probably was afraid it'd look like he was trying to influence content."

"Oh, he was afraid, all right," Vanderlaan said. "Afraid he'd have to defend his obscene tastes and behavior."

Sheesh, he made it sound like Roman orgies. "Well, thanks." Zoe waved a good-bye and returned to her terminal, where she made a note of the conversation and attached it to her e-mail. A pretty good haul for just a single search. Still, it seemed like there should be a way to get even more. The *University Record?* Were the *Ann Arbor News* archives on-line? She thought for a minute, then logged off and headed down the back stairs, stopping at the sports desk to grab one more piece of now-cold pizza.

Barney McCormack didn't look up when she opened the door to the computer room on the ground floor. He remained hunched over a computer that wasn't even the same species as the ancient Macs in the city room. Zoe waited a minute, then knocked on the side of the door.

"Anybody home?"

"For you, always." Barney scooted his chair back from the desk. The *Daily*'s system administrator wore his usual faded tee and torn jeans. "Does this mean you've finally succumbed to my charms?"

"Absolutely," Zoe agreed. "I'm a sucker for knobby knees. Unfortunately," she put her hand on her heart and a soulful expression on her face, "I'm a slave to work. No time for pleasure."

"A likely story. So this is a business call after all. Oh, the sorrow." He sighed deeply. "All right, what can I do for you this time?"

"I'm looking for information about some people." She stopped, unsure of how to proceed. "I've done a search of the *Daily* archives, but I don't know where else to look."

"Well, what sort of information are you looking for?"

"I don't know. Anything." She waved a hand. "They're all alumni, if that helps."

"Maybe. Are you looking for things like grades, degrees, that sort of thing?"

"Not really. At least, not unless there's something hinky about them."

"So what you're really looking for is dirt?" he asked shrewdly.

"I guess so, yeah." The words made her uncomfortable, but she had to admit they were true. "Not *necessarily* dirt," she added. "I've got a list of people and I'm trying to see if there's any connection between any of them and a woman named Lindsay Summers."

"Let me see the list." He took the sheet of paper from her and scanned it. "You say they're all alumni?"

"Right."

He looked off into space for a few moments. "Okay." He scooted his chair back to the computer. "Come back in a couple of hours."

"What are you going to do?"

"Well, there's e-mail . . . or maybe a couple of administrative file servers . . ." He cocked his head at her. "You sure you want to know?"

"Probably not." She shook her head. "Okay. Thanks, Barney." He didn't reply; he was already engrossed in his search.

# TWENTY-ONE

The sound of the shower through the half-open door only made Anneke nuzzle deeper into her pillow. Through the window, the muted rattle of a cable car and the less-muted blare of horns seemed to encapsulate San Francisco, old and new and beautiful and ugly and just slightly mad. She had a sudden desire to get out of the tourist areas and prowl the neighborhoods, where real people presumably led real lives.

"Are you awake?" Karl sat down on the bed, his crisp dark hair still slightly damp from the shower. She reached up and brushed away a droplet of water.

"I'm glad you're not going bald," she said.

"I thought about it for a while," he said solemnly, "but I decided against it." He brushed his hand along her cheek, down the hollow of her neck and moving under the quilt and along her body. She shivered with pleasure and reached up her arms.

"Ooh, nice. Why don't we pretend we're on our honeymoon, Lieutenant?"

"I think we could just manage that." He untied the belt of his terry cloth robe and let it drop to the floor.

"I think you've already started."

"Not to worry. I'm sure you can catch up with me." He grinned and slipped under the blanket. "Why don't I—oh, *damn*."

The knock on the door was loud and forceful. So was the obscenely cheerful voice that sang out: "Room service."

"Just a minute," Karl called. He sat up and laughed ruefully. "I called down before I got into the shower," he said to Anneke. "I thought we could have a nice quiet breakfast in bed."

"It figures." She reached for her robe, trying to quell her annoyance. "Everything about this honeymoon's been interrupted by food."

Still, it was nice to sit in the privacy of their room and sip coffee, and nibble on small croissants, and read the newspaper in peace. She read the coverage of last night's Maize-and-Blue scrum, giggling at the reporter's description of Richard's triumph. For triumph they'd declared it: "Never before has a demonstration been catered so deliciously."

When they were done with breakfast, Karl checked in with Wes Kramer in Ann Arbor while she showered and dressed quickly. She was determined to spend today, at least, doing honeymoon things—as soon as she could decide exactly what those things were.

"Just let me check my e-mail and then we can get out of here," she promised.

"No rush. It's still early." Karl flicked the TV remote and turned to a local news program, and she listened with half her attention as she logged on and downloaded her mail. There was another sizeable message from Zoe, and as she read it through her eyes widened.

"Karl, look at this."

"What?"

"It's from Zoe. It's—"

"Hold on a minute." Karl held up his hand, gesturing to the TV. Anneke heard the words "Maize and Blue" and turned to face the screen.

What she saw made her mouth drop open. It was film obviously taken earlier, because it was full dark—dark, that is, except for the glaring lights of fire engines clustered in front of the restaurant.

". . . your basic Molotov cocktail." The speaker was a man in a dark blue uniform, whether police or fire official Anneke couldn't tell. "It was thrown through a window at the back of the building—luckily they had a sprinkler system that contained the fire."

The scene shifted to daylight, and a pretty, dark-haired woman standing in front of the Maize and Blue, a professionally serious expression on her face. "The identity of the dead man has not been released pending notification of next of kin, but we have been told he was an employee of the restaurant."

"My God." Anneke got up and moved over to the edge of the bed to see the screen better.

"We talked to the owner of the Maize and Blue, Richard Killian, just a little while ago," the television reporter said.

The camera shifted again. This time it was Richard with the reporter, standing on the front steps of the restaurant. Standing exactly where he'd stood last night, only this time, instead of a beautiful tray of hors d'ouevres, he held a twisted and charred piece of metal in his hands. This time, instead of a triumphant smile, his face wore an expression of bitter anger.

"It's a basketball hoop from Yost Field House, the last game played there before the team moved to Crisler Arena." He held up the piece of metal. "At least, it used to be. But that doesn't matter." He tossed the piece of metal aside, and it clanked to the ground. "I'd give up the whole place rather than have anyone else die here." He almost seemed to mean it, Anneke thought.

"Do you know how soon you'll be able to reopen?" The pretty reporter held up her microphone.

"Reopen? Hell, I don't know." Richard stared at her as if the question hadn't occurred to him. "There wasn't that much damage, actually—mostly to a storeroom and a private dining room."

"Do you have any idea who did this, or why the Maize and Blue was targeted?" the reporter asked.

"Truly, I haven't the smallest clue." Richard shrugged. "I don't suppose even the *most* disgruntled Buckeye would carry a rivalry this far, do you?" he blurted, and then had the grace to look embarrassed.

"Do you think it had anything to do with last night's demonstration?" the reporter persisted.

"Hell, *I* don't know." He ran his hand through his hair in a distracted gesture. "Over a culinary disagreement?" Richard sighed. "You'll have to ask the police those questions."

The screen flicked back to the reporter standing live in front of the restaurant. "So far the police will only say that they're investigating," she said. "And that's the latest word from the bombing site," the reporter said. "Back to you, Joe."

"Good God." Anneke stared at Karl as he flicked the remote to turn off the newscast. "Karl, it doesn't make any sense. Does it?"

"You mean, is it connected to Lindsay Summers's murder?" he deconstructed her protest. "I think we have to assume it is."

"But . . ." She paused, framing her objection. "The death, probably. Maybe. But the bombing? Why would any of those people want to destroy the Maize and Blue?"

"Well, but no one *did* destroy the Maize and Blue," he pointed out.

"That's true," she said thoughtfully. "In fact, the bomb

itself didn't do much damage at all, did it? Was it pure luck that it took out a storeroom and left the kitchen undamaged? Oh, the whole thing is ridiculous," she protested. "Can you see any of those people skulking around in the middle of the night with a jar of gasoline in a paper bag? I mean, how would any of them even know how to make a Molotov cocktail?"

"How did you know it was a jar of gasoline?" he asked.

"But that's just—oh. I suppose so." She glanced at her laptop, its phone cord still plugged into the wall, connecting her to everything she'd ever want to know about bomb-making.

"We really can't make any sense of it until we know who the victim is. And how he died."

"I suppose you're right—arguing ahead of data again. Oh. Karl, I almost forgot. Wait till you see what Zoe's come up with." She disconnected her laptop and passed it across to him, waiting impatiently while he read Zoe's message.

"Interesting," he said finally. "We need to give all of this to Braxton."

"I know. Let me dump it to a floppy. We can print it out downstairs and drop it off at his office."

"I doubt that he'll be in his office," Karl said.

"Oh, God, I suppose you're right." She sighed. "But once we talk to him we're getting out of there. I'm as loyal an alumna as anyone, but I absolutely refuse to spend one more day of our honeymoon at that damned restaurant."

"I agree." He laughed at her expression. "We'll just talk to him for a few minutes, give him Zoe's findings, and leave."

"Promises, promises," Anneke muttered.

# TWENTY-TWO

Richard was sitting on the steps leading to the patio when Anneke and Karl arrived at the Maize and Blue. No, make that lolling, Anneke decided; whatever anger and sorrow had affected him earlier, he seemed to have recovered his usual sunny disposition. He was leaning back on his elbows, his jeans-clad legs stretched out in front of him, and he was grinning boyishly at the same pretty television reporter who'd interviewed him earlier. They seemed to be discussing—surprise, surprise—food.

". . . Cherries Jubilee is so twentieth century," the woman was saying. She was perched on the step next to Richard, leaning forward slightly with her arms wrapped around her knees. In that position, her short skirt just about covered her rear end, and the view went pretty much to the top of her thighs. Which she was perfectly aware of, Anneke concluded, feeling unaccountably bitchy. She glanced at Karl to see if he'd noticed, or was still noticing, for that matter. He intercepted her glance and winked at her, and she giggled. What the hell, a free show is a free show; let him enjoy it.

"Then you absolutely must try the banana-caramel tart at Loco." Richard kissed the tips of his fingers, a gesture that, even for Richard, was unpardonably affected. "Exquisite, I promise you."

"We-ell," the woman drew out the word, "I've always been a big fan of bananas." She looked up at Richard from beneath lowered lashes; Anneke fought back the urge to stick her finger in her mouth and pantomime violent sickness. Instead, she kept her mouth shut and silently followed Karl across the sidewalk, stepping carefully over wide puddles of water presumably left by the fire hoses.

"Good morning, Richard," Karl said.

"Lieutenant!" Richard jumped to his feet, rearranging his pale gray leather jacket, along with his expression. From hound on the prowl, he instantly became angry citizen. "Do you believe this?" He waved an arm. "And not a soul saw anything. I ask you." What he was asking was unclear. "Lenore," he turned to the woman on the steps, "this is Lieutenant Karl Genesko, of the Ann Arbor Police Department. Oh, and his wife, Anneke Haagen. This is Lenore Garcia, one of the rising stars of Channel Ten News."

"Glad to meet you, Lieutenant." Lenore Garcia rose gracefully to her feet, displaying another few yards of tanned, nylon-encased leg. She ignored Anneke. "Are you working with the San Francisco PD?" she asked, her eyes sharp.

"My wife and I are friends of Richard's." Karl neatly sidestepped the question.

"Why don't you go on inside." For once in his life, Richard took a hint. "I'll be along in a bit."

Anneke held her breath as they climbed the stairs and stepped inside the Maize and Blue, but the big dining room looked the same as ever. The only thing that struck her was the smell.

"Ugh." She made a face. "Essence of wet fireplace."

"It could be a lot worse." Karl stopped and sniffed. "There's hardly any gasoline smell."

"That's because there wasn't a whole lot of gasoline." Peter Braxton emerged from the kitchen, wiping his hands together.

"Oh?" Karl sounded interested.

"Right." Braxton nodded, agreeing with something Karl had implied.

"Amateurs usually use too much fuel, not too little." Karl made the explanation for Anneke's benefit.

"But a professional would have used the right amount," Braxton said.

"Unless this *was* the right amount." Karl and Braxton shared a moment of consideration. "Who was the victim?" Karl asked.

"His name was Eddy Takahashi. He was a temporary busboy. And before you ask, yes, he was working here the day Lindsay Summers was murdered."

"But he wasn't regular staff, then? How'd he come to be working here that particular day?"

"I don't know yet."

"Do you know the cause of death?"

"Not yet. In fact, I don't know much of anything yet, to tell you the truth." Braxton looked tired; he'd probably been here half the night, Anneke reasoned. She tried to feel sympathetic and failed; at least he wasn't on his honeymoon.

"Well, we have some information for you from Ann Arbor," Karl said. He turned to Anneke, who withdrew a disk and a sheaf of paper from her purse. Braxton took it without any indication of breathless anticipation, and ran his eye down the pages; instead of pleasing him, Zoe's material seemed to make him even gloomier.

"So now we have more possible motives." He looked at Anneke as he folded the papers and put them and the disk into his jacket pocket. "Do you—" He broke off as Marcy Liu emerged from the kitchen.

"Got someone you might want to talk to, Inspector."

"Oh?"

"At least Killian can't throw me out this time," Barbara Williams snapped. She appeared suddenly behind Sergeant Liu, escorted by two uniformed patrolmen.

"We picked her up prowling in the alley out back," one of them said.

"I wasn't *prowling*." She peered around the dining room, ignoring her uniformed escort.

"And just what were you doing in the alley, Ms. Williams?" Braxton nodded to the uniforms, who took a few steps backward but remained in the room, standing against the wall on either side of the kitchen door. Almost as though they might prevent Barbara from bolting, Anneke thought.

"Saw the report on the news this morning, and I wanted to see what was going on. Thought maybe Cody Jarrett would finally have time for me. For my article." She looked up at the ceiling and then back to Braxton. "I don't see much damage."

"You sound disappointed," Braxton said.

"More damage'd make a better story." She shrugged.

"Oh, right. For your 'article,' " Braxton said. "Refresh my memory, will you? Just what article was that, again?"

"I told you. I'm writing an article about the food wars."

"For the *Chron*, you said?"

"Either *Chron* or *Bay Guardian*. Haven't decided yet."

"Ah. Of course. Would it surprise you to learn that no one at either publication has ever heard of you?"

"I *said* I was working freelance."

"Let's cut the crap, Ms. Williams." Braxton's voice sawed the air. "The only things you've ever written in your life are threatening letters, isn't that right?"

"Don't know what you're talking about." Barbara's eyes wandered about the dining room. Anneke, startled, glanced at Karl, but he only shook his head.

"Well, maybe the name Vegan Militia will refresh your memory?" Braxton asked. Barbara blinked at him, her expression, if anything, only more sullen. What on earth is this all about? Anneke wondered. "All right, Ms. Williams." Braxton shrugged elaborately. "Take her downtown," he said to the uniforms.

"You can't do that!" Barbara showed emotion for the first time.

"Oh, but I can." Braxton smiled. "You're a material witness to a murder, and a suspect in a firebombing." He jerked his head, and the uniforms each took hold of one of Barbara's arms.

"This is false arrest!" she shouted. "You can't do this! We'll make you pay for this!" She was still shouting as they half led, half dragged her out.

"I take it your background check on Barbara Williams turned up something," Karl said when she was gone.

"Right. Although I'm damned if I know what to do with it." Braxton turned his eyes from the door. "It seems that our Barbara Williams, girl reporter, is actually a fairly high-level functionary of the Vegan Militia."

"One of those neo-Nazi groups?" Anneke wrinkled her nose in disgust, but to her surprise Braxton began to laugh.

"Not exactly," he said, chuckling. "This one's dedicated to, and I quote, 'the end of animal exploitation and the elimination of all animal products from the daily lives of the human race.'"

"Oh." Anneke grinned. "Well, but an animal rights groups isn't exactly a threat to public safety."

"Maybe not in Michigan." Braxton was abruptly sober. "But in California some of them are plain nuts. And this particular group is categorized as armed and dangerous."

"Armed and dangerous?" Anneke could hardly credit the description. "An organization of vegetarians? Who on earth would they attack, the corner meat market?" When Braxton didn't answer, she stared at him. "Are you serious?"

"Ask yourself this," he said. "If there was an epidemic of poisoned meat at your local supermarket, would you be so inclined to grab a package of hamburger on your next shopping trip, or would you maybe decide you'd just as soon have a veggie burger?"

"Is this group—"

"Or if people started attacking dog-walkers the way they attack women wearing fur coats, how many people would decide they'd just as soon not be pet owners?" He stopped. "Excuse me, this is San Francisco; the politically correct term is 'pet guardians.' "

"Wait a minute." Anneke held up a hand. "I get the hamburger thing—at least, I kind of understand where vegetarians are coming from—but why would anyone attack pet owners? I mean, they care for animals, don't they?"

"The animal liberation people argue that even pet guardians—yes, that's the official usage by the city of San Francisco—exploit animals, that all animals should be free of human interference and constraints." Braxton sounded like he'd been boning up on the subject, which he probably had.

"What are they supposed to do, live off the land?" Anneke waved a hand. "Pretty hard to graze, in all this concrete."

"Don't ask me." Braxton shook his head. "I'm no expert on these groups. I can tell you, though, that there are a couple of them that the antiterrorism division's keeping an eye on."

"Terrorism." The word struck Anneke with force. Terrorists and firebombs seemed to go together. "Do you think—?"

"Beats me." Braxton answered the question she didn't complete. "Right now your guess is as good as mine."

# TWENTY-THREE

"This is outrageous." Elisa Falcone's high heels *tap-tapped* across the parquet floor, with its big Block M inlay at the center. She wore a camel's-hair coat belted at the waist, and a small matching beret perched rakishly on her carefully coiffed hair. Three delicate "scatter pins" adorned her lapel. "Inspector, the police need to do something about those people."

"What people do you mean, Ms. Falcone?" Braxton asked with an air of weary patience.

"You know perfectly well what people I mean. Those radical animal groups are no better than any other terrorists, but this city has been coddling them as though they were a religious order." She looked toward the kitchen. "Is Cody here yet?"

"He was here earlier, but he's gone home."

"I thought the kitchen hadn't been damaged." Elisa made it sound like an accusation.

"It wasn't."

"Then why can't he open?" She glared at Braxton. "Are you closing us down because of those creatures?"

"No one's closing down anything," Braxton said. "This is a

crime scene—a murder scene, in fact," he reminded her. "Once we're finished with our investigation, the Maize and Blue can completely ignore the death of two people and proceed with business as usual."

"Please don't try to guilt-trip me, Inspector." Elisa didn't back down an inch. "It should be obvious by now even to the police that we're all the victims here. It's the Maize and Blue, and Cody, that are the real targets. If I seem less than sympathetic, it's because I refuse to let terrorists win. Not to mention," she added caustically, "that I do wonder which of us is going to be next."

"Inspector?" One of the uniforms stuck his head through the kitchen door. "There's a guy here who wants to talk to you?" At Braxton's nod, the uniform stepped aside and George McMartin stepped through the door, looking around as though inspecting for damage.

"What can I do for you, Mr. McMartin?" Braxton asked.

"You can find out who's trying to put us out of business." The words were sharp, but George's heart didn't seem to be in them. He sniffed the air, wrinkling his nose as though he'd just smelled month-old hamburger, but even that seemed a cursory exercise, as though he were distracted by other concerns.

"We're doing our best," Braxton replied. "As long as you're here, Mr. McMartin, perhaps you can clear up something for me."

"Clear up something?" George sounded nervous.

"You said you'd never heard of Lindsay Summers until she showed up here, isn't that right?" Braxton asked.

"Yes. No. I mean, no, I'd never even heard of her before this," George said jerkily. "Why?" He twitched his shoulders, as though pulling himself together.

"And yet, Lindsay Summers reviewed your latest book in the *Michigan Daily*, didn't she."

"She—What?" George seemed genuinely startled. "Are you serious?"

"You didn't know that?" Braxton's voice held amused disbelief.

"Oh, George." Elisa shook her head.

"Oh, Elisa," he mimicked. "Don't be silly. Lindsay Summers wasn't on the *Daily*."

"Did you read their review of your book?" Braxton asked.

"Of course." George laughed. "They trashed it. Well, they would, wouldn't they? They had to prove that they weren't intimidated because the author was a board member."

"And do you remember who the reviewer was?" Braxton persisted.

"No." George shrugged. "It didn't . . ." His voice trailed off and his face fell in horror. "But . . . you mean it . . . but how?"

"Don't sputter, George," Elisa said cattily.

"Inspector, I didn't know!" George waved his hands frantically. "I swear I didn't! I mean, why would I remember? And anyway, it was just a local review, I certainly wouldn't *kill* someone over a bad review, that's ridiculous." He ran down finally, his face red and sweating. If he wasn't telling the truth, Anneke thought, he was one hell of a great actor.

She thought Braxton agreed, although his demeanor didn't change. "So you weren't—" He stopped as the uniform appeared at the kitchen door once again.

"Two more of 'em, Inspector," he said, standing aside to let Blair and Noelle through the door.

"It's about time," Elisa snapped. "What took you so long?"

"We've been meeting with the Connor Finch people," Blair said. He glanced at Noelle.

"They're not reconsidering, are they?" Elisa asked sharply.

"No, not at all." Noelle smiled. She was dressed for success in a navy power suit worn with a wildly colored floral silk blouse. Her mass of auburn hair was piled on top of her head, held back by an elaborate hand-crafted gold-and-silver barrette. She patted Blair's arm. "We have everything under control." Anneke wondered if Noelle was only referring to the finances.

"Ms. Greene." Braxton zeroed in on her. "You denied knowing Lindsay Summers before Saturday morning, is that right?"

"That's right." Noelle looked wary but not especially worried.

"Isn't it true that you and she had an exchange at a rally in Ann Arbor?"

"Nope." Noelle shook her head.

"Then you didn't write a letter to the *Michigan Daily* calling Lindsay Summers a food Nazi?"

"Yes, I wrote it."

"Ms. Greene, I recommend that you not play games," Braxton warned her.

"I'm not playing games, I'm answering your questions." Noelle grinned. "Sorry, I've spent too much time with lawyers in my young life. Inspector, you asked me on Saturday if I'd ever met Lindsay Summers, and my answer, then and now, is no. I never met the woman in my life before Saturday. What's more, I never had any personal communication with her. She made her statements to the *Daily*, and I made mine the same way, and that was the end of it." She laughed. "If I went around offing everyone who didn't appreciate my bountiful charms, I'd never have time to get any work done."

"I see." Anneke had the feeling Braxton didn't altogether believe her, but he didn't pursue it. Instead he turned to Blair. "Mr. Falcone, do you also still maintain you had no connection with Lindsay Summers?"

"Would you define 'connection,' Inspector?"

"Blair!" Elisa stared at him. He waved a hand at her, a peremptory gesture that made her purse her lips angrily.

"Why don't you just tell me about the thing you think *isn't* a connection, Mr. Falcone?" Braxton sounded impatient. "This isn't a game."

"I'm aware of that, I assure you." Blair's dark, heavy-featured face was grave. His eyes drifted to the ceiling as he weighed his words. "Let me say, first, that I also never met Ms. Summers face to face. And, as Ms. Greene did, I assumed that was the intent of your earlier questioning." Braxton snorted under his breath, and Blair gave him a sharp look before continuing. "I will admit—no, I will *agree*—that our paths did cross superficially, also in much the same way as Ms. Greene has described." He stopped.

"Well?" Braxton snapped. "Let's have it, Mr. Falcone."

"Please, Inspector. I'm perfectly willing to tell you what you want to know, but there are certain confidentialities I need to work around."

"You mean your negotiations with the University of Michigan to take over their stadium food service."

Blair was good, but then they already knew that. Not good enough to control his autonomic nervous system, however; his expression remained as gravely noncommittal as ever, but his face turned several shades whiter, so that his dark eyes seemed to stare out of a bleached and mottled landscape. Still, to Anneke's surprise it was Noelle who broke.

"Busted." She laughed aloud. "My congratulations to the Ann Arbor police." She faced Karl and performed an ironic bow. "Who'd they rubber-hose to get it? And how on earth did they know enough to ask the right people the right questions?" She sounded genuinely perplexed.

"Michigan Stadium? Oh, Blair, that's a wonderful idea!" Elisa clapped her hands together happily. "Imagine the boost that would give Cody's cuisine."

"We're a long way from any kind of agreement." Blair had regained his control. "So far, we've merely discussed it privately with one or two people. Apparently someone didn't understand the definition of 'confidential.'" He turned to Karl. "I suppose there's no point asking how your people got this information?"

"I'm afraid not." Karl shook his head, and Anneke stifled a giggle. How angry would Blair be if he knew his project had been outed by a nineteen-year-old undergraduate and a computer geek? She carefully didn't allow herself to wonder how Zoe had gotten the information in the first place, although she'd have given long odds that Falcone Venture Capital, Inc., might profit from improving its firewall.

"Well, I don't suppose it matters all that much." Blair waved a hand. "In any case," he said to Braxton, "I can't imagine what it has to do with what's been happening here."

"Wasn't Lindsay Summers's Healthy Food Initiative already targeting the stadium?" Braxton asked blandly.

"Oh, for heaven's sake. That's ridiculous," Blair sputtered. "You can't possibly imagine I'd commit murder over something like that. Besides, she wasn't the chair of the organization, she was only providing them with research data."

"I know that." Braxton nodded easily. "But I'm surprised that you do, considering your earlier statement that you'd never even heard of her before Saturday."

"Oh, Christ." A muscle at the side of Blair's jaw jumped, and his hands balled into fists. "Look, Inspector—"

"Blair." Elisa's voice held a sharp warning. "I think you ought to call Daniel, don't you?"

Blair took a deep breath. "For once in your life, Elisa, I think you're making sense. Inspector, I believe I'd prefer to continue this with my attorney present."

"Certainly." Braxton inclined his head. "Shall we say—" he consulted the thin gold watch on his wrist "—two o'clock this afternoon in my office?"

"Fine." Blair rubbed a finger along his temple, as though

fighting a headache. "Until then, I think I'd better get back to my office."

"I'll go with you," Noelle said.

"Remember, Blair," Elisa called as they headed toward the door. "We're having dinner with the Ellmans tonight at Watershed, and it took us three weeks to get a reservation."

# TWENTY-FOUR

"So you're still saying Ann Arbor isn't a small town?" Peter Braxton shoveled scrambled eggs and chunks of sausage onto his fork.

"What do you mean?" Anneke took another sip of coffee. They'd accompanied Braxton, who hadn't yet had breakfast, to a waterfront café that looked like it had been there since the earthquake—the first earthquake—and, like the workingman's café it assuredly was, provided portions large enough to feed the average Marine battalion.

"Then why the hell are there so many connections between a group of random people?" Braxton waved his loaded fork in the air before putting it in his mouth. He looked tired and irritable; a day-old growth of beard shadowed his face, and Anneke realized he'd probably been dragged out of bed in the middle of the night. No wonder he was so hungry.

"They're not really random," she pointed out. "They're all actively involved with the University, and they're all actively involved with food. In fact," she said thoughtfully, "it's food that really brings them together. Oh, they all come at it from different perspectives, but they're all obsessed with it."

"Obsessed is a pretty strong word."

"Maybe. But I honestly think it's accurate. They spend all their time thinking about food, working with food, analyzing food, tasting food, judging food. If that doesn't qualify as obsessing, it's the next best thing."

"In case you hadn't noticed," Karl said, nibbling on a piece of thick sourdough toast, "Anneke isn't what you'd call a foodie."

"In San Francisco, everyone's a foodie." Braxton finished a last morsel of sausage and managed a smile. "Around here, if you need to make small talk, you talk about restaurants. It's our version of talking about the weather." He sighed and pushed his empty plate aside. "I never thanked you for the information, by the way. That was good work."

"Zoe'll be pleased to hear it," Karl said.

"That's another thing." Braxton shook his head. "Who the hell is this Zoe, anyway? And should I ask how she got all this information, or should I file it under 'don't ask, don't tell'?"

"Zoe is . . ." Karl spread his hands and turned to Anneke. "Would you like to field this one?"

"Not a chance." She laughed. "How do you explain a force of nature? And as to your second question," she told Braxton, " 'don't ask, don't tell' is probably a good idea. Especially the material about Blair."

"Yeah, that's what I thought." He drained his coffee and signaled the elderly waitress for a refill. When it was poured, he leaned back and sighed. "Too bad she didn't turn up anything about Barbara Williams."

"What *is* her story, anyway?" Anneke asked. "How does someone become a—what, an animal terrorist?"

"Hard to say. The Baltimore police did a little more digging and turned up a suggestion of abuse when she was a child, but apparently not enough to pull her into the social-work system.

She showed up in San Francisco a couple of years ago, working with the Vegan Militia. She's been involved in a couple of demonstrations, but that's about it."

"That still . . ." Anneke thought for a minute. "Has the Vegan Militia targeted restaurants before this?"

"Not that we know of."

"Then why now? And why the Maize and Blue?"

"For that matter, why Lindsay Summers?" Karl asked. "I think we can assume that the famous 'article' was just a smoke screen, but if so, what was Williams's purpose in contacting Summers in the first place? And did she really just come across her work on the Internet, or was there some prior connection between them?"

"She could have hung out in Ann Arbor before she came out here," Anneke mused. "Ann Arbor does get its share of runaways, after all." She looked a question at Karl, who shook his head.

"They haven't found any trace of her so far, but of course that doesn't mean it's impossible, only that there's no record of her. Still, now that we know more about her, I'll ask them to dig deeper."

"I don't suppose this Zoe of yours can turn up anything?" Braxton laughed without humor. "Maybe she can unearth a cell of the Vegan Militia back there."

"I'll certainly ask her." Anneke took his semi-ironic question at face value. "I'll e-mail her as soon as we get back to the hotel."

"Of course, we still don't know if Williams, or the Vegan Militia, is even relevant to the murders," Karl pointed out. "If this Militia was responsible for the bombing, they're more than usually incompetent."

"I know." Braxton sighed. "They simply could have provided someone with a convenient scapegoat."

"But that would mean the real bomber knew about the Militia," Anneke said.

"Not necessarily," Karl said. "There were a dozen different groups taking part in the demonstration last night. The real murderer could have figured that at least one of them was far out enough to be suspected."

"Which is perfectly true." Braxton drained his third—or was it fourth?—cup of coffee and stood up. "We've got enough nutballs in this city to populate a small planet. And I'd better get back to hunting for this one."

# TWENTY-FIVE

"Great stuff, Zoe. Be advised that the San Francisco police are convinced you're a witch." Zoe chuckled as she read Anneke's e-mail, then groaned over the next sentence. "Now, if you can get any information about one Barbara Williams, age 22, originally from Baltimore, member of a radical animal-rights group called <I swear I am not making this up> the Vegan Militia, they'll put you in for beatification."

Zoe hit Reply and typed: "Do you know how many Barbara Williamses there are in the world? Beatification won't do it— and anyway, what would a Nice Jewish Girl do with it?:-) If I come up with anything I want an autographed Steve Mariucci poster and the title of Empress of Ann Arbor."

She hit Send, wrote "Barbara Williams," "Baltimore," and "Vegan Militia" on a piece of paper, stared at it for a couple of minutes and shook her head. This was no job for an amateur; this was a job for SuperSysop. But when she trotted down the back stairs to the computer room, there was a note from Barney pinned to the door reading: "Gone until tonight." Damn; she hated waiting.

She climbed back up, and as she reached the top of the stairs she saw a figure she recognized coming slowly down the aisle. He stopped when she caught his eye, and for a minute Zoe was afraid he was going to bolt, but he visibly squared his shoulders and continued on until he reached the city desk. He ignored the editor in the slot, who looked from him to Zoe without curiosity and returned to marking up copy.

"Hi." Zoe tried to keep it nonthreatening. "It's Harry, isn't it?" The skinny guy she'd met at the public health school—the one who'd defended Lindsay Summers. The one who she was pretty sure had been in love with Lindsay. Did she maybe have something for her?

"Yeah. Harry Bernhardt." He jerked slightly, as if he were sorry he'd given her his last name.

"Come on over here." Zoe led him around the big oak cabinets and dropped into a chair at one of the terminals, nice and casual. Harry took the chair at the adjoining terminal and perched stiffly on its edge; he had a large manila envelope clutched in both hands that he pressed tightly against his lap.

"I've never been in here before." He looked around the cavernous city room. "Didn't realize it was so big."

"Yeah, it's pretty nice." Zoe nodded and smiled. She felt like she was trying to coax a frightened dog out from under a porch.

"I didn't know—" He stopped and ran a hand through his mouse-colored hair, so that chunks of hair stood out at strange angles. Zoe stifled a desire to laugh. "Here." He slapped the manila envelope on the desk in front of her so abruptly that she jumped.

"What is it?" Zoe picked up the envelope, feeling a prickle of excitement.

"It's— Just read it, okay?" He stood up.

"Wait." Zoe was torn between wanting to see what was in the envelope and wanting to question its owner before he could escape.

"I'm not going anywhere." He produced the semblance of a

tired smile. "I just don't want to sit here watching you read. I'll go get myself a Coke and come back in a few minutes."

"Okay, sure." She didn't much want to read whatever-it-was while being watched, either.

The manila envelope was slit across the top, its flap still sealed. Zoe upended it and let its contents spill out onto the desk. Inside were two more envelopes, standard business size, unsealed, lumpy with something small and square inside. She opened one at random; inside was a microcassette and a few sheets of paper. She unfolded the paper and began reading, but as soon as she'd read the first few lines she stopped. She opened the second envelope; it, too, contained a tape and some sheets of paper.

She stood up, carried all the papers over to the business department's side of the city room, and rapidly fed them into the copier. She held them carefully by the edges, trying to avoid fingerprints as much as possible, but she made sure she got good, clear copies of all seven pages. Only then did she return to her chair and begin reading in earnest.

"I didn't know what to do with them." Harry was back, carrying a bottle of Coke.

"How did you get them?" Zoe slid the papers and tapes back into the manila envelope, her mind whirling with questions.

"About a month ago Lindsay asked me if I'd keep an envelope for her—said her roommate was a snoop and she had some personal things she wanted kept private."

"Sure, that's reasonable." It was a reasonable story, anyway; everyone had roommate horror stories. Except Zoe knew damn well that Jill Sainsbury, Lindsay's roommate, would have had zero interest in snooping. Sainsbury wasn't the one Lindsay was protecting the tapes from.

"Yeah, that's what I thought," Harry said gratefully.

"So you just shoved the envelope in a drawer and forgot about it until now," Zoe offered.

"No." Harry shook his head, rejecting the easy way out. "As

soon as I heard she was dead I opened it and read the transcripts. I even listened to the tapes, to make sure it was really Lindsay and Carr talking. Only I couldn't decide what to do. Lindsay . . ."

"Sure." Zoe repeated the word soothingly. She could understand why someone who cared about Lindsay might not want those tapes made public. Because the Lindsay Summers in the transcripts of those tapes was a vicious, conniving, blackmailing bitch.

The first transcript had begun abruptly, as though Lindsay had suddenly thought to start taping:

> L: . . . can't walk away from me that easily.
>
> G: It won't serve any purpose to get hysterical, Lindsay.
>
> L: Oh, that's just so typical. Any time a woman gets angry, the guy accuses her of being hysterical. If you think I'm just going to fade away like a good little girl, you're the one who's crazy. You made me promises, and you're going to keep them.
>
> G: Will you get it through your head that my wife is the one with the money? I won't be able to keep any promises to anyone if she leaves me, and if I don't stop seeing you that's exactly what she's threatened to do.

Then there was a second conversation:

> L: Once I'm in Washington, she won't have to know anything about us.
>
> G: Don't be an idiot. Washington is the gossip sink of the world. I'm not going to risk my career for something like that.
>
> L: Something like what? A quick and dirty screw? That's all it was to you, wasn't it?

G: That's not what I meant. But you know perfectly well I can't afford a scandal, and my wife is prepared to create one.

L: Maybe I am, too, Griff. Did you ever think of that? How far would your precious political career go if one of your students filed a sexual harassment complaint? Especially in Ann Arbor, where they take their academic ethics seriously.

G: Sexual harassment? Shit, I'd have had to beat you off with a club, you bitch. Besides, I really don't think you want to do that, Lindsay. Sure, it would finish me. But it would finish you, too. Women who file sexual harassment complaints have a funny way of not getting the good faculty jobs, you know? Sometimes they don't even get their dissertations approved.

The second transcript was even more revealing:

G: All right, I've removed Bergman from your committee.

L: Good. He was being a real prick about research design. Who did you replace him with?

G: Marguerite Lomax, from the nursing school. I think I can convince the grad school people that nursing is related to the topic, since it deals with health issues. And she wouldn't know a Likert scale from a bell curve. Satisfied?

L: Oh, not even a little bit. This is just a start, Griff. I'm still thinking I'd like one of those big, powerful congressional committee jobs, you know? I hear they have more policy impact than most weenie congressmen anyway. I'll just keep thinking about it and get back in touch soon.

Christ, they deserved each other, Zoe decided; she felt dirty just from reading the transcripts.

"She wasn't really like that, you know," Harry said.

"She must have felt really hurt." Except the words on the transcripts didn't sound like emotional pain, Zoe thought; they sounded more like wounded vanity. Still, you couldn't always tell from the printed page.

"Exactly," Harry said eagerly. "And remember, this was the second time she'd been dumped by someone who was supposed to be in love with her."

"The second time?"

"Yeah, her ex-husband. She was real bitter about him—said he'd run out on her when she got pregnant. That's why she had to have the abortion. I mean, she was a student with no job, no money, and nobody to lean on. How could she raise a kid by herself that way?" He seemed to be trying to convince himself more than Zoe.

"Rough," Zoe murmured, more to keep the stream of information flowing than to comment.

"It was after that that she really went a little over the top on the whole food thing, you know?" He waited for her nod. "I think it was all about control. She wanted to be sure she was the one who was the user, instead of being the victim."

"It's possible, sure," Zoe said.

"I think that's why she behaved the way she did with Carr," Harry went on, warming to his theory. "I think most of what she said was just a way of getting control again, of not letting him control her."

Or maybe, Zoe thought, unforgiving of psychological alibiing, she really was just a manipulative bitch. Aloud, she said: "So when you told me Lindsay was the one who broke it off because she'd found someone better, you were just trying to protect her?"

"No." Harry shook his head. "That's really what she told

me. I guess she just didn't want to admit she'd been dumped again," he said sadly.

"Poor Lindsay." Zoe wasn't sure whether the words were hypocritical or not. She picked up the envelope of tapes and transcripts. "These have to go to the police, you know."

"I guess. I would have done it right away, but everyone said Carr was in Washington when she was killed. And if he definitely didn't kill her, why drag her name through the mud for nothing?"

"Because you can't be sure about what matters and what doesn't in a murder investigation until it's over." Zoe sounded tendentious even to her own ears. "Besides . . ." She paused. "Look, Harry, you knew I was a reporter when you brought these to me."

"Yeah." He nodded. "Even if Carr didn't kill her . . ." He didn't finish the sentence; he didn't have to. "Can you take care of it all?" He gestured at the envelope.

"Sure. Although the cops will need to talk to you, you know."

"I know." He sighed and stood up. "Thanks."

"Don't mention it." As he sketched a wave and started to turn away, she had a sudden thought. "Harry? I don't suppose the name Barbara Williams means anything to you, does it?"

"Barbara Williams? What about her?"

# TWENTY-SIX

"We are still going home tomorrow, aren't we?" They were standing halfway up a flight of wooden steps that seemed to climb forever. To their right, another, shorter flight led to a row of houses that disappeared into the early-morning fog. There was a street sign at the intersection of the two staircases, and numbers on the houses that faced the wooden walkways.

"Getting homesick?"

"Not exactly." Anneke gazed at the homes set along the staircases, tucked into small gardens. "How on earth do they manage?" she wondered aloud. "They probably can't even get a pizza delivered." She laughed and shook her head.

"It would take a hell of a big tip, at least."

"It's beautiful, though, isn't it. I think," she said slowly, "that I'm tired of being a tourist. After a while it feels . . . superficial, somehow. I keep wondering where the real people are, how they live, what it's like."

"It's the old academic argument—breadth versus depth." Karl nodded. "You can know a little bit about a lot of things, or a lot about one thing. Travel is the same way. You can see the surface of a hundred places, or spend a long time getting to know one or two places well." He took her hand. "You're a depth person."

"I guess I am." She considered the statement. "Is that a good or bad thing, do you think?"

"I don't know that you need to assign a value judgment to it, do you?" He smiled down at her. "I think I prefer depth also."

"That's good. I guess the important thing is that we both share the same approach." She turned to take in the breathtaking view. "I'll be glad to get home. I just wish . . ."

"What?"

"I hate to leave an unsolved problem, that's all."

"Sometimes they never get solved," Karl pointed out.

"I know. Poor Richard. Oh, I know he's a hound, but he's such an entertaining one." She laughed briefly. "I hate to think of him twisting in the wind like this." She was silent for a moment. "Karl, why don't we take another look at Lindsay's files? Maybe there's something there we missed."

"If you like. Your laptop's in the car, isn't it?" When she nodded, he said: "I know just the place."

Ten minutes later they were ensconced at a tiny sidewalk table outside Caffè Puccini, in North Beach, eating raspberry rings and drinking enormous lattes out of cups the size of young soup bowls. Next to them, an elderly man and a young Asian woman were holding a conversation in rapid-fire Italian, while Pavarotti's "Nessun Dorma" drifted from speakers overhead.

Anneke's laptop was open on the table. "If there's anything here, it would be in her dissertation files, wouldn't it?" She asked the question rhetorically, already scanning the file list. "Here—chapter-by-chapter outlines. Even the abstract is already written. She was further along than I'd realized. Except . . ." She turned to Karl, puzzled. "Wasn't she just beginning her field research?"

"I think so. Why?"

"Because she didn't have any data yet, but this dissertation is nearly finished. Even the conclusions chapter—she just left the actual numbers blank. Look." She pressed keys to display the file. " 'The presence of high-fat food choices on the menu is itself one of the key determinants of poor food choices,' " she read aloud. "And here: 'More than XX percent of subjects said they generally ate the entire portion of food served to them, regardless of the amount. Only XX percent said they ate only until hunger was satiated.' She uses that in the Recommendations section, too." She paged down and read: " 'The size of restaurant portions should be regulated by law to prevent unmanaged overeating. Second helpings may be provided for larger diners.' And won't that be nice for you." She laughed at the expression on his face before turning back to the screen and switching to the chapter titled Statistical Methods, which she read with growing interest.

"But it's absolute crap," she said at last. "Karl, this is pure statistical garbage. I mean, you can't analyze Likert-scale data this way. And you can't just run correlations on a dozen different unrelated variables. It's just . . . nonsense." She waved a hand. "How could she possibly expect to get this past any self-respecting dissertation committee?"

"Maybe it wasn't—self-respecting, I mean," Karl said thoughtfully. "Carr was her committee chair, wasn't he?"

"Yes. You know," she said slowly, "it isn't just sloppy. It's . . . completely wrong. Karl, they had to be in it together," she said.

"In what together?"

"Cooking data to produce the results they wanted. She puts together this pseudo-statistical crap, and he shoves it past the committee. Once it gets to Congress, who's going to quibble about bad statistical methods? Most people don't know a factor analysis from a Fig Newton." She closed the dissertation folder and opened the one labeled "Legislation." She read for a couple of minutes before nodding rapidly. "Look. These are her notes for Carr's 'Healthy Food' bill. There's the recommendation to regulate restaurant portions, and another to require at least fifty percent of all restaurant menu choices to be 'healthy.'" She gave the word an ironic twist. "And each recommendation has a 'conclusion' from Lindsay's dissertation appended to it, *with* supposed 'statistical analysis' as supporting data. Phooey." She leaned back and glared at the screen.

"Is there anything there about site selection?" Karl asked after a moment.

"Let me look." She reopened the dissertation folder, scanned its contents, and clicked on a file. "Here's her original research proposal. Here: 'Interviews will be conducted at sixteen restaurants, selected for demographic, stylistic, and dietary breadth.' That doesn't tell us much. Oh, here." She clicked on another file. "Here's a description of her interview sites. She's even included the menus with each entry." She turned the laptop slightly so Karl could see the screen, and read through the list. "Look at this—four bars. Hardly what you'd call diverse culinary styles. Three Italian restaurants, a couple of steakhouses. No seafood restaurants, you notice, which I'd guess would skew lighter."

"No Asian, either. Or Mexican. Or even what they call fusion, which also tends toward lighter and fresher foods. She had a very limited notion of diverse cuisine, didn't she?"

"Either that, or she was purposely selecting restaurants that would give her the results she wanted." Anneke snorted. "Read her description of the Maize and Blue. 'Food type: Nouvelle Midwest—pseudo-chic rendering of middle-class comfort food.'" Despite herself, Anneke giggled; Lindsay hadn't been too far off target.

"Still, it doesn't mean she was particularly targeting the Maize and Blue." Karl pointed to the description of a restaurant in Terre Haute called Indiana Belle, and Anneke giggled anew as she read it. "Working-class Big-Night-Out restaurant. Motto over the front door reads: IF IT AIN'T FRIED, IT AIN'T FOOD." She read the rest of the descriptions, surprised at Lindsay's sharp humor, less surprised at its nasty edge. When she was finished, she sighed. "It doesn't really tell us anything, does it? At least, nothing about the people at the Maize and Blue."

"Not really, no. There really isn't any reason to suspect she was specifically targeting the Maize and Blue. I think it's entirely likely that she chose it simply because of the University connection." Karl leaned over her shoulder and pointed to a folder labeled "Food Initiative." "Let's take another look at these."

"That's the Healthy Food Initiative directory," she said, clicking on the icon. "It's just a campus organization."

"No it isn't, actually. It was started by students, but it's a full-fledged local organization. With, I might add, a full-fledged local agenda."

"Oh, goody, just what Ann Arbor needs. Another group telling us how to live." She perused the short file list as she spoke, passing up a file titled Vending Machines and another titled Dorms; she could only imagine Zoe's reaction to a dorm menu crafted by Lindsay Summers. She clicked finally on a file titled Resources, hoping for a list of local or even national supporters, but was disappointed to discover that it was nothing but a bibliography. Articles from scholarly journals; testimony at congressional hearings; items culled from newsletters and the Internet and other oddments, several of them semi-anonymous. There was one article by someone named "Humanitas," and a white paper from another with the initials VM.

"Nothing I can see," she said at last. "Not unless one of our suspects is named Velma McSorley. Or Vittorio Mendoza."

"Why?" She pointed at the entry on the screen, and he stared at it for a moment. "VM," he said aloud.

"My God." The penny dropped. "Do you think . . . ?"

"Vegan Militia?" He spread his hands. "It's pretty tenuous."

"But it's the connection between Lindsay and Barbara Williams. It has to be—look at the title. 'Flesh-Eating: The Profit Margin.' I wonder where the actual document is."

"Well, tenuous or not, we'd better let Braxton know." Karl took out his cell phone, pushed the power button, and waited for it to cycle on. But before he could enter more than a couple of digits of Braxton's number, the phone rang. "That's why I had it turned off." He grimaced and pushed the talk button. "Genesko here . . . yes, Zoe . . . yes . . ." Then for what seemed like forever he sat and listened while Anneke tried desperately to read his expression. It was something major, that she was sure of.

Finally, he said: "All right. Hold on." He took his wallet out of his pocket and extracted Peter Braxton's business card. "First, I'd like you to fax the transcript to the San Francisco Police Department—I'll pick it up there. And if you would, fax your notes about Barbara Williams, too." He rattled off the number. "Then take the whole package to Wes Kramer." He listened again for a while. "No, no twin brother. Sorry, Zoe, but Griffith Carr really was in Washington, in full view of a congressional committee meeting." He chuckled. "Yes, he's every one of those things and probably more, but he *didn't* kill Lindsay Summers. . . . Yes, we'll be home tomorrow. . . . Steve Mariucci?" He cast a puzzled glance at Anneke, who broke up laughing. "Whatever you say."

He ended the call and immediately dialed another number, while Anneke squirmed with impatience. "Inspector Braxton, please . . . Peter? Karl Genesko. You'll be receiving several pages of fax from Ann Arbor in the next few minutes . . . no, from Zoe Kaplan . . . yes." He chuckled. "You're not going to believe this."

# TWENTY-SEVEN

Maybe he wasn't the murderer, but Griffith Carr qualified as a world-class, gold-medal, Olympic-caliber slimebucket. And Zoe wanted to be the one to bag him.

It was already after noon by the time she got through talking to Genesko, and *Daily* staffers were beginning to filter in to the city room. Including, unfortunately, city editor Wayne deLoach.

She thought about it for a bit. The Griffith Carr story belonged to city side. Rhea Brown had been covering the Summers murder investigation, and doing a nice job, and Zoe, who was usually pretty good about protocol, knew she should turn over her notes and let Rhea take it from there. Only, she didn't want to. She examined her motives carefully; no, it really wasn't about bylines or glory; it wasn't that she was out to avenge Lindsay Summers, either. Mostly, she decided, it was that she was the one Harry had trusted, and she just didn't feel like she could pass that over to someone else.

She thought about it for a couple of minutes more. Finally

she got up and walked over to the sports desk, where Gabriel Marcus was gobbling a Big Mac, pounding on his computer keyboard, and scribbling on a sheet of copy paper, all at the same time.

"Got a minute?" she asked him, dropping into a chair.

"Mmff," he said around a mouthful of special sauce and sesame-seed bun. He put the hamburger down, scooted his mouse around the desk for a minute, scribbled another note, and took a gulp of Coke before giving her his attention. "Sure. What's up?"

"I've got a biggie," she said.

"Oh?" His eyes brightened.

"Yeah, except it's not sports. It is big, though," she went on with a rush. "It's got everything—politics, academic corruption, even sex."

"Politics? You mean Griffith Carr?" Gabriel's eyes opened even wider. "Did he kill that girl?"

"Unfortunately, no. But he did a few other things that are going to get his ass kicked out of the U."

"Wow." Gabriel whistled appreciatively. "You sure you've got it nailed? What'd Wayne say?"

"Oh, he's nailed, all right. But I haven't talked to Wayne yet. I just got the stuff. Look, would you give him a message for me? Tell him I'll have a major exposé of Carr, *with* supporting documents, for tonight's paper."

"He's here," Gabriel pointed out. "He's in the senior edit office."

"I know. I want to talk to Carr first, get his responses. Just tell Wayne, okay? See you later." She grabbed her backpack and trotted down the back stairs without waiting for him to protest.

True to her promise to Genesko, she biked first to City Hall, where she dropped Harry's manila envelope at the front desk with instructions to pass it along to Wes Kramer. Only then did she turn her bike toward Griffith Carr's district office, pumping her legs energetically. She'd done her civic duty; the Ann Arbor police had the hard evidence. But she damn well wanted to get to Carr before Wes Kramer—and a dozen other reporters—beat her to it.

Not until she stood in front of the office door did it occur to her that he might not be there. Well, only one way to find out. She discovered her heart was beating a tattoo as she turned the knob and stepped inside.

Gloria McGyver looked less than thrilled at her arrival. "What do you want, Ms. Kaplan? I'm extremely busy—I was out sick last week and I still have a great deal of work to catch up on."

She looked kind of pasty, at that. "Is Congressman Carr in?" Zoe asked sweetly.

"I'm afraid he's far too busy to see you today. If you'd care to make an appointment?" McGyver reached for the elegant leather calendar book.

So he was there. Zoe took a deep breath. "I think he really will want to make time for me." She reached into her backpack, withdrew the sheet of paper she'd prepared, and handed it to McGyver. It was a copy of one page of the transcript, folded into thirds and taped shut. "Would you just give this to him, please?"

McGyver stared at the paper in her hand like it was a dead bug. "Don't be ridiculous," she said.

"Ms. McGyver, I'm about to publish some extremely damaging material about Congressman Carr. I'm here to give him a chance to rebut. If he doesn't want to, that's his prerogative. But believe me, he won't thank you if the first he finds out about it is by reading tomorrow's *Daily*."

The look on McGyver's face could have killed several small animals. Without a word, she stood up and stalked across the room to the closed door marked J. GRIFFITH CARR, U.S. CONGRESS. She entered without knocking and shut the door behind her.

Zoe could hear murmurs from behind Carr's door, and once or twice she thought about wandering nearer to see if she could pick out words. In the end, she stayed where she was, and it was only moments later that McGyver emerged from the office, holding the door open and looking angry enough to chew glass.

"Ms. Kaplan?" Griffith Carr's face was shuttered, but Zoe noted a muscle jumping at the side of his jaw. "Please, come in."

Showtime. She followed him through the door and looked around. It wasn't any fancier than the outer office; if anything, it was even messier. Stacks of papers covered the battered wooden desk and spilled onto chairs and file cabinets. He swept a collection of bound legislation booklets off one chair and motioned her to it before going around the desk and sitting down in the worn leather chair.

"Now." He picked up the page of transcript, looked at it, and put it back down. "I'm afraid I don't understand this."

So that's how he was going to play it. "It's part of the transcript of some tape-recorded conversations between you and Lindsay Summers," Zoe said bluntly.

He picked up the sheet of paper again. " 'Just remember,' " he read aloud, " 'if you bring me down you get nothing. Nada.' " He dropped the paper and shook his head. "I'm sorry, Ms. Kaplan, but there must be some mistake."

"There's no mistake, Congressman. I've heard the tapes." She reached down and pulled a notebook and pen from her bookbag, holding them ostentatiously to be sure Carr got the picture. "Do you deny you were having an affair with Lindsay Summers?"

He leaned back in his chair and looked at her, expressions flickering over his thin, ascetic face too fast for her to analyze. She had the feeling he was trying to psych her out, trying to figure out what would work. Finally he said: "Did you ever see *Fatal Attraction*?"

Sheesh. "Yeah. The movie that gave every cheating husband a sympathy play."

"How old are you?" he asked.

"Nineteen."

"Of course. Only a teenager could be quite so rigidly judgmental." He picked up the sheet of transcript and crumpled it into a ball. "For the record, I have no comment at this time, Ms. Kaplan."

"Are you saying that Lindsay entrapped you? Is that why you helped her get substandard work past her dissertation committee?"

"Which part of 'no comment' didn't you understand, Ms. Kaplan?" He reached for the intercom on his desk. "Should I ask Ms. McGyver to escort you out?"

"Never mind, Congressman." Zoe stood and picked up her backpack. "I guess I'll just have to go with what I've got. You can read the full transcript in tomorrow's *Daily*."

"Wait." He motioned to the chair. "Sit down, please." She did as she was told. "This is going to be a big story for you, isn't it?"

"Big enough." She nodded, waiting to see where he was going.

" 'Big enough.' " He repeated her words scornfully. "Only for a kid with no ambition. And I think you have a *lot* of ambition, don't you?"

"I've got my share." What the hell was he offering her?

"How would you like a *real* exposé, in a *real* newspaper?"

"Such as?"

"There's a major sting operation going on in the House even as we speak." He leaned forward, baiting the hook. "I can give you the details, get you in touch with the people involved, *and* set you up to write it for the *Washington Post*."

"The *Post*? No way." The *Washington Post* was one of the few papers left in the country that Zoe respected.

"Absolutely." He nodded rapidly, sinking the hook. "You offer them what I give you, and tell them to call me for confirmation. Then you tell them they can't have the rest of it unless they let you write it." He beamed at his own cleverness.

"Sure, that'll work." Zoe nodded. "Every big newspaper's gonna let some nineteen-year-old kid carry the ball on a sensitive political scandal."

"I'm telling you, it will work, with my word to back you up. Remember, I'm a congressman."

"Oh, I remember." She stood up again. "Sorry, *Congressman*, but no thanks."

"Dammit, do you have any idea what you're doing? This is a tight district. Do you *want* it to go Republican in this election? Don't you *care* about health issues, and the environment, and the poor?"

She shook her head in disgust and turned to leave, but one question occurred to her. "How do you know I'm even a Democrat?" she asked.

"Because a Republican would have grabbed the *Post* story," he said bitterly. He waved a hand at the door, and Zoe saw the tremor of his fingers. "Go on, get out."

She unlocked her bike and pedaled at a deliberate pace back to the *Daily*, working out her story in her head as she rode. The story was in the transcripts, of course, especially without comment from Carr, but there were other angles. She should talk to local political leaders about the effects on the election, and definitely someone in the administration about the sex-with-a-student issue. She was still mulling it over as she hit her brakes and jumped off the bike in the parking lot behind the *Daily*.

"Ms. Kaplan?" Zoe, deep in thought, jumped and spun around at the sound of her name. Gloria McGyver stood outside the back door waiting for her. "May I speak to you?"

"Sure." Was McGyver about to spill? "Come on in."

"No." McGyver darted a glance behind her at the old brick building. "I'd rather . . . Look, I know I can't stop you from publishing those transcripts. But shouldn't you at least have the whole story?"

"I gave Congressman Carr the chance to tell his side of it,"

Zoe pointed out. "If you have something to add, I'll listen." She took out her notebook and pen once more, but McGyver shook her head.

"Not something to say, something to show you. I have some documents in my car." She sighed heavily. "I think the best thing is for you to see for yourself. It won't save him, but at least you'll have the truth." She walked to a white Volvo station wagon, drawn up at an angle behind the first row of cars, motioning to Zoe to follow. "It's in the back seat." She opened the door and looked inside. "Damn. I put everything into a file folder, and it must have slid under the front seat." She started to bend into the car and then stopped, reaching around and massaging her lower back. "Damn this back. Would you get it?"

"Sure." Zoe stepped around her and leaned into the car. She didn't really expect much; McGyver was probably making a last-ditch effort to play her. But whatever it was, she'd better take a look at it.

It was her last coherent thought before the world exploded in pain.

# TWENTY-EIGHT

"Dunno." Peter Braxton leaned back in his chair, his immaculate Bruno Magli loafers propped on his desk. "It's enough to hold Williams, but I don't think there's enough hard evidence for the D.A." He played absently with the diamond stud in his ear. "I wish the poison were something traceable."

"What was it?" Anneke asked.

"An infusion of yew. You can brew it up in your own kitchen, from stuff you can pick from your own backyard."

"We have a yew bush out front," Anneke said, startled. "Is it really that poisonous?"

"Apparently so." Braxton nodded. "And it acted even faster than usual on Summers, because she was so thin and didn't have any food in her stomach."

"Well, at least you have evidence of a direct connection between Lindsay and Barbara."

"Thanks to Zoe." Karl looked grim. "The AAPD should have turned it up."

"You can't really blame them," Anneke found herself defending his colleagues. "After all, Harry was apparently the only one except Lindsay who met her. And he didn't seem to think anything of it. Zoe said he was surprised when she asked."

He'd only met Barbara Williams that once, Harry had told Zoe. He'd gone to Lindsay's apartment—her old apartment, not the current one—to pick up some lab notes, and found Barbara there with Lindsay. Zoe's faxed notes were admirably detailed:

> Z: What were they doing?
> H: They were just drinking bottled water and talk-
> ing. Lindsay had some sort of article or some-
> thing and she was asking Williams about it.
> Z: Do you remember what the article was?
> H: I don't know. Something about the economic
> consequences of meat production. I think Barbara
> was some sort of rabid vegetarian, because she was
> talking about how milk cows are mistreated and
> how they were all exploited, that kind of thing.
> Anyway, Lindsay was going along with her, which
> is why I remember it.
> Z: Lindsay wasn't a vegetarian?
> H: Nah. She didn't eat red meat, of course, but she
> ate fish and chicken and sometimes even a hard-
> boiled egg. But she was just letting Williams rant.
> It was really kind of funny, you know? Here's this
> ugly, lumpish chick going on and on about how
> only total vegetarians are healthy, and here's
> Lindsay, who's so beautiful and everything,
> and . . . ah, shit.
> Z: Did they talk about Barbara getting in on Lind-
> say's research?

H: No. Wait, maybe. Williams said something about "when you do San Francisco," something like that. And she said they could get a lot of people to support Carr's Healthy Foods bill, that San Francisco was more enlightened or something like that. I guess that's why Lindsay was stringing her along.

Z: And that was the only time you saw her?

H: Yes.

Z: Did Lindsay ever mention her again?

H: No.

Zoe's notes ended there, but it was enough. Braxton had interrogated Barbara again, this time with some ammunition, and the woman had broken down—to a point.

"Are you sure yourself that she did it?" Anneke asked.

"I think so, yes." Braxton nodded, as much to himself as to her. "Once I told her we had evidence that she knew Lindsay Summers, she pretty well gave it all up. All the background, anyway. She still denies actually committing the murder."

"How did the Vegan Militia come across Lindsay in the first place?"

"According to Williams, one of the members—she won't give us any other names, by the way—saw an article about Griffith Carr on some vegetarian Web site. It mentioned Summers's research, and they thought it might give them ammunition. Remember," he noted parenthetically, "these people really do believe meat kills. Anyway, they checked it out a little bit, and finally Williams agreed to approach her. That was the meeting in Ann Arbor that this guy Harry walked in on.

"According to Williams, she came away convinced Summers was on their team. She went back to the Militia with the good news that they had a friend in Congress, that Lindsay's research—and Carr's bill—was going to sound the trumpet for vegetarianism. And then she found out she'd been scammed."

"How did she find out?"

"Same way. One of their members was doing research on the Net and came across a paper Summers was working on. Not even published—she'd just loaded it into her own home directory for Carr to look at, if you can believe it."

"Oh, I can believe it." Anneke laughed. "A lot of students use the Internet that way. They set up an orphan page—one with no links into it—and they seem to think that makes it private. They don't realize that searchbots can find it. And of course, mostly it doesn't matter because no one else is interested anyway."

"Well, in this case someone else definitely was. Seems Summers was working on an 'ideal diet,' and it contained fish and milk and eggs and all sorts of 'disgusting things,' according to Williams. Apparently the rest of the Militia was really bent out of shape, and they blamed Williams for letting herself be scrammed. Which, of course, she was. Summers not only betrayed her, she also made her look like a fool among her veggie friends."

"How did Barbara come to be at the Maize and Blue?"

"She wanted a firsthand look at Summers's research. Once the Militia realized they were just being used, they wanted information they could use to discredit her, along with Carr's bill. She says she actually told Summers she did want to do an article about her research for some veggie newsletter, and Summers said okay."

"Do you think she acted on her own?" Karl asked. "Or did her organization plan it with her?"

"Good question." Braxton shrugged. "Doubt that we'll ever know for sure, but if I had to guess, it'd be that, yeah, some of the others were in it with her."

"But why would they?" Anneke asked. "I mean, Barbara had a personal motive—Lindsay made a fool of her—but would this organization kill someone just out of revenge for lying to them?"

"Beats me." Braxton sighed and swung his feet to the floor. "Who knows how crazy some of these people are? Maybe they thought if they killed her it would stop Carr from introducing his bill."

"If they're as paranoid as you say," Karl put in, "they may have thought Lindsay knew too much about them. Do you have any idea how much Williams told her?"

"No." Braxton looked thoughtful. "That's not a bad line to pursue."

"What about the busboy?" Anneke felt a small wave of guilt that she'd forgotten about him.

"You mean, why kill him?" Braxton shrugged. "We have to assume he saw something and she found out about it."

"Was he the one assigned to our table?"

"Actually, no." Braxton gnawed his lower lip. "He was a floater, moving from table to table wherever they needed an extra pair of hands. And in fact he was apparently assigned to the other side of the room. Still, that doesn't mean anything. He could have been passing the table—or even just happened to look in that direction—just at the wrong moment." He shrugged. "I doubt we'll ever know."

"Who was he?" She felt a sudden need to know more about him, this anonymous victim whose death seemed to be just a sidebar.

"His name was Eddy Takahashi. He was a student at San Francisco State, studying film and media. He worked as a part-time busboy for three or four local restaurants, picking up tuition money. Everybody had nothing but good things to say about him, no problems anywhere he worked. A good kid, by all accounts."

"Not the sort of person to try blackmail?" Anneke probed.

"Not from what we've picked up, no. But that doesn't mean he didn't let something slip by accident. The famous 'knowing something he didn't know he knew,' if you get what I mean." Braxton sounded a bit defensive, Anneke thought.

"Still . . ." She paused. "Was he a vegetarian? Or involved with any food causes?"

"No to both." Braxton shook his head. "Just a poor guy who was in the wrong place at the wrong time."

"I suppose." She wished she could put her finger on just why she felt so dissatisfied. "And Carr's definitely off the hook."

" 'Fraid so. In this case, the ironclad alibi really is ironclad. Vouched for by four congressmen, half a dozen congressional aides, and a dozen other people."

"The poison couldn't have been put in something she carried here with her? Vitamins, aspirin, something like that?"

"Nope. Toxicology report showed it was definitely in the tomato juice." He peered at her. "What's your problem? Something we should know?"

"No." She shook her head. What *was* bothering her about the resolution she'd so wanted? "It was an incredible chance to take, though, wasn't it?"

"What? Slipping her the poison in public? You're the one who pointed out how easy it would have been during a big moment in the game." Braxton sounded annoyed. "What's more, Williams was sitting right next to her. It was a lot less risky for her than for anyone else at the table."

"That's true, isn't it?" She shook her head irritably. "I guess I'm just . . ." She threw up her hands.

"I think mostly we're both ready to go home," Karl said. "Congratulations, Inspector." He stood up and held out his hand.

"Thanks." Braxton shook hands, his face relaxing into a

smile. "But if we're handing out bouquets, the biggest one goes to this Zoe of yours."

"Which reminds me," Anneke said, grinning. "We need to make one more trip down to Forty-Niner headquarters. An errand for the empress."

# TWENTY-NINE

Someone was using her head for a blocking sled. She tried to jerk away, and a bolt of pain lanced through her. She whimpered and twisted, trying to escape. Maybe if she asked politely? She tried to speak, but her tongue refused to behave, producing a series of grunts instead of words. They sounded funny, and she giggled despite the pain.

"Good, you're awake." The voice seemed to come from a long distance away. Zoe started to open her eyes to see who was talking to her, but it was too much trouble. "Don't play games," the voice warned her. Like she was planning a fast round of hopscotch, Zoe thought, snickering to herself. "All right, then."

The water caught her full in the face. Some of it went up her nose, making her sneeze, and the sneeze made her head feel like it was exploding.

"Hey!" She sputtered and coughed, suddenly awake and fully conscious. "What the hell was that about?" She started to scramble to her feet, but her muscles didn't seem to do what she told them to. Only then did she realize that she was lying on the floor on her side, her hands tied behind her, her ankles tightly bound, and her whole body wrapped around with rope. She scooched sideways, trying to figure out where she was, and who was throwing water at her.

Gloria McGyver stood in the middle of a small, square room, one of those tiny rooms that could only be the third bedroom of a three-bedroom ticky-tacky suburban house. It had blank white walls and blank wood doors and a single window with a cheap curtain of some nubbly material.

And it had way too much stuff in it. From her position on the floor, Zoe could see an ugly beige sofabed, a chipped glass-topped coffee table, two scarred wooden captain's chairs, a blue-painted table, and a tall black-lacquered cabinet painted with elaborate Japanese scenery—at least, she guessed it was Japanese. There were also vases and bowls and figurines and boxes and every kind of beleaguered flotsam, all of it on top of the kind of olive-green shag rug she'd only seen in an Austin Powers movie. It was, Zoe concluded, your basic "spare room," the place where things you can't quite throw away go to wait until you can.

It took her a minute to recognize one particular pile of flotsam as the contents of her own backpack.

"Hey! That's my stuff." Why had she dumped out her bookbag in Gloria McGyver's spare room? For that matter, why was she *in* Gloria McGyver's spare room? The pain in her head made it hard to think clearly. Why was McGyver standing there with that grim expression on her face, and that large and wicked-looking kitchen knife in her hand?

"What the hell is going on?" Reality swam gradually into view, leaving Zoe aware but confused. She struggled to get up, but succeeded only in scraping her elbow against the coarse rug. "Lady, are you nuts?"

"Where are the tapes, Ms. Kaplan?" McGyver ignored both her question and her struggles.

"The Summers tapes? You mean this is about those stupid tapes?"

"You know perfectly well what this is about." McGyver's lips were pressed into a thin line. "I want those tapes. And since they're not in your bookbag or in your dorm room—I took your keys and searched your room while you were unconscious—I assume you've left them somewhere at the *Daily*. Where are they?"

"You searched my dorm room?" Zoe twisted against her bonds, outraged. "You are a species of lunatic, you know that?"

"Where are the tapes?" McGyver repeated.

"You're out of luck, lady." Zoe felt a wave of satisfaction; for once, doing the right thing had been the right thing to do. "You want them?" she said savagely. "Okay, you go down to City Hall, and you go into the police department, and you ask for them. Because I gave those tapes to the cops before I ever walked into your office."

"Nonsense." McGyver barked out the word. "You're a reporter. I know your type. You wouldn't turn them over until you'd gotten your pound of journalistic flesh."

"Well, you're wrong. That's exactly what I did. So you may as well knock off the game and let me out of here."

"Ms. Kaplan, don't try to play me for a fool." McGyver took a step closer, holding out the knife threateningly. "If the police had those tapes, they'd have been on our doorstep already."

"They probably just haven't gotten around to it." Zoe shrugged, awkwardly because of the ropes. "They know Carr didn't kill Lindsay, so it's not at the top of . . . I mean it's not . . ." She clamped her teeth shut, partly to keep from saying more, partly to keep them from chattering in fear. The pounding in her head must have muddled her thought processes; how else could she have been so dim?

"That's true." McGyver nodded. "I made sure the congressman would be in Washington. And of course it never occurred to anyone to suspect *me*. So now, as soon as I have those tapes, the whole sordid Lindsay Summers episode will be over and we can get back to the country's business."

Maybe the police really were on top of the tapes, Zoe thought. Maybe Wes Kramer was already interrogating Griffith Carr. And what if he was? No way it would lead him here. She felt her body shaking, and realized with a kind of surprise that she was absolutely terrified, so frightened that she couldn't think straight. And she was going to have to do some fast thinking. To buy herself some time, she asked:

"How'd you do it? You couldn't have been at the table with her, could you?"

"Of course not," McGyver said scornfully. "How could you poison a glass in front of a table full of people? Besides, she knew me. I just stayed in the crowd around the bar."

"Then how?" Zoe persisted. She was buying time, but she was also curious.

"I thought she'd ask for a special order—Lindsay couldn't eat what ordinary people ate." McGyver's tone was vicious. "I watched the waiter talk to her and then go into the kitchen, so when he finally came out with her juice I waited until he had to work his way past the bar. So many people were jammed in against the bar that he was watching his feet, not the tray. I had it in a little vial, and I just moved my hand over the tray and upended the vial."

"But what if she hadn't ordered anything special? Or the waiter had gone in some other direction?"

"Then I'd simply have done it somewhere else." McGyver shrugged. "The bar was ideal, because it threw suspicion on a whole group of San Francisco people and turned the spotlight away from Ann Arbor. But if necessary, I'd have done it in her hotel room. So long as she was killed somewhere other than Ann Arbor or Washington, at a time when the congressman had a perfect alibi, it didn't really matter."

"Yeah, but the waiter did see you, didn't he?" Zoe asked. "That must have been the guy who was killed in the firebombing." Poor guy; talk about just being in the wrong place at the wrong time.

"No." McGyver's face darkened. "That was my own mistake, I'm afraid. As soon as I got there I went into the ladies' room to change clothes—take off my blouse and put on a Michigan T-shirt and baseball cap. So I wouldn't be noticed," she explained. "I'd flown in from Tokyo earlier that morning, and somehow my passport fell out of my purse and I never realized it. The next day the Takahashi boy called to tell me he'd found it."

"So he was trying to blackmail you? Tough." Zoe tried to pour sympathy into her voice.

"No." McGyver shook her head. "He was trying to be helpful. He'd noticed the Japanese visa and he was interested. He just wanted to know where I'd been, what I'd thought of Japan. He offered to mail it back to me, but I told him I was returning to San Francisco the next night, and arranged to meet him at the Maize and Blue when he got off work. I had to tell the congressman that I was sick, of course." She sighed deeply. "I feel badly about that; I don't like having to lie to him."

She really was nuts, Zoe concluded. She felt a stabbing pain in her shoulder and tried to wriggle herself into a more comfortable position.

"Don't bother trying to get loose, Ms. Kaplan," McGyver said. "That's brand-new clothesline, good and strong."

"I didn't know anyone still used clothesline." Sheesh, why was she talking about clothesline at a time like this?

"That doesn't surprise me," McGyver said scornfully. "You kids don't care what your appliances do to the environment as long as it saves you a little work. Toss your clothes into an electric dryer, don't worry about the tons of hydrocarbons that power plants spew into the air, then go off to your raves and snort your drugs and let other people worry about the future of the earth." Her face contorted. "You just don't care about anyone or anything but yourself, do you?"

"Hey, I recycle. And I ride a bike instead of driving." The conversation was getting more and more surreal. "I can't very well use a clothesline in a dorm, you know." She wriggled again; whatever else clothesline was good for, it was doing one hell of a job keeping her immobilized. She searched her memory for any hostage-in-jeopardy scenario she'd ever heard of, fictional or real, and went for an oldie but goodie. "I have to go to the bathroom," she said plaintively.

"Isn't that a shame." McGyver shrugged. "Tell me where the tapes are, and maybe we can move on."

"I'm not kidding." Zoe poured anguish into her voice. "I've really gotta go. And if you make me do it in my pants, it'll get in your rug and you'll never get the smell out."

At least it seemed to make McGyver stop and think. Finally, without speaking, she approached Zoe, leaned over and sliced through a coil of rope with her knife. Zoe felt the ropes loosen and flexed her shoulders gratefully. Her hands were still tied behind her back, and her ankles were still bound tightly together, but at least she wasn't trussed like a Thanksgiving turkey.

McGyver walked across the room and opened one of the flat wooden doors. "Across the hall."

"How am I supposed to get there?" Zoe asked.

"You can crawl." McGyver stood unmoving, arms folded. Zoe started to protest, but one look at McGyver's face told her she couldn't play her much further. Shrugging, she scooched along the floor toward the door, collecting a nice assortment of rug burns along the way. She finally found herself on a tired-looking strip of vinyl, her nose a few inches from the porcelain base of a toilet, in the noxious blue beloved of late-fifties housewives.

"Now what?" She twisted around to peer up at McGyver, who made a cluck of annoyance.

"Roll over onto your stomach," McGyver directed. Zoe did as she was told, and felt two hands drag her halfway erect, so that she was kneeling on the ugly floor in front of the toilet. She realized McGyver had put the knife down for that couple of seconds, but by the time it occurred to her it was too late. And anyway, what could she do tied up this way?

Even before she'd worked this out, her head still muzzy, McGyver had gripped her by the arms once more, hauled her onto her feet, and spun her around. She overbalanced, nearly fell, and collapsed onto the toilet seat, still fully clothed. By the time she got her bearings, McGyver had the knife in her hand, its tip pressed against her belly button.

"Stand up, Ms. Kaplan. Very, very slowly." Silently, Zoe obeyed. "I'm going to pull your clothing down, and then you'll sit down again. If you do anything foolish, I won't hesitate to use this knife. It can do a great deal of damage and still leave you able to tell me where you've hidden those tapes."

This was getting too stupid. Zoe wished now she'd never tried the bathroom game. "For Pete's sake," she said, "don't you just have a gun you can point at me?"

"A gun!" McGyver yanked viciously at Zoe's blue jeans, the knife scratching at her stomach. "That's so typical. I wouldn't have a gun in my house. Do you know how many young people—children, teenagers, people your own age—are killed by guns every year in this country? Do you know the damage caused by our culture of violence?" She dragged the blue jeans down to Zoe's knees with one hand, and Zoe wished suddenly that she'd worn something besides an old, graying pair of cotton underpants. She'd have felt embarrassed, except that McGyver didn't seem to be paying any attention.

"You really don't understand how important Congressman Carr is to this country." McGyver panted slightly as she dragged on the despised underpants. "That's the whole problem with people your age. You're so cynical you don't believe that one man can make a difference, and so judgmental you think human peccadilloes matter more than the crucial issues of our time." With a kind of gasp, she yanked Zoe's underpants down and shoved her to a sitting position on the toilet. "Congressman Carr is going to make a real difference, if people like you don't drag him down because he doesn't meet some exalted standard. And I'm going to be there with him. He promised me, and I'll make sure he keeps his promise." She stood up straight, moving the knife so that its point was against Zoe's throat. "Now do what you have to do and let's end this."

This wasn't the way it was supposed to go, Zoe thought desperately as she forced out a tinkle or two. In a thriller, the hero would follow some carefully placed clues and ride to her rescue. Only, this story didn't seem to have a hero. The only person who knew where she had been going was Gabriel, and that wouldn't help much. Even if he tried to track her down, Carr and McGyver would just say she'd been to the office and left. And the fact that her bike was locked up behind the *Daily* would confirm their story.

Dammit, it wasn't fair. She'd done everything absolutely by the numbers. She'd turned the evidence over to the cops, she'd made sure someone knew where she was going, she'd even been assured that the guy she was going to confront *wasn't* the murderer. And look where it got her—trussed up like the heroine in a bad sweeps-week TV movie. It didn't raise her spirits any to recall that all fem-jep movies had happy endings—they probably had better writers.

"All right, you're done." McGyver flicked the knife against her jaw. "Stand up. You can hobble back into the other room."

"I can't." Zoe tried moving her feet, but they were bound too tightly.

"Then you can crawl again." McGyver shoved her down ungently onto her knees, causing Zoe to squeak as pain shot through her legs. She wanted to ask McGyver to at least pull her pants up again, but she figured it wouldn't do any good. She scooched some more, out of the bathroom, across the hall, back to the overstuffed room. If they find my dead body, she thought, they're going to wonder how I got these rug burns on my ass. The notion made her giggle, then laugh, then clamp her teeth together tightly. She didn't dare give way to hysteria. She had to *think*, dammit.

"That's far enough." McGyver stopped. "My patience is running out, Ms. Kaplan." She flicked the knife against Zoe's cheek. "Where are those tapes?"

"I *told* you . . ." Zoe stopped, seeing the trap at last. Suppose she did convince McGyver that the tapes really were in the hands of the police? Then there'd be no reason to keep her alive, would there? And one way or another, McGyver had to kill her; the tapes didn't point to her as a murderer, only Zoe could do that.

So she couldn't insist that the cops had the tapes; and she couldn't turn over the tapes; and no matter what she did, McGyver was going to use that knife on her in the end.

So how the hell was she supposed to play it?

# THIRTY

"To the Maize and Blue." George McMartin raised his champagne flute and held it out across the table, looking for someone to clink glasses with. The table, of course, was laden with food, half a dozen varieties of cakes, pastries, and other diet nightmares.

"To Cody." Elisa raised her glass.

"Nah." Cody Jarrett shook his head. "But at least all this did give me some ideas for some special diet recipes." He waved his fork, which held a chunk of chocolate cake. "What do you think of it?"

"This is a diet recipe?" George, who'd eaten a sizable piece of cake with every evidence of relish, looked warily at the remaining crumbs on his plate.

"You couldn't tell? Great." Cody looked pleased. "It's low-fat *and* sugarless; the icing's a kind of take on chocolate mousse, with buttermilk instead of cream."

"Cody, stop thinking about recipes—this is a celebration," Noelle said cheerfully. She raised her own glass high in the air. "To Karl Genesko, linebacker and gentleman." She winked at

Karl, and then all of them were clinking and sipping and laughing, giddy with relief.

Well, not all of them. Jeremy Blake pulled at the cuff of his Blake's Fitness windbreaker and stared into the far distance.

"Jeremy?" Mimi put her hand on his. He blinked and turned to her, attempting an unconvincing smile. "We know Lindsay was lying," Mimi murmured. "Don't let it get to you—don't let *her* get to you again."

"It's not that," Jeremy said somberly. "I know you believe me that I didn't have a clue she was pregnant. It's just . . . I might have had a son, or a daughter, that I never even knew about."

"Jeremy?" Karl looked perturbed. "Didn't you talk to Inspector Braxton?"

"About what?" Jeremy and Mimi both turned to face him.

"Dammit, I thought you knew," Karl said. "What Lindsay told that boy in Ann Arbor was a lie."

"Yes, we know." Mimi curled her fingers around Jeremy's. "Jeremy would never have done something like that."

"No, that's not what I mean." Karl shook his head. "The whole thing was a lie. I've seen the autopsy report, and Lindsay Summers was never pregnant."

"Oh, thank God." Mimi whispered the words, then raised her voice. "That bitch. That absolute, unconscionable bitch."

"Poor Lindsay." Jeremy colored slightly and glanced at Mimi; for all his exaggerated muscle, he looked younger than she did. "I know, I know. But she made herself even more unhappy than she made other people." He stared into the distance once more. "You know, when I thought about having a kid, it felt weird. It was like Lindsay had taken something away from me that I never even knew I wanted. Maybe . . ." He looked at Mimi and grinned suddenly, and her eyes widened before a smile worked its way onto her face.

"Hey, we're having a celebration here." Noelle laughed and raised her glass. "To young love."

"Hear, hear." Blair clinked glasses with her and drank. Blair looked different somehow; he was wearing a deep gold silk shirt under a brown suede vest; he'd rolled his shirt cuffs above his wrists, and he seemed more relaxed than he ever had before.

"Is everything ready to go, then?" Richard's eyes sparkled; he had the gift of optimism, Anneke thought with something like envy.

"Ready and waiting," Noelle said. "The financials will be in place by the end of the week, and you can start signing options as soon as the ink's dry." She glanced at Blair, who winked at her. Elisa, resplendent as always in a cream-colored blazer, didn't seem to notice; Anneke wondered how she could possibly miss what was going on between her husband and the other woman. Because Elisa couldn't imagine Noelle as the Other Woman, she concluded. Elisa, safely barricaded behind her thin, toned body, simply wouldn't take Noelle seriously—wouldn't take a *fat* woman seriously—as a romantic or sexual rival until it was far too late. Anneke knew she should feel sympathy for the betrayed wife—well, she thought she should, anyway—but in this case she couldn't do it. She liked Noelle; she didn't like Elisa; and there was no point beating herself up over it.

The conversation turned to the future, the glittering plans for Cody Jarrett and Nouvelle Midwest. Everyone drank champagne, and celebrated, and put the ugly facts of murder and firebombing out of their heads.

So why, Anneke asked herself, did she feel so dissatisfied?

"Problem?" Karl read the expression on her face.

"Not exactly." She worried at her thoughts for a moment. "I think it's the busboy," she said finally.

"What about him?"

"Okay, let's assume Barbara Williams killed the busboy—Eddy Takahashi, wasn't it?" She felt suddenly guilty for referring to him as "the busboy," as though he were a chess piece instead of a person. "Anyway, let's assume she killed Takahashi because he'd seen her, or found out somehow that she'd murdered Lindsay Summers. So the firebomb was to make it look like he wasn't the actual target? But then why make it such a damp squib of a firebomb? Especially considering how much she hated the Maize and Blue. Why not really blow the place out?"

"Possibly sheer incompetence," he suggested.

"Except you and Peter Braxton both agree that amateurs usually use too much explosive, not too little." She chewed on her lip. "Besides, wouldn't she have aimed for the kitchen, or at least the dining room? Why carefully firebomb a storage room where she'd do the least damage?"

"The only answer to that is the old truism that criminals usually don't think things through as carefully as detective fiction suggests. It's likely that she just killed him where she met him, and didn't plan much further than that."

"Maybe," Anneke acknowledged. "I suppose Barbara wasn't the brightest bulb on the tree, was she?"

"Please, this is a celebration. I don't want to hear that woman's name ever again," Richard interrupted, shuddering delicately. "I knew there was something peculiar about her. She made the hair on the back of my neck stand on end, I swear to it." He seemed quite proud of his reaction, as though it were a tribute to his Irish intuition. Which, Anneke supposed, it might well be.

"All right; never mind." Anneke shrugged off her misgivings and tried to enter into the spirit of the occasion. "So you're just about finished planning the expansion?" she said to Noelle.

"Oh, I never actually *plan* to expand." Noelle ran her hands down her lush body. "It just seems to happen." She laughed uproariously, and most of the others joined in. Only Elisa looked on with a patronizing smile. Noelle reached for a whipped-cream-covered tart; so did Blair; their hands bumped and the small pastry tipped over, covering their fingers with whipped cream.

"Hey." Noelle made a face and flicked her fingers at Blair, catching him neatly on the cheek with a dollop of whipped cream.

"Oh, you want to play rough, do you?" He laughed and scooped a mound of white fluff out of the tart which he flipped expertly in Noelle's direction. Noelle ducked; Richard didn't.

Richard scraped the sticky stuff off his face and looked at it. He looked from Noelle to Blair, both of them laughing uncontrollably. Then, without speaking, he reached toward a platter of individual raspberry soufflés and dug out a large pink mass.

"Richard . . ." Mimi's warning was spoiled somewhat by the giggle that followed. Richard looked at her consideringly, as if measuring trajectories.

"Don't you dare," she squeaked.

"Don't worry, I'll protect you." Jeremy picked up a hefty chunk of the diet chocolate cake. "Don't even . . ." Whatever he was going to say was stifled by the large blob of raspberry soufflé that caught him square in the face.

"Hey!" Mimi yelped in mock outrage. "You can't do that to my guy." She reached for another whipped-cream tart. "Prepare to die."

Prepare to duck, you mean. Anneke started to back away from the table, afraid that she was too late. She was; before she could react, a chunk of chocolate-mousse icing splatted directly into her face.

"Are you going to let them do that to me?" she demanded of Karl.

"Absolutely not." He was grinning widely as he reached for a butterscotch tart.

"Give me one of those." She picked up one of the raspberry

soufflés and looked around for a target, ducking to avoid a chocolate missile. Richard, she decided; definitely Richard . . .

By the time they'd showered, and washed the food out of each other's hair, and done several other enjoyable things in the shower, the fog had lifted. They drove back toward the beach, to watch the tiny shore birds and happy dogs and the vast, oblivious ocean. Anneke checked her watch; this time tomorrow they'd be home. In fact, this time tomorrow it would be three hours later. She laughed to herself at the paradox of time zones.

"Karl?" The thought hit her suddenly.

"What?"

"Exactly what time was Griffith Carr in that committee meeting in Washington?"

"If I remember correctly, all morning. Why?"

"Because morning in Washington would be . . . No, it's the other way around, isn't it?" She made a face as she puzzled out the time difference.

"No, it wouldn't work." Karl shook his head, following her line of thought. "If he was in committee until noon Washington time, that would be nine A.M. San Francisco time. And it's a five-hour plane flight. But nice idea. Not that I blame you for wanting it to be Carr, but he really is out of it. Besides," he pointed out with a smile, "we were there, remember? If Carr had been there, we'd have seen him."

"He could have been there in a Michigan jacket and cap and we wouldn't have noticed. Oh, all right, all right." She laughed. "Anyway, it's not that I want it to be Carr. Well, all right, I suppose I do. But dammit, he's the only one with the real motive."

"Motive is in the eye of the beholder, I'm afraid," Karl replied. "People have killed over a parking spot."

"Yes, but those are flash killings. I mean, they're heat-of-the-moment things, not as premeditated as this one was. I know, I know, now you'll tell me about someone who poisoned a neighbor because his cat dug up a flowerbed." She sighed. "Never mind." She looked out the window. "What are those?" As the big Explorer crested the hill before the steep run down to the beach, she saw a cluster of jagged peaks at the horizon.

"The Farallone Islands." Karl steered around a huge articulated bus and stopped at a red light. "They're a nature preserve."

"How far out are they?" Anneke shaded her eyes and peered into the sun.

"About twenty-five miles."

"So far? They look close enough to touch. A trick of the light, I suppose." She leaned back against the seat and let the sunset glow seep into her skin. "It almost feels like, if you just squinted a little, you could see all the way to Japan." The big car started up again, downhill and around the long, sweeping curb. The Farallones disappeared below the horizon, as invisible as Japan.

Japan . . .

"Karl."

"What?"

"Griffith Carr wasn't the only one whose career would go down in flames if Lindsay went public with her accusations."

Instead of answering, he swung the big car into a parking space facing the surf. "His administrative assistant, you mean." He turned in his seat to look at her. "Zoe said she was hoping to transfer to Washington with him after this next election."

"And when Zoe talked to her two days after the murder, she said she'd just gotten back from Tokyo." Anneke looked out across the vast water. "A quick stop-off in San Francisco—who'd notice?"

"Even if she did," he pointed out, "how could she have done

it? We eliminated any outsiders in the kitchen, and we know she wasn't at the table."

"I don't know," Anneke said fretfully. "We're missing something. We have to be." She cast her mind back to the morning of the murder. Something, some possibility hovered at the back of her mind, but she couldn't for the life of her dredge it up. "Can you check her flight, at least?"

"I suppose it can't hurt." Karl rubbed his hand across his chin for a moment, then pulled his cell phone out of his pocket. "Let me call Wes and have him check it out." He punched buttons on the tiny phone, and Anneke listened with impatience to the one-sided conversation. "Wes? Good, you're still there. . . . Quick question—did you do a check on Gloria McGyver? . . . Yes, I know. . . . Sure . . . Would you check with the airline, find out if her flight included a layover in San Francisco? . . . Yes, I know the case is settled, I'd just like to clean up a couple of loose ends, if you don't mind. . . . We'll be back tomorrow afternoon." He hung up. "It's the longest of long shots, you know," he said to Anneke.

"I know." She nodded. "And I promise, that's my last word on the subject." She opened the car door. "Let's take one last walk on the beach."

# THIRTY-ONE

Her head still felt like someone was playing concerto for guitar and jackhammer. She needed time to think. Time. "What time is it?" she asked.

McGyver consulted her tiny wristwatch. "Six o'clock."

"You're kidding," Zoe said, startled. It'd only been around noon when she'd left Carr's office.

"Yes, and my patience is running out." McGyver flicked her cheek with the knife again, harder this time, and Zoe felt a stab of pain and something damp trickling down her cheek.

"Ouch! Hey, that hurt."

"It was supposed to. The next one will hurt even more. Now where are those tapes?"

"I left them with my boyfriend at the *Daily*," Zoe blurted. Now where did that come from? she wondered. And who the hell am I going to feed to her?

"And his name?" McGyver demanded.

"Barney McCormack." It was the first *Daily* name that popped into her head. Now why him, and not Gabriel? Of course; because Barney was going to be gone until evening. If she'd had the emotional energy for it, she'd have felt proud of her cleverness.

"Where can I find him?" McGyver went on inexorably.

"He's the sysadmin—the computer guru," Zoe explained. "He works in the computer room in the basement. He's got the tapes there, in this big manila envelope. He doesn't know what they are, either, just that I asked him to keep them for me." Now that she had decided what to say, she was babbling; she clamped her jaws together to shut herself up.

"You'd better be telling the truth," McGyver warned her.

"Of course I'm telling the truth. Once you have the tapes, you don't need me anymore, right? And it'd only be my word against yours, and you're an important woman so they'd believe you. Please, just go get the tapes so you can let me go?" She heard the whimper in her voice; good. She was going for a frightened-little-girl riff, which wasn't that much of a stretch considering how scared she really was. But if McGyver bought into it, she'd be more likely to wait around for Barney to show up instead of coming right back. Right now, all she wanted was to buy some time.

"All right." McGyver moved out of her line of vision, and Zoe squirmed herself around on the floor to see what she was doing. "Lie still," the woman snapped, and Zoe obeyed.

"All right. Stand up." Zoe started to ask how she was supposed to do that, but McGyver grabbed her roughly by one arm, dragged her to her knees once more, and pulled her upright. The knife was pressed firmly against her throat as McGyver forced her backward against the big Japanese cabinet; in a moment, Zoe felt herself trussed all over again, tied up to the cabinet with more coils of clothesline. She wriggled experimentally, and felt the cabinet wobble.

"I wouldn't do that if I were you," McGyver said. She spoke matter-of-factly, without emotion, like she didn't really care a whole lot. "It's a beautiful cabinet, but one of its feet is broken. If you don't remain very still, you'll bring it down on top of you. And it's *very* heavy." She stepped back, examining her prisoner. "I wish I could have you write him a note, but I'm not going to risk untying your hands." She cocked her head, looking even more sparrowlike. "I'll take your wallet," she decided, rummaging among the pile of Zoe's possessions. "I'll tell him you forgot it and ask him to return it to you." She took one last look at Zoe. "I'll be back as soon as I have the tapes."

"You were right about the flight connections, anyway." Wes Kramer's voice sounded tinny through the cell phone. "She had a six-hour layover in San Francisco Saturday. What's more, there was an earlier flight back to Detroit that she could have caught but didn't. Still, it probably doesn't mean anything, you know. Odds are she just wanted to spend a few hours sightseeing."

"I know. And I hate to give you added work just on a hunch." He glanced at Anneke, who felt herself reddening. It was her hunch, after all, and Karl was climbing awfully far out on a limb for her.

"Well, we'll talk to her. It's on my way home anyway, and I'm just about ready to cash in for the day."

"Thanks, Wes." Karl broke the connection. "You were right about the layover in San Francisco," he said to Anneke.

"Which, as you so rightly pointed out, doesn't mean a single damn thing." She sighed. "The thing is, if she did it, *how* did she do it? She wasn't at the table; she wasn't in the kitchen; and there wasn't any other . . ." The scene clicked in then, suddenly, and Anneke couldn't imagine how she could have been so dense. "The waiter." She plucked at his sleeve with a sudden urgency. "We need to talk to the waiter again."

Zoe waited until she heard the garage door open, the sound of a car engine, the garage door slamming shut. She waited another couple of minutes, forcing herself to remain still against every instinct in her body that wanted to struggle, and scream, and generally panic. She took a deep breath, forcing herself to be calm, to think. If she could figure out something to think *about*. Now that she'd bought herself some time, what the hell was she going to do with it?

She should have been able to do something before. She was young and reasonably strong; how the hell could she have let herself be manhandled and trussed up by a middle-aged woman who didn't even have a gun? She ran over the sequence of events in her mind, but she couldn't see when she'd have had a chance to fight back. She felt tears start to leak from her eyes and fought them back. Think, dammit.

She was standing upright with her back against the Japanese cabinet. Her hands were behind her back, tied tightly with clothesline; her ankles were tied together just as tightly. More clothesline was looped around and around her body and around and around the cabinet; she and it were lashed together as effectively as if she were chained to a dungeon wall.

She pulled against the rope, wondering if it might stretch, and felt the cabinet wobble ominously at her back. She stopped and waited for it to steady itself, fear-induced sweat popping out under her arms and at her crotch. She wished she could pull up her pants, more for comfort than for modesty; it felt weird somehow. She giggled, then gulped back incipient hysteria.

All right. If she struggled in any way she'd bring the cabinet down on top of her; she'd just be trading death by knife for death by furniture. Well, not exactly; there was too much stuff in the room for the cabinet to fall flat to the floor. In fact, if she and it fell straight forward the upper portion of the damn thing would land on the coffee table.

Would that do any good? She thought about it for a minute and shook her head, carefully so as not to jiggle the cabinet. She wouldn't be pinned under it, but she'd wind up just sort of hanging from it. Besides, the coffee table was glass and the cabinet would probably just break right through it and she'd wind up on the floor anyway. Well, no; the chrome base would probably hold it. . . .

Glass. For the first time, the bubble of an idea began to form in her mind. Glass. She narrowed her eyes, trying to ignore the pounding in her head. If she could use the cabinet to break the glass, could she use an edge of broken glass to cut through the rope?

She wiggled the cabinet experimentally and recoiled in fear as she felt it begin to overbalance. She wasn't sure she even had the guts to do it, never mind whether it would work or not. And besides, there were too many ifs—if the glass tabletop actually broke; if the base held the cabinet up; if she could even reach a shard of the glass. Too many ifs . . .

She lunged forward, refusing to give herself time to think, refusing to give the fear time to take over. She plunged forward, the heavy cabinet on her back propelling her toward the floor, her eyes squeezed shut, the scream inside her silenced by the breathlessness of terror.

The crash of the cabinet and the crack of glass were less loud than the pounding of her own heart. She found herself face down and half-suspended a foot above the olive green shag rug, the top of the cabinet resting on the ruins of the glass-topped coffee table. To her joy she was able to bend her legs and settle down on her knees, giving her the first feeling of stability she'd had since her ordeal began. Now, if she could just . . .

Too late she recognized her mistake. The glass tabletop had broken, all right; broken utterly, into pieces that lay all around her on the floor. Out of reach, useless, as unattainable as the moon. And finally Zoe broke, and wept tears of pain and terror, thrashing against the implacable ropes and the heavy weight of the horrible cabinet on her back, sobbing with fear. And almost not hearing the creaking sounds of the monstrosity lashed above her.

The cabinet was creaking. She hurled herself against the ropes and felt something give, and jerked her body back and forth, frantic beyond hysteria, feeling the cabinet move like something alive, back and forth, her muscles aching, and back and forth again, over and over, until with a final angry *snap!* one corner of the cabinet gave way and the whole thing seemed to fold into itself with a sigh, collapsing sideways and pulling her with it to the floor. She felt the ropes loosen, and she scrambled desperately along the floor, hands and feet still bound, until finally, finally, she was crawling free.

The glass. Her mind was suddenly clear, focused, her whole body in overdrive. She scooched along the floor, found a large, jagged piece of glass, then had to turn around to pick it up, fumbling with it behind her back. Still on her knees, she jiggled over to the sofa and crammed the glass into the crevice between seat and arm. Sat down; backed up until the rope holding her wrists was pressed against its edge; sawed up and down, up and down, wondering how long she'd taken, how much time she had left.

She felt the rope snap, and then she had to pull and pull before the coils were loose enough to finally—finally!—release her hands, but when she reached down to untie her ankles her arms refused to work, and she wasted more precious time working the circulation back into her fingers before she could fumble the final knots free. She tried to stand up, but her knees buckled under her, and she had to drag herself to her feet using the arm of the sofa for support.

She pulled up her pants with still-shaky hands and went out into the hall, every nerve ending still quivering. She stopped for a single second to get her bearings, identifying the front of the house and heading as fast as she could for the door, trying to ignore the throbbing in her legs. She had her hand on the doorknob when she heard the sounds of a car pulling into the driveway.

She whimpered, frozen at the door, nearly at the end of her strength. She looked around wildly, hobbled back down the hall as fast as she could. The kitchen—there had to be a back door—there! Choking back a sob, she flung herself at the latch, hurled the door open, and plunged outside. The slam of a car door carried through the night air, and footsteps tramped heavily toward the house.

Zoe fled.

# THIRTY-TWO

".. . and then I just walked to the police station." Zoe took a handful of the weird San Francisco trail mix and shoved it into her mouth, trying not to notice the collection of small scratches on her wrist. Scratches from sawing glass against the rope that bound her wrists, cuts she hadn't even known she had. At least the doctor had said they'd fade eventually.

"If it hadn't been for you, I don't think she'd ever have been found out." Anneke intercepted a look from Berniece Kaplan, who nodded gravely. Zoe's mother was right; the girl needed to talk about her ordeal, and she needed reassurance. "And an innocent woman might have been executed."

When she showed up at the police station, staggering, bleeding, and calling for Lieutenant Kramer, there'd been several minutes of Keystone Kops activity. Zoe had dissolved into mildly hysterical laughter when she discovered that the footsteps she'd heard outside the door had been Kramer himself rather than McGyver. And it took her too long to tell them that McGyver herself was probably standing outside the door to the *Daily* computer room, impatiently waiting for a nonexistent manila envelope.

By the time McGyver was brought in, under arrest and deathly silent, Zoe was long gone, scooped up by Bernie and taken back to the house in Birmingham. Bernie had been shaken enough by the phone call from the police; she was even more shaken when Zoe had gone with her without a word of protest, not even wanting to stay and find out how it all ended.

Now, three days later, they were sitting in the big living room of Karl and Anneke's Burns Park house at Bernie's request, answering each other's questions. It was a nice house, Bernie Kaplan decided; comfortable and mildly elegant without being in the least pretentious. It was familiar to Zoe, of course; familiar and above all, safe. Zoe hadn't exactly wanted to come back to Ann Arbor right away. It was Bernie who'd insisted.

She glanced at her daughter now, relieved to see her turn her attention to Wes Kramer. If Zoe was back in reporter mode, Bernie knew she was going to be all right.

"She must have been nuts." Zoe took another handful of trail mix, looked at it, and put it down on the coffee table in front of her. "Well, she was nuts." She reached forward and selected a pecan and put it in her mouth. "She did all that in a crowded restaurant? Anyone could have seen her."

"She says she was sure no one would." Kramer shrugged. "Went on and on about 'the anonymity of the middle-aged woman.' " He moved uneasily, casting a glance at Karl. "Still, we shouldn't have ignored her like we did."

"Below suspicion," Anneke said suddenly.

" 'Scuse me?"

"*Below Suspicion*. It's the title of a mystery novel by John Dickson Carr. He's referring to a housemaid—it's set in Victorian times," she explained parenthetically. "Just as there are people who are above suspicion, there are people who are below it—below the official radar, you might say. That's where Gloria McGyver was."

"Besides, a lot of people dropped the ball on this one." Karl's lips were tight. "I was there myself when that waiter was interviewed the first time."

Jason Blethridge had been interviewed again, and again he'd insisted that he went straight from the kitchen to Lindsay Summers's table. Only this time he'd given them a bit more detail.

"I remember it was when Truesdale made that great run," he said, "and the whole place went crazy and I had to slow down going past the bar and I almost tripped over some old woman, but I never spilled a drop." Had he stopped to watch Truesdale's run? No; well, not really. He might have slowed down for a couple of seconds, especially when Truesdale made that juke move around the linebacker. Wasn't that something? By which they understood that practically anyone could have dumped practically anything into the glass of tomato juice on his tray while that play had been going on.

"We figured out that everyone at the table could have been distracted by the game," Anneke said, "only we forgot to apply the same logic to the waiter."

"Is he going to be able to ID her?" Zoe asked.

"Probably not," Wes Kramer said. "And he didn't see her drop the poison in the glass anyway. Your evidence is going to be the key."

"I really didn't act like the idiot in a bad TV movie, you know." For the third time, Zoe defended herself against an accusation no one had made. "I mean, I took the evidence to the police, *and* I made sure someone knew where I was going, and on top of that, everyone said no way Carr could be the murderer."

"Zoe?" Anneke caught the girl's eye and held it. "You didn't take a single step wrong. And you're too bright to fall into blame-the-victim mode, all right?"

Zoe took a second, then grinned suddenly. "Okay, I guess you're right." Bernie, who'd been telling her the same thing for three days, shot Anneke a look of gratitude. It always sounded better coming from someone who wasn't your mother. "Pass me another one of those pasties?" Zoe asked.

Anneke pushed the platter toward her, started to take one herself, then firmly pulled back her hand. She was still trying to lose the six pounds she'd gained in two San Francisco weeks. She fully intended to wrap up all this food and send it to the dorm with Zoe.

For Richard, upon hearing of Zoe's ordeal, had sent—of course—food, a passionate outpouring of trail mix and pasties, Michigan dried cherries and smoked Lake Superior whitefish and even an entire box of venison steaks. The phrase "coals to Newcastle" apparently hadn't occurred to him. He'd also sent, specifically for Anneke, a two-pound jar of Callista's chocolate syrup, which she'd tasted experimentally, concluding that if it wasn't better than sex, it was a damn close second.

And he'd sent one other thing, something Anneke had promised to get and hadn't had time for. Now she reached behind the sofa and pulled out a large, flat package which she handed to Zoe. "I believe I promised you this."

Zoe ripped off the brown paper covering and gazed with delight at the signed poster of Steve Mariucci.

"Oh, wow. Will you look at those eyes?"

# AFTERWORD

No, I am not making up the notion of a "fat tax." There is indeed more than one proposal for legislation to force Americans to eat the way the public health establishment has decided they should. If you want to know more, check out the following URL:

http://www.nutritionaction.org/reports/tax/

Begin rant:

If you think it's okay for the government to control people's lives to make them healthier and safer, consider your own activities, your own pleasures, before you commit. Do you enjoy bike riding? Lots of accidents there. Inline skating? Ditto Do you drink a lot of coffee, or Coke? They've been trying for years to find some health risk in caffeine, and believe me, eventually they will. Do you play computer games? Bad for eyes, and morals, and social interaction. Think they're not going to get around to you, when they're done with the rest of us? Power trips lead to more and greater power trips, and control addicts are never, ever satisfied.

End rant.

Yes, this book contains—wait for it—a recipe. And that sound you hear is my friends, all of them, falling off their chairs laughing at the notion that I even know how to read one, let alone (sort of) creating one.

After I finished my third (I think) book, I got the edited manuscript back with a mildly plaintive margin note from my editor. "Doesn't Anneke *ever* cook a meal?" she asked.

To which I replied: "About as often as her creator." Which is to say: Only if all the delis go on strike and the pizza delivery boy runs his car into a lamppost. I admit it. I'm one of those people who recognize only three food groups—caffeine, nicotine, and anything cooked by someone else. I'm the only person I know who has to dust her stove.

On the other hand, I never said I *couldn't* cook; I only said I *didn't* cook. And every now and then, when the moon and three or four planets are in exactly the right configuration, I get this peculiar urge. . . .

Which seems to be what happened here. Nouvelle Midwest, it should be reasonably obvious, is a total invention of my own. So is Cody Jarrett's "Cotswold Fusilli." But the more I wrote about Cody's gourmet take on macaroni and cheese, the better it sounded. And since it *was* my own invention, the only way to have some was to actually get down there in the trenches with the butter and the pasta and the Cuisinart and the boiling water.

This, then, is the result, and not half bad, if I do say so myself.

**CODY JARRETT'S
COTSWOLD FUSILLI**
*(Not for the cholesterol-conscious)*

## Make the pasta a day ahead:

| | | | |
|---|---|---|---|
| 2 | Tbs. butter | 1 | tsp. salt |
| 2½ | Tbs. flour | ⅛ | tsp. pepper |
| 2 | cups milk | 3 | Tbs. fresh chives (don't |
| ½ | lb. shredded Cotswold | | cheat and use the dried kind) |
| | cheese (you can substitute a | ½ | cup sour cream |
| | good double Gloucester if | ½ | lb. fusilli, broken into one- |
| | necessary, but the result | | inch pieces |
| | won't be as good) | ¼ | cup unflavored bread crumbs |

*Make a white sauce:* Melt butter in heavy saucepan over low heat, mix in flour, and stir for about one minute. Add milk all at once and simmer for three minutes, stirring continuously. Add shredded Cotswold and stir until melted. When sauce has thickened, remove from heat and stir in salt, pepper, chives, and sour cream.

Break fusilli into one-inch pieces and cook according to package directions. Drain well and pour into a large bowl. Pour sauce mixture over fusilli and mix well.

Pour the mixture into a buttered loaf pan and sprinkle with the bread crumbs. Bake at 357°F for 40 minutes or until a knife inserted into the center comes out clean. Remove from oven, cool, and refrigerate several hours or overnight.

When ready to serve, remove from loaf pan and slice into eight slices.

### Make the cheese sauce:

| | |
|---|---|
| 2 Tbs. butter | pinch cayenne pepper |
| 2 Tbs. flour | |
| 1 cup milk, room temperature | 2 Tbs. butter for pan-frying the |
| ½ cup shredded Cotswold cheese | fusilli |
| | fresh chives for garnish |

In a heavy saucepan, melt butter over low heat. Stir in flour and stir for two to three minutes. Slowly pour in milk, add the cayenne pepper, and simmer, stirring constantly, until sauce thickens. Add cheese and continue to stir until cheese is melted and sauce is thick and smooth.

In a heavy frying pan, melt two tablespoons of butter over medium heat. Place slices of the fusilli loaf in the pan and fry gently until lightly browned on both sides. Arrange on platter, overlapping the slices slightly, and pour cheese sauce over all. Sprinkle with fresh chives.

*Serves 4. This is wonderful with fresh asparagus.*